Also by Kate Parker

The
Detecting
Duchess

Kate Parker

JDP PRESS

The Detecting Duchess copyright ©2017 by Kate Parker

ISBN:978-0-9964831-6-2 [print]
ISBN:978-0-9964831-7-9 [e-book]

Published by JDPPress
Cover Design by Kim Killion of The Killion Group, Inc.

Dedication

To Jennifer Enger for naming this book, and the many people I've met during Georgia's adventures, including Ruth Nixon, Sherri Hollister, Lori Caswell, Shelley Giusti, Jill Marsal, and Faith Black. You, the readers, have made this journey special.

CHAPTER ONE

I wouldn't have noticed the young woman when she entered my bookshop except for the silk shawl in bright red wrapped around her neck and shoulders. Against the soot-stained city with its grimy buildings and darkly dressed inhabitants, she stood out like a beacon.

She glanced at me, the nearest person to the door, and said, "I need to speak to Georgia Fenchurch."

"I'm Georgia Fenchurch," I said as I stepped toward her. She wore a dull, dark blue muslin dress in a style often seen on upper servants or shop clerks. No pleats or tucks, no lace at the cuffs, and minimal puffiness in the upper sleeves. A plain gown.

And then I glanced again at her red silk shawl, which made the outfit anything but plain.

She glanced around Fenchurch's Books, currently occupied by half a dozen shoppers, my manager Grace Yates, and myself, without any apparent interest in the books. Her voice was pleasant and well-modulated, but accustomed to being heard across wide spaces. "We need to speak in private."

That drew the attention of everyone in the shop, all of whom suddenly appeared to find the book in their hands fascinating while they leaned toward us in anticipation of some juicy gossip.

I suspected this woman either wanted a handout to keep quiet about some made-up scandal she would threaten to spread across London, or she wanted to warn me against marrying into the aristocracy lest my soul perish. I'd faced down these sorts of threats since my engagement to the Duke of Blackford had been announced. The most annoying threats were of a different sort, issued by aristocrats who didn't want to see a duke marry someone in trade. "What does this concern?"

"My name is Eugenie Munroe." She handed me a plain calling card on cheap stock. "I need you to find a former investigator for the Crown. Grayson Burke."

I hadn't expected a missing person investigation to drop into my lap eight days before my wedding. I also hadn't expected the jolt of excitement I felt rush through my veins at the thought of working on one more Archivist Society case unfettered by matrimony.

I loved Blackford with all my heart, but marriage and childbearing and the duties required of a duchess would end the freedom I had as a spinster bookshop owner.

What I couldn't do was expose my role in the Archivist Society. It was unacceptable for any woman to investigate murder, missing persons, and robbery. It was unthinkable for a duchess to do so. "Let's go into my office."

"No. I fear I've been followed. I could be trapped

indoors and bring danger to your shop. Let's go for a walk."

"Did you see anyone following you?"

"No, but I suspect they're there."

I had a suspicion she was crazy and this investigation would turn out to lead nowhere.

It was a pleasant June day in the year of our Lord 1897, neither hot nor rainy. With the bookshop now managed by Grace Yates, I had the freedom to go for a walk or call on bored aristocrats whenever I wanted. In other words, I was in the position to follow the whim of this young woman and carry out our interview outdoors.

My friends told me I would get used to not having the constant demands of Archivist Society cases and the press of bookshop business. I hoped they were right. Already I found myself missing the excitement. "All right, let's go out."

I put on my hat, kept on my book-handling white cotton gloves, and followed her out onto the pavement. Clouds swept across a blue sky, driven by what was only a light breeze along my street. This side street, sheltered by buildings four and five stories high, received only a couple of hours of direct sunlight even in summer. Despite the breeze and the shade, it felt uncomfortably warm.

"Why did you seek me out?"

"Gray, Mr. Burke, said if anything happened to him, that I should go to you and you alone." She twisted the strap of her handbag with both hands as she stared at the pavement.

That instruction was strange. The Archivist Society worked all of our investigations as a group, calling in as many members as needed for each task. We tried to keep our individual names away from anyone's notice. "I don't know Mr. Burke." How did he get my name?

"He knows you. He said I should consult you and no one else."

I thought I should make my position clear from the start. "I'm to be married in a few days. If we don't find Mr. Burke quickly, I will have to drop out of the investigation. But never fear. The rest of the Archivist Society will serve you well."

"He said *you*. He said to come to Fenchurch's Books and speak to you." Her tone passed beyond stubborn to mulish.

"The ladies who work in Fenchurch's Books are also members of the Archivist Society," I told her. "They can help you."

She glanced at me and shook her head. "I am sure they're capable, but Mr. Burke said you're the best at what you do. And we must try to find him as quickly as possible. I'm certain he's in danger. Grave danger."

"What sort of danger?" I was expecting something as nebulous as her stalker.

"When he disappeared, Grayson Burke was chasing a murderer who'd stolen a fortune from the Egyptian government. This murderer is now focused on stopping Mr. Burke."

Oh, my. She wanted me to conduct a massive,

complex investigation by myself in a few days. It was impossible, even though it sounded fascinating.

I decided I would have to tell her "no." We had only taken a few steps from my shop. All I had to do was tell her I couldn't do it and go back to the bookshop.

The shove came from behind. I stumbled a step or two before the force knocked me to the pavement. I landed heavily, my hands and knees screaming in protest.

By the time I caught my breath and could call out, I saw a large man in a black cape and tall black hat pulling Miss Munroe's bright red scarf tightly around her neck.

She wheezed, "Help."

She grabbed at the silk with both hands, her head tilted back in an effort to breathe. His hands were large, powerful, and by the time I got back on my feet, Miss Munroe was slumping, her hands sliding away from her neck.

I threw myself at his back, grabbing at his face from behind with my fingers, all the while screeching like Dickens with his tail stepped on. In the distance, a bobby's whistle blew.

"Help me!" I shouted.

The attacker released his grip on Miss Munroe's scarf. At that instant, I saw the flash of a knife blade.

I clutched at his cape in an effort to stop him. He swung an elbow back and struck me in the chest above my corset. With that blow, he shook me off like a raindrop as I staggered, gasping in pain.

He strode away, keeping his face averted. I never

caught a glimpse of his features.

Miss Munroe sprawled on the pavement the moment he released her. I began to yank the scarf away from around her neck as a bobby finally arrived. Other people on the sidewalk stood frozen, looking on in shock.

Between us, the bobby and I freed her neck and then lay her on her side. I quickly looked her over and found a knife slit in her bodice, but no blood. Feeling around in the slit, I discovered the knife had struck a corset stay. The corset seemed to be damaged, but the blade hadn't penetrated.

She gasped and then coughed before she could take a breath. I exhaled deeply with relief when her deathly shade changed to a normal color. The bobby and I helped her to sit up.

"Did you see his face?" I asked.

She shook her head, still gasping.

I looked around at the bobby and the bystanders, but everyone shrugged or said, "No."

"Did you see which way he went?"

Again, people looked up and down our narrow street blankly, shaking their heads.

Miss Munroe focused on me and croaked, "Help me. He said he'd kill me."

CHAPTER TWO

Grace rushed out of our shop to join the crowd on the pavement, and with the bobby's help, she and I got Miss Munroe back to my bookshop office. She refused to see a doctor. While I sent the bobby off to report the attack, Grace brought her a cup of tea.

Once she drank it, Miss Munroe looked from one to the other of us and sobbed, "Someone stole a fortune in gold from the Egyptian government. Now this person wants to kill both Mr. Burke and me to keep his treasure."

"Do you know who has it or where it is?"

"No, I don't. And neither does Mr. Burke. That's why we were hunting for the thief. Only, he's found me." The teacup shook so badly I took it from her hand.

What was going on? "Did you see your attacker?"

"No. I was talking to you. Then you cried out and the man grabbed me from behind and began to choke me. I felt him strike me with something as I lost consciousness."

"A knife. Your corset stopped the blade. You're very lucky."

"Who would do this to me?" She sounded baffled.

"You heard him speak. Did you recognize the voice?"

"I was too busy trying to breathe. But I did hear his words very clearly. He said, 'I will kill you.' Oh, please. I need your help." She sounded near tears.

Dickens, the mouser for our block, rubbed against Miss Munroe's hem before jumping onto the desk where he sat proudly, not one paper on the stacks of invoices and bills disturbed.

He was on his best behavior today.

She sniffed and gave a shaky smile, appearing to recover from the shock. "Oh, how beautiful. He looks like Bastet come to life."

"Bastet?" I asked.

"An ancient Egyptian god in the form of a cat. It's your cat's aristocratic stare that gives him the look of an ancient god."

"Dickens thinks himself an aristocrat, and we are all his servants. Don't tell him he resembles a god, or there will be no living with him." I smiled at her before giving Dickens a warning look. He yawned in reply.

A cool breeze came in from the top of the open window facing the alley. Sitting amidst the disorder in what had long been my office calmed me. My trembling from the shock at the violence of the attack eased.

"If everything's all right, I'll go back into the shop," Grace said. "Call if you need me."

I nodded in reply. "Now," I said, facing Miss Munroe, "perhaps you'd better start telling me about this theft."

"I need to start further back than that." She gave me

a smile that made her features quite lovely. Dark brown eyes, brown hair the color of chocolate, and the glow of youth on her cheeks. The red silk scarf, now twisted and wrinkled, set off her coloring to perfection. I guessed she was in her early twenties.

"My father is the vicar in Little Chipwith Bridge in Yorkshire. His brother worked in Cairo for many years for the British government. Because this past season, from October to the end of May, was to be his last, I begged my uncle to let me come along as his secretary. He and my father agreed. They thought it would end my desire to travel. To be an explorer."

She smoothed her skirts before she looked at me and said, "I met Mr. Burke the night my uncle was murdered."

My fingers rose to my mouth. "Oh, Miss Munroe. I'm very sorry about your uncle. Please, lead me up to that night with anything that's important."

She settled more comfortably into her chair as if to tell me a story. If it weren't for the attack, I would wonder if it was a tale. "My uncle, Bradley Munroe, was a trusted British government official in Egypt for many years. Since languages and mathematics have always come easily for me, after Oxford I went out to Egypt, acting as my uncle's secretary. I quickly learned to speak Arabic better than most of the people at the Residency."

"The Residency?"

"The British Consul-General's residence and the offices of the British officials in Cairo."

"A small group, then."

"No. The Residency is huge, and still all the officials were packed in practically on top of each other. As far as I could see, life went along quite normally for the British officials and their families until the first of May. On that day, a shipment of gold from the Egyptian treasury, meant to make a payment on the debt owed by the Egyptian government to various European banks, was stolen."

I felt my eyes widen. "This must have been a valuable shipment."

"It was. In the neighborhood of a million British pounds."

I gasped. For a bookshop owner, well, for everyone, a million pounds was a breathtaking amount. An income of a thousand pounds a year was enough to maintain a house in London, raise a small family, and employ two servants. To my knowledge, most of the British diplomats in Cairo earned about that much.

Surely no one could spend all that money in a lifetime.

I tried to picture moving all that gold. "Surely this would be too much for one person to carry."

"They couldn't. The gold coins filled a chest about so big built of polished wood. I suppose it must weigh much more than a man." Her gestures indicated a box well over two feet long in all directions.

"The chest, coins and all, was switched either by Egyptian soldiers in the government treasury building while being moved from the vault to the assembly room where it was handed over, or after the Caisse de la Dette Publique officials, charged with accepting the gold and guarded by British soldiers, took possession of the chest and removed it from the building." She twisted her fingers as she spoke.

"Someone must have seen the theft."

"Everyone was questioned and claimed to have not seen a thing."

That path was blocked. "When was the theft reported?"

"I soon heard, in fact all of Cairo soon learned, that the Caisse officials returned a short time after they left. They said the box contained iron nails. They complained that they'd been swindled and demanded a second payment. The Egyptians refused, saying they gave the Caisse officials gold and they must have stolen it. Dire consequences were threatened on both sides. The bankers and treasury officials nearly came to blows."

"That's the type of story that would get around quickly." I tried to picture such a thing happening in London, and couldn't. "How long had they been transferring gold this way? Did they do this very often?"

"Georgia. What on earth happened?"

Both Miss Munroe and I turned our heads toward the commanding baritone coming from the doorway.

I gave Blackford a smile. This case was one where his expertise would come in handy. "Miss Munroe, this is my fiancé—"

"Mr. Ranleigh," he finished, giving her a respectful bow.

Mr. Ranleigh? What was going on that Blackford didn't want the woman to know he was a duke, and one of the most powerful men in the empire?

She rose and gave him a curtsy.

"Sit down, Miss Munroe. I hear you've had a terrible shock." Blackford perched on my desk and scratched Dickens behind the ears. The traitor purred.

"How did you hear?" I demanded.

"Mr. Grantham told me."

Detective Inspector Grantham? This subterfuge could only mean Blackford didn't trust my client one bit.

"I'll speak to you later, shall I?" Miss Munroe said, starting to rise.

"Oh, no," I said, waving her back into her seat. "Please feel free to speak in front of Mr. Ranleigh. He is likely to know the background of this theft."

"Have you traveled to Egypt, Mr. Ranleigh?" she asked.

"Yes," Blackford said. "Please continue."

"You were about to tell me how often the Egyptian government transferred funds from its treasury to the Caisse, I think you called it," I said.

"Twice a year, in a ceremony that's never altered."

"About twenty years ago, Egypt nearly went bankrupt, owing more to European bankers than they could possibly pay back," Blackford told us. "The Caisse de la Dette Publique was formed with representatives of various European interests to collect twice-yearly debt payments and split it among the various creditors according to a formula they, the Europeans, worked out."

"With this much gold missing, I'm surprised someone hasn't started a war." I stared at Blackford. Either he wasn't involved or, more likely, he wouldn't tell me if he were.

"This theft has put Egypt in a bad position with both the English, who effectively control their land as a colony and who lent Egypt a great deal of capital, and the Ottoman Empire, who are the official rulers of Egypt. Diplomats are racing between capitals trying to avert bloodshed," he replied.

Miss Munroe nodded. "The Egyptians want it proven that the English are the thieves. The English have never trusted the Egyptians. The other European countries are waiting to see if this weakens the British hold on Egypt so they can move in."

"And the Ottoman Empire sits in Constantinople doing nothing while sending out conflicting demands to the Europeans and the Egyptians," Blackford finished.

I could see how a theft of this magnitude could rapidly turn bloody. "What did they do to find the treasure?"

"The consul-general, Lord Cromer, appointed my uncle to lead the investigation. My uncle was very honest and fair. Everyone, English and Egyptian, trusted him." There was a little hitch in her voice, but she quickly swallowed and continued.

"My uncle realized Mr. Hathaway, the head of the committee working to modernize the Egyptian tax code, was in the best position to steal the gold. Hathaway worked out of the Egyptian treasury building where the gold is stored. He knew the building layout and every detail of the transfer. And he had permission to go everywhere in the building at any time."

"Surely this wasn't the only British official your uncle suspected," Blackford said.

"Well, no. But given what happened later, he was the best suspect." She set her handbag on her lap as if ready to rise.

There was a lot more I wanted to hear. "Wouldn't the rest of Mr. Hathaway's committee know as much and have as much access? Who else was on it?"

"The other English member of the committee is the secretary of the mission, a sort of junior minister in charge of reports, an aide to Lord Cromer. Sir Antony Derwaller. He had too many other duties to pay much attention to this committee. There is a French member of the committee, but he came down with a tropical fever a week before the theft and was unable to leave his bed, much less take any part in a robbery."

"What about the Egyptians? After all, it is their treasury," I said.

Miss Munroe gave a gentle shrug.

Blackford glanced at us both and said, "All of the Egyptians working in the treasury are being closely watched by the other Egyptians. Anyone found to be involved will immediately forfeit their life."

"Has there been any sign of any involvement—?"

Blackford shook his head. "Not after the guards who moved the payment from the vault to the ceremony were murdered."

It was a brutal solution, and still no one had found the treasure.

I decided to try another line of questioning. "Your uncle thought Mr. Hathaway was guilty. Did he find any evidence?"

Miss Munroe turned her soft brown eyes on me. In a voice barely more than a whisper, she said, "More than a week after the theft, he searched Mr. Hathaway's room and found a packet of coded letters."

"If they were coded, why did your uncle think they concerned the theft? They could have been of an amorous nature, or espionage, or some secret business we know nothing about," Blackford said.

"Did Mr. Hathaway know anyone had been in his room?"

"Mr. Hathaway must have found out, but he never said a word to my uncle. I believe they were the reason my uncle was murdered."

"That makes no sense. Even if he found out, the letters were in code. Your uncle couldn't have read them," I said.

"Your uncle stole them so he could translate them," Blackford said, shaking his head.

I could see the danger with that action immediately. "Once Hathaway discovered they were missing, did he find out who'd been in his room? Did he say anything to your uncle? Threaten him?"

"I wish it had been that simple." She sounded quite bereft.

"What did the notes say?" My curiosity had me sitting forward, listening to every word. They had to have been incriminating to have led to murder.

"They were in code," she repeated. "As much as my uncle and I tried to unravel them, it wasn't until after the Queen's Birthday celebrations that Gray—Mr. Burke and I managed to decipher one of them. It turned out to be the name of a ship and a cabin number."

Hardly something to put into code or kill someone over. "Where was your uncle when he was killed?"

"He was in his room at Shepheard's Hotel. I discovered my uncle's door ajar and went in." She shuddered and then continued. "My uncle lay on the tile floor, his head bloodied from a blow. When I knelt down next to him, my uncle slipped the letters out of his pocket and gave them to me."

"Did he name Mr. Hathaway as his attacker?"

"No. He said, 'I didn't think it was him.' Those were the last words he spoke. Then I screamed for help."

I felt certain either his attacker wasn't Hathaway or he'd expected someone other than his killer when he opened the door and had been surprised. "What happened after you screamed?"

"Various hotel employees, Mr. Burke, Colonel Gregory, and other hotel residents arrived. Someone went for a doctor. The doctor who arrived had been treating another hotel guest. He and Mr. Burke tried to save my uncle's life, but to no avail."

"Mr. Burke helped the doctor?" She hadn't mentioned this talent before.

"Yes. He plans to attend medical school. He'd worked with an army doctor in India. He's ever so clever."

This gave me another hint on how to find the elusive man.

"It was in the days following my uncle's murder that I learned Grayson Burke had come to Cairo as a special agent for the queen and government, a crown investigator, to find out what had happened to the gold."

"So Mr. Burke came to Egypt after the gold went missing." I wanted to get this timeline straight. "How long after the theft occurred was your uncle murdered?"

"Two weeks."

"How long had Mr. Burke been in Cairo at that point?"

"One week."

"Did your uncle and Mr. Burke work together at all?"

"Yes, for a few days before my uncle died. My uncle never introduced me to Mr. Burke. I think he was trying to protect me from any danger."

Really? "Why did he think you'd be in danger?"

Her stubborn expression was at odds with her innocent-sounding "I don't know."

I was certain she was lying. What had she done to put herself in danger in Cairo? And was today's attack the first?

Blackford wasn't going to sit there while she feigned innocence. "What was the next thing to happen after your uncle was killed?"

"The two Egyptian guards who'd moved the gold at the treasury during the ceremony were killed."

How many more murders would be associated with this theft? The story was so fantastic I was growing skeptical. But she had been attacked, and her attacker meant business. My stinging knees and palms testified to that. "When was this?"

"After Mr. Burke and I began investigating together. A few days after my uncle's death. One guard was stabbed on the night Mr. Burke and I spoke to him; the other guard died hours before we traveled to his village to question him about the transfer. They were the only two guards involved in moving the gold. The gold was on a small cart. It didn't take more than two men to move the chest because of the cart."

This sounded like a good time for a couple of men to hide the gold and replace it with something else. But if they were both dead, they must have acted on someone else's orders. "Were they ever out of sight of everyone else while they had the gold?"

"Yes. They had to walk down a hall and up a ramp from the vault to the gallery where the Europeans were waiting."

"How long were they alone, out of sight with the gold?" Blackford asked.

This could well be when the gold was stolen. But it didn't help us find Miss Munroe's attacker if both of the guards were dead.

"One minute, perhaps. Certainly less than two," she told us. "And the guard we spoke to said a ghost had smashed a door open into his face and had given him a bloody nose. He was stunned for maybe fifteen seconds."

Blackford faced me. "I'm certain that would be long enough for the other guard and his accomplice to swap the casket containing gold for one holding nails."

"An accomplice played the role of ghost and hit the guard in the face with the door." I nodded. That made sense. "Miss Munroe, what was behind the door that hit the guard?"

"Treasury records. Mostly tax records being utilized by Mr. Hathaway and his committee."

"Another reason why your uncle suspected him?" I asked.

She nodded.

"Did anyone know you and Mr. Burke were questioning the two Egyptian guards?" Blackford asked. Then he turned to me and raised his eyebrows. He was growing as skeptical of Miss Munroe's tale as I was.

"Grayson didn't make a secret of why he was in Cairo, and in the crowded city streets, anyone could have followed us."

Grayson again. Miss Munroe had grown closer to the investigator she now sought than she had admitted. There was no point in pressing her on her feelings. They were too obvious. The only obvious thing in her entire story.

And I still didn't fully understand what had happened in Egypt. "How much of an investigation did your uncle carry out? Did he question the guards?"

"Yes. He and all the other investigators for the Egyptians and the Europeans were turning up everywhere around the city, asking everyone questions. They all heard the story about the ghost, too. However, the other guard and the captain of the guards laughed off the story as an excuse for the guard's clumsiness."

"Were the guard and the captain involved?"

"My uncle thought their involvement was likely. He suspected the accident was where the switch was made, but it created a diplomatic problem he was unable to solve."

Blackford leaned forward, his interest increased. "What diplomatic problem?"

I sighed. Could this crime get any more complicated?

Miss Munroe gestured with her short, narrow fingers. "If the gold was taken before it was handed off, the Egyptians would need to repay the gold. But if it were Englishmen who stole it, as my uncle suspected, then the Egyptians, except perhaps the guards, were innocent. The English government, or the banks, could either get it back from the thieves or take the loss."

"A huge loss," Blackford mumbled, glaring at my floor.

"Yes."

Oh, dear. At least I understood the importance of the investigation Miss Munroe was involved in, but not why she now feared for Mr. Burke's safety. Especially since she was the one who'd been attacked. "Who did your uncle suspect was involved besides Mr. Hathaway?"

"He had no idea. We both tried to watch him, to see who he spoke to or sent notes to, but no one stood out as a conspirator."

I gave her a hard look. "Was there any chance Mr. Hathaway knew you were watching him?"

"No." She shrugged. "Maybe. I don't know."

It didn't sound like uncle and niece were very careful. "Then what happened?"

"Eventually, Mr. Burke and I, by pooling our efforts..." She slid into silence. Then she began again. "After the Queen's Birthday, 24 May, when all the Europeans were leaving Egypt for cooler locations, Mr. Burke and I translated one of the notes that mentioned a particular stateroom on the *Minotaur,* a ship sailing from Egypt to Southampton. It turned out to be the stateroom reserved for Mr. Hathaway."

I waited in silence, wanting to hear more.

"Mr. Burke and I sailed back on the *Minotaur.* Burke searched Mr. Hathaway's cabin and his trunks in the hold. Nothing. And once we docked in Southampton, Mr. Hathaway was killed."

CHAPTER THREE

"What?" So much for the prime suspect in this tale of theft and murder. This whole story made no sense. If Hathaway was the culprit, then who killed him? "Where? What happened to him?"

"Grayson left the ship early to follow Mr. Hathaway. He saw Hathaway on the docks headed toward the Southampton railway station and followed at a distance. When he, Mr. Burke, caught up to Mr. Hathaway, he was dead, lying in an alley between two huge storage barns. When I finally found him, Mr. Burke told me to find a bobby and report the murder of Mr. Hathaway. Then Mr. Burke left."

Oh oh. "Did he kill Mr. Hathaway?"

"No." She scowled at me in annoyance.

"Are you certain?"

"Of course."

"Did you kill Mr. Hathaway?"

"No!" She sounded horrified that I would ask that question. "I'm the daughter of a vicar."

"That doesn't mean that you couldn't kill a man."

She folded her arms over her chest and jutted out her chin. "I believed Mr. Hathaway was behind my uncle's murder, but I couldn't have killed him. However, I would have loved to hand him over to the authorities and watch him hang."

Perhaps. I reserved my judgment on that. "When did you next see Mr. Burke?"

"I haven't seen him since that day. That's why I need you to find him." She sounded desperate.

I glanced at Blackford, who nodded. I rose. I doubted I could find the missing man before my wedding. "Thank you, Miss Munroe. I'll talk to the Archivist Society and organize them in an immediate search for Mr. Burke."

She rose, her eyes flashing with anger. "No. He said I should come to you, and you alone. If you won't help me by yourself, I'll have to find Mr. Burke on my own. It's probably too late anyway." She turned to leave.

Blackford put a gentle tone into his voice. "Are you certain you don't want a few of us looking for him? We are very discreet."

"I don't want whoever attacked me today to find him by following an entire society around London. Particularly if Gr—Mr. Burke has found a safe hiding place." She started out the door of the office.

"Wait. Are you well enough to travel around London alone? You were just attacked. Savagely attacked," I added.

"I'm from Yorkshire. We're hearty people. If you change your mind about helping me, I'm staying at Mrs. Allen's on Queen Square."

With that, she stomped away.

When I moved to follow her, Blackford put out a hand to stop me. "Let her go."

"What do you think of her story?"

"The story of the theft matches the reports coming out of Cairo. But neither of us have time to chase all over London looking for a missing man who may not even be in the country. If she won't allow this to be handled by the full Archivist Society, let it go."

He punctuated his comments by taking me into his arms and giving me a kiss that left me weak in the knees. I finally let him go with a sigh.

By the time we entered the shop and Blackford gave me a jaunty wave as he set the bell over the front door jangling, Miss Munroe was long gone.

I walked over to Grace, who raised her eyebrows.

"That attack was real enough, but I feel like I've gotten only half the story. Why does she want me to hunt for this missing man without involving the rest of the Archivist Society?" And why, if I were going to work on one last case as an unmarried woman, did it have to be on behalf of someone who wanted to keep us in the dark?

"She needs your help, Georgia."

"She needs *our* help. The trouble is, she doesn't want it."

Grace gave me a hard stare. She'd seen how bruised and frightened Miss Munroe was. "Then you'll have to bring her around."

I loosed a loud sigh and nodded. Grace was right. "I guess I'd better try to talk to her. But first, I'm going to follow one easy lead. She mentioned Burke's desire to attend medical school. Could it be as simple as checking with the ones in London to find him?"

I used our reference books to find the short list of local medical schools. By visiting each one and using my connection to the Duke of Blackford, who I said was looking for an old friend, I was able to discover that Grayson Burke had not enrolled in any medical school in London.

I determined to write to the medical schools in Edinburgh and elsewhere that evening, but first I headed out toward Bloomsbury, where Miss Munroe was staying. Being accustomed to London and its nightmarish traffic patterns, I reached Mrs. Allen's house in a short time and asked for Miss Munroe.

"Have you changed your mind?" she demanded as soon as she came to the door.

I tamped down a flash of anger. She'd said she wanted my help, but she wasn't making it easy for me to want to help her. "So far I've learned Grayson Burke has not enrolled in a London medical school. I'll work on finding him until my wedding, but it would be helpful if I brought in the Archivist Society. With several of us looking for him, we'll find him faster. And you said speed was imperative."

She seemed to consider this for a moment before she stepped back, reluctance in her expression. At Mrs. Allen's suggestion, she led me into the drawing room.

I decided to try to put her at ease. "How did you end up staying with Mrs. Allen? Her home seems nice."

"Her sister is a parishioner of my father's in Little Chipwith Bridge."

"Have you traveled to London before?"

"Just in passing through."

"You mentioned you studied in Oxford. Do you still see any of your friends from that time?"

"I was a charity student. I didn't have any real friends."

She continued to stand there with her arms folded, unwilling to do more than just answer my questions as briefly as possible. I gave up. "Your attacker thinks you know something. Did you see anything out of the ordinary on the Southampton docks?"

"Not on the docks, exactly. The odd thing was the shipping labels for Mr. Hathaway's statues. They were changed after his death. He had twenty crates, each with a large statue of Bastet or Anubis that Mr. Hathaway had wrapped and packed to ship to his relatives in Gloucestershire." She remained standing, as if she couldn't decide how cooperative she wanted to be.

"Statues? Anubis? Is this a gift one normally brings back from Egypt?" I couldn't picture them, and now I was even more confused.

"Maybe one or two, but not as many as Mr. Hathaway bought. I've mentioned Bastet is an ancient cat god. Anubis is an ancient god in the form of a jackal or dog. The statues were hollow and sold in the markets in Cairo for next to nothing. There was nothing special about them except their size. They were about three feet tall and bulky."

"Did you check to see if the gold was hidden inside the statues?" It seemed obvious.

Miss Munroe must have decided on cooperation because she walked over to sit on a stuffed chair. "Yes. Grayson opened the crates while we were on the ship. All the statues seemed empty. Completely empty. That's when I saw the tags on the crates said to ship on to Gloucestershire.

Once Mr. Hathaway was murdered, the tags had been changed. I saw them in the left luggage room at Waterloo Station marked to await pickup. Only Mr. Hathaway's fellow thief would have changed the labels."

I walked to the open window. "Why not Mr. Hathaway himself?"

"I saw the labels shortly before he died. They hadn't been changed then."

I left the window where I was enjoying the breeze and sat across from her on a small sofa, nodding for her to continue. When she didn't, I said, "Perhaps the police did that."

"When I picked up my sea trunk in Waterloo Station, the crates were sitting nearby. They'd been changed." She leaned toward me. "I asked a porter and he said someone had rewritten them with pen and ink. They didn't carry any official seal or mark, so it wasn't done by the railway people or the police. But the porter didn't seem concerned about the change. He said people change their minds all the time."

She sat facing me with her hands kneading her silk scarf. "I've never known a dead man to change his mind," she added.

I couldn't argue with her logic about dead men, but I didn't understand where her thoughts were headed. "Why are the statues important?"

"I thought it had something to do with the gold. The gold wasn't hidden inside them, but maybe they're a clue to where the gold is hidden."

"What sort of clue? Where would it lead you?"

She looked at me with wide brown eyes. "I don't know."

Statues of cats and dogs seemed like a strange clue to me. I decided to leave that for the time being. "What did you do after you found the tags changed?"

"I sent a telegram to Lord Salisbury and went home to Yorkshire. I hoped—"

"Wait. Why Lord Salisbury?" Prime minister for the third time, he was a busy and influential man. I couldn't see him getting directly involved with the details of an investigation, even one this potentially dangerous to Britain's interests.

And why would a vicar's daughter be presumptuous enough to send a telegram to the prime minister?

"Mr. Burke said he was his employer. If I wanted to get in touch with him, I should contact Lord Salisbury. And I wanted both of them to know about the change to the shipping tags. I thought it was important. Don't you?"

Burke certainly worked for the highest levels of our government. *If* this were true. All I said aloud was, "It could be important. Go on."

"I hoped Mr. Burke would get in touch with me to say they'd recovered the gold or found my uncle's killer, or maybe found the statues with one of Mr. Hathaway's relatives, but all I've heard is silence. Finally, I convinced my father I was going to visit a college friend and traveled to London."

Her expression said she'd just confessed a sin. "Lord Salisbury's private secretary told me the crates had been misplaced from the left luggage room, and Mr. Burke was unavailable. There was nothing they could do to help me, so I should go back to Yorkshire. I didn't believe him."

"Why not?"

"He didn't look me in the eye."

I understood her disbelief. I'd faced that style of lying often enough before. "I know you want me to get in contact with Mr. Burke, but how exactly do you think I can proceed without the help of the Archivist Society?"

"I want you to find Mr. Burke without alerting anyone. I think if you can find him, he and I should be able to find my uncle's murderer. If you can't, then the killer has probably killed him, too."

Considering the number of corpses already in Miss Munroe's story, and now the attack on her, it seemed possible Mr. Burke had met the same fate. I needed to check with the Metropolitan Police for men who'd died by violence in the past month. "Do you have a photograph of Mr. Burke?"

She shook her head.

"A sample of his handwriting?"

"No. Nothing to show he was ever alive. Real." She seemed close to tears, but she sniffed into her handkerchief and then straightened her shoulders.

She showed all the signs of being in love with Mr. Burke. Had he gone off on another assignment to escape hurting her feelings by telling her he didn't love her? "And he only gave you Lord Salisbury's address to send any messages to him?"

"Yes." She studied me for a moment. "I know what you're thinking, but I assure you, he is not trying to avoid me."

This vicar's daughter was certainly unusual. She traveled to Egypt and then had searched for her uncle's murderer in a foreign land. "Do you know anything about Mr. Burke's family? Do you know where he comes from originally?"

"His mother died when he was quite young, and he has an older brother. And Colonel Gregory told me his father is mad and locked up in the countryside somewhere."

"Colonel Gregory?" Was this another member of the British contingent at the Residency? Had he been a friend of Mr. Hathaway or Mr. Munroe?

"I'm sorry. Of course you wouldn't know who he is. He's the head of the Egyptian police. The inspector-general of their police. An official of the khedive—the king of Egypt—but in some sort of agreement, the head of the Egyptian police is always British."

"Please. Continue." I couldn't wait to hear what she'd tell me next. And whether it was believable.

"Colonel Gregory was in Shepheard's Hotel visiting a friend the night my uncle was murdered and so came right away. It was clear from the start that he and Mr. Burke didn't like each other. It turned out they had served together in India when they were both in the British army."

"Have you tried to contact Colonel Gregory? He sounds like someone who might be able to tell us more about Mr. Burke's family and where he came from."

"I tried, but my telegrams to him in Cairo go unanswered. All the British officials leave Egypt at some time in the summer months. If he left, he could be anywhere. Sailing the Mediterranean, enjoying the spas of Europe, hiking in Scotland. He could be in London for all I know."

"No one in Cairo keeps track of where everyone goes in case someone is needed?" It only seemed practical to me.

"No. Anyone who stays to do anything, can't. It's soon 120 degrees, and in Western clothing, you can't survive. So little is done by anyone, Egyptian or European, in summer that they hardly need a government."

"It sounds horrible."

"Oh, no. It's incredibly beautiful. Beyond the irrigated fields and villages on either side of the Nile River is the desert. The sun sets fiery red over the sandy cliffs beyond the green fields across the blue water of the Nile from Cairo." Her eyes half-closed as she described her memories.

"And the sky is so blue. Not always gray with fog like here. Have you ever seen the pyramids?"

"No." Perhaps, with Blackford…

"The pyramids, rising up from the desert, are magnificent. It's hard to believe they are older than Rome. The souk, or market, in old Cairo has the scent of a hundred spices and the sound of a thousand voices. The buildings have intricate mosaics of small tiles and lots of arches. And the call to prayer from the minarets at sunrise and sunset is haunting. I'd love to go back, but of course, that's now impossible."

"Why?"

"My uncle is dead. I'm a vicar's daughter. This was my only chance at adventure. And now it's gone."

I hoped the Archivist Society wasn't my only chance at adventure. But then, I hoped everything with Blackford would be exciting. I brought my thoughts back to the point of our conversation. "What else did Colonel Gregory say about Mr. Burke and his insane father?"

"Only that his father attacked women and had to be locked up. He said I should stay away from Mr. Burke because he might have inherited his insanity."

"That sounds like an old-fashioned belief." Colonel Gregory sounded like he was trying to cause trouble between the two lovebirds. If indeed that was what they were. My guess was yes.

"I can't find him on my own in the next week," I told her. "If you want Mr. Burke found before he's killed, you need to let me call in the Archivist Society. We have an almost fifteen-year history of finding missing people and capturing murderers, but only because we work together."

She gave me a defiant look.

"It's your choice. Do you want our help or not?"

"Are you sure you won't get him killed when you hunt for him?"

"We've been successful all these years. You're going to have to trust us."

I could see in her eyes when she made up her mind. "Yes. Just be careful."

"We will. Is there anyone else you can think of who might give us information about Mr. Burke or his background? Is there any other detail you can think of?"

She smiled at the image in her head. "He has dark hair, blue eyes, and a lovely smile. He must be about six feet tall and quite strong. And very handsome."

"I look forward to meeting him." And finding out what he really looked like. "Did he mention any other family members? Grandparents, aunts, uncles, cousins?"

Her eyes widened. "Oh, dear. I think he told me once that his grandfather was something very grand. A baron or a baronet or a bishop or a cabinet minister."

That certainly covered a lot of possibilities. I rose and said, "I'll look into it. I'll get in touch with you when I learn something. Please understand that the rest of the Archivist Society will be involved in helping locate Mr. Burke, particularly after my wedding."

If she didn't know I was marrying a duke, I certainly wasn't going to tell her. The fewer who knew, the better, had become my guiding principle, and Blackford had made it clear he didn't want her to know.

She nodded, stood, and then gripped my lower arm to detain me. "Please find him as quickly as possible. I'm worried. There's a murderer loose in England."

Probably more than one, but there was no sense making her even more frightened. There was only one killer she was interested in.

"You feel quite recovered from the attack?" I asked her.

"Yes, quite, thank you."

"The Archivist Society and I are glad to take this on for you. We'll let you know as soon as we learn anything." I stopped in the front hall and studied her face. "Is there nothing else you need to tell me? No other detail that might explain the attack on you today?"

She looked me in the eye and said, "No. Absolutely not."

I didn't believe her.

I returned to the shop to find Grace stacking newspapers and periodicals. She looked up and said, "Will she let us help her? That attack was certainly real enough. Did she give you any leads?"

"I think so." I walked over to our copy of Debrett's and looked up the name Burke. I found a Lord Burke of Arlkenny Castle, County Armagh. "Miss Munroe mentioned an important grandfather, and this man is certainly old enough."

Grace looked over my shoulder and then scowled. "The name's familiar. Look through old copies of the newspapers and see if there's something there. Or ask Lady Westover and Lady Phyllida. They'd be sure to know."

"How recent was the story in the papers?"

She brushed a stray strand of blondish hair out of her face and then pressed her hands into her back. "It's warm in here today. I'd love a cooling breeze."

"The newspaper article?" I reminded her.

"Quite recent, but I don't remember exactly when or the details. Whether or not the story is of any importance, I know the ladies will want to see you."

"They want to see me nearly every day. I think they're more excited about this wedding than either Blackford or me." I closed my eyes, tired from the endless round of parties and dinners that were more in hopes of creating other matches during the London season than in honor of our upcoming wedding.

I opened them to see Grace with a sympathetic expression on her face. "We're all excited for you and we all want to share in your good fortune. Too bad there aren't several of you to divide among all your friends."

"Then Blackford wouldn't know who he was marrying." I had to smile at the thought. "If anyone else comes looking for me, I'm going to Westover House."

I hoped I could find information for Miss Munroe there. If Lord Burke of County Armagh was Mr. Burke's grandfather, Lady Westover and Aunt Phyllida would be sure to have lots of answers to this mystery.

CHAPTER FOUR

I wasn't a duchess yet. I traveled like the rest of the middle class on an omnibus from Charing Cross Road to near Mayfair and walked the rest of the way, glad the day wasn't rainy. I knocked on the shiny black front door of Lady Westover's home and was shown upstairs into the first-floor drawing room.

Lady Phyllida, known to me as Aunt Phyllida during the years she lived in my flat while hiding from aristocratic gossip, was seated near an open window. She grasped my hands when I walked over to her. She hadn't been young when we'd met on an early Archivist Society investigation and the years were catching up with her, particularly in the swollen joints of her fingers.

"Are your hands painful?" I asked, looking closely at them.

"I've had to give up most of my cooking," she told me. "Cook is very kind and makes some of my old recipes from time to time. Sit down, Georgia, and tell me what is new with you before I begin to wallow in nostalgia. Would you care for tea?"

I'd been flirting with nostalgia since I set foot in the bookshop that morning. "Yes. I'll ring for it, shall I?"

Aunt Phyllida gave me one regal nod.

I walked across the drawing room to the bell pull, avoiding Lady Westover's large attacking ferns. "I remember how wonderful the meals were at the flat when you lived with Emma and me. You raised her, much more than I did."

"She was thirteen when you rescued her from that housebreaking gang. She was already halfway to adulthood. And now she and Sumner..." Aunt Phyllida couldn't quite make herself say Emma was increasing. She looked pleased, but she was flame red.

The maid came in, saving Aunt Phyllida from finishing her thought as she asked for tea to be brought up.

In the years when she would have married and raised a family, Phyllida had been trapped in slavery to her mad brother, the Earl Monthalf, who'd brought prostitutes home and then butchered them. It left her shy and fearful, and while she'd become more independent since then, there were still things she wouldn't discuss.

Usually, she was safe from hearing about such subjects. No one mentioned childbirth or its cause in polite society. Murder was only alluded to in general terms.

I looked around the drawing room at the ferns and flowers on every table, in every corner, next to every chair, and by each windows, products of Lady Westover's greenhouse in back of the house. "How is Lady Westover?"

"Very well. She'll be down in a moment. You don't mind that I'll stay here with her for the foreseeable future, do you, my dear? She relies on me, and I've come to rely on her."

"Not at all. Especially since you managed to keep all her plants alive while she was ill. With a talent like that, she'll never let you leave. But if you ever change your mind, Blackford and I would love to have you join us."

"I know that and appreciate it, but you'll be newlyweds. You won't need me chaperoning you."

I gave her a smile, picturing Blackford's reaction to a chaperone after the wedding. His fury would probably bring on a snowstorm in midsummer. "I do need some information. A case has come in by way of the bookshop today."

"A case? You don't have time for a case. You're about to be married." Aunt Phyllida sounded scandalized.

I wished people would stop thinking of me only in terms of my wedding.

I was saved by Lady Westover entering the room. I rose and walked over to her as she marched in, her cane as much of a prop as an aid. She was still thin from the terrible pneumonia she'd had the previous winter, which had brought Aunt Phyllida into her household to nurse her and keep the household in order.

"My maid said you'd arrived, Georgia. I'm so glad to see you. How are the wedding preparations progressing?" She grabbed one of my hands, squeezing it, and then moved over to the sofa, where she sat as gracefully as a debutante.

The tea arrived, and as it was poured, I thought, *I'm a bookshop owner. I don't belong in this world*. "How are you doing, Lady Westover?" I asked as I sat on a nearby sofa and took a sip of my tea.

"Fine. How did the interview go with the lady's maid?" she asked me.

Oh, dear. I'd hoped she wouldn't ask me. "I'm afraid she wouldn't do. Much too strident."

"Oh, no." I could tell Lady Westover didn't believe me.

"Oh, yes. Quite opinionated."

"That's what you said about the other two."

"I'm sorry, Lady Westover, but I don't need an opinionated lady's maid."

"You certainly do," Lady Westover said.

"Hmm," Aunt Phyllida said.

We both stared at her.

"Don't pay any attention to me," she said and smiled.

Lady Westover turned her attention back to me. "What's wrong, Georgia?" Her gaze was probing.

"Wrong?" I echoed. I didn't want to answer that question. At least not honestly. Unfortunately, Lady Westover would keep at me until I told her the truth.

"She has a new investigation," Aunt Phyllida said.

"I see." Lady Westover raised an eyebrow. "Out with it, young lady. Never before has a new investigation caused you to look pitiful."

All right. If they wanted to hear my complaints, they

were welcome to them. "Sir Broderick can't come to the wedding. He hasn't been out of the house in more than a dozen years since the—accident that landed him in that wheeled chair. I wish we were getting married in the drawing room instead of St. Ethelbert's down the street from his home."

"But my dear. You couldn't fit in all the dukes and Archivist Society members who are attending, much less everyone else," Lady Westover said as if I were a small child.

"Don't forget the Marquess of Salisbury," Aunt Phyllida added.

"I'd forgotten about the prime minister. Why does he have to come? All that protocol." I ended in a wail.

"You must realize he and Blackford are good friends. These are the circles you'll move in for the rest of your life." Lady Westover sounded very stern. "Therefore, you need an opinionated lady's maid."

Leave it to her to bring the conversation around to her point of view.

"What if I don't want to?" As soon as it came out, my cheeks heated. I'd promised myself not to admit that to anyone. I loved Blackford. Being a duke was part of who he was. That was just my least favorite part. "I want to move to the colonies. The United States. Europe. Somewhere I can be Blackford's wife without all those eyes staring at me in judgment."

"Don't be childish," Lady Westover said. "You'll always be judged, whether you're a duchess or a bookshop owner. You might as well be a duchess."

I wanted to pout, and then curl up in bed, pull the covers over my head, and sleep for a week.

Aunt Phyllida joined me on the sofa. "Oh, Georgia, you're just having pre-wedding panic. I understand it happens to every bride. I can't think of any two people more suited to each other than you and Blackford. Besides," she said as she gave me a smile and an airy wave of one hand, "when you leave St. Ethelbert's, you'll outrank the prime minister."

That thought shocked me enough that no sound came out of my mouth until I murmured, "Oh, dear Lord."

"Pull yourself together, dear, and tell us about your new investigation," Lady Westover ordered, sounding like a judge handing down a hanging verdict.

Anything to take my mind off the wedding. "I understand from Grace there was some news about a Lord Burke recently. Would you remember what it was?"

"It didn't make much of a stir in London, but it must have been quite a wonder in Ireland," Aunt Phyllida said.

"Lord Burke and his heir were wiped out in a single night. A fire in their castle." Lady Westover looked over the rim of her teacup at me. "What is your interest, Georgia?"

Was that why Grayson Burke hadn't contacted Eugenie Munroe? Had he died in the fire?

When I didn't respond, Lady Westover said, "What does your investigation have to do with the Burkes?"

I took a sip of tea to give me time to decide what to say. "I'm not certain. A young lady has come to us, trying to locate a young man who said his name was Grayson Burke." Explaining the connection to Egypt and a fabulous theft would only confuse the issue.

"That's not a name familiar to me," Aunt Phyllida said, instantly transforming into Lady Phyllida Monthalf before my eyes. "A cousin, perhaps?"

"Irish family relationships are so difficult to understand," Lady Westover added. "He could be some random person with the last name of Burke. I believe it's common in Ireland."

"What happened to Lord Burke and his son?"

"There was a fire in the castle. Completely destroyed the interior. The stone walls survived. Lord Burke was quite elderly. I remember him being a fine figure of a man when I was just a girl," Lady Westover said. "His son was also home and they both died, along with the son's valet and a groom who tried to put out the fire."

"Wait. Wasn't there a fifth body they weren't able to identify?" Lady Phyllida said.

"I believe you're right," Lady Westover said. "A tragedy for the family. And they haven't been able to locate the new Lord Burke."

"Could he have been the fifth body?" I asked, looking for the simplest explanation.

"It's possible," Lady Phyllida said, "but I think someone said he was out of the country. Young people travel so much these days."

Blackford had said we'd travel around the continent for our honeymoon. I was looking forward to that. Seeing new places. Learning new things. Traveling among foreigners who weren't as concerned with my pedigree. Avoiding aristocrats who didn't find me aristocratic enough for a duke. Avoiding taunts and snubs from aristocrats who'd made our engagement painful.

Turning my mind away from those cuts and back to the investigation, I asked, "What do you know about the Burke family? Are they a large tribe of red-haired Irishmen?"

"Lord Burke wasn't as a young man. Dark-haired, as I recall. I believe he only had the one son who in turn had two sons. Or possibly three. It's been ages since anyone mentioned them," Lady Westover said.

"Probably because the son was mad," Lady Phyllida said, sounding like chatty Aunt Phyllida again. "I don't know what form his madness took, but—"

"He attacked women. Just like your brother. That's why everyone tried to avoid mentioning details when you were around, Phyllida," Lady Westover said.

"It's not likely I'll shatter like a vase, Amelia."

"This was a few years ago. You might have at that time."

Phyllida drew herself up and folded her arms over her chest. "That was then and this is now. Please tell Georgia all the details that you remember."

It was a measure of how much Aunt Phyllida had recovered from those dark times, and how close the friendship between the two women had grown, that she could freely speak her mind.

"The trouble is I don't remember many details. He was completely mad. Went around exposing his—er, his nether regions." She blushed. "At balls and large parties. To young women," came out too quickly. "They decided the best thing to do was lock him away in the family castle. He escaped once and attacked a young woman in the village. Nearly raped her right on the main street."

"How dreadful," Lady Phyllida said.

"They doubled the locks and guards after that."

I stared at Lady Westover. "Was anyone else in the family insane?"

"Not that I've heard. His father was a tyrant, but very attractive. And apparently sane."

I was glad for Miss Munroe's sake that madness didn't run in the family. She appeared sweet on the young man, whether or not he deserved it. "Do they know what started the fire?"

"No. Apparently, it started in the drawing room. The fireplace wasn't banked properly or a lamp was left burning. The mad son and his valet were locked in for the night and no one could reach them to let them out. Lord Burke died of smoke inhalation in his sleep. It must have been terrible." Lady Westover shook her head.

I could see that another talk with Miss Munroe was in order. "When you knew him as a young man, did Lord Burke have younger brothers or cousins?"

"Oh, dear." Lady Westover set down her teacup and closed her eyes. When she opened them, she said, "I seem to remember a young man—well, he was my age, not a young man any longer, who was visiting London with the handsome Lord Burke. I don't remember if he were a brother or a cousin. Some sort of relation. I have no idea what happened to him."

"Was Grayson a family name?"

"Not that I know of."

"Do you know the name of the new Lord Burke?"

"James."

It was too bad James Burke was traveling. He might have information on his brother, cousin, or distant relation named Grayson Burke.

"Where are you going tonight?" Aunt Phyllida asked, having discussed the Burkes and deaths enough for one visit.

"Blackford and I are having dinner at the Robson-McLains. When we return from the continent, I'm going to owe a dinner invitation to every lord, lady, and financier in London."

"Of course, dear. And every one of them is going to want to see how you've put your stamp on Blackford House."

Both of the ladies looked at me and smiled. Inwardly, I cringed. I couldn't see changing a thing in that beautiful house. And I wasn't certain Blackford wanted me to, either.

Since Lady Westover and Aunt Phyllida were ready, we went out together to pay social calls on one or two ladies who were at home to callers on that day. I was used to shelving books, discussing books, and selling books at this time of day, not sitting in a drawing room discussing the weather. I found it tedious.

The weather was dry, so we walked the two blocks to Lady Ashwin's townhouse. Above the treetops in the square, the clouds seem to sail across the sky as they rolled in from Ireland. The parks looked cheerful, with manicured flower beds everywhere and children playing under the watchful eyes of nurses.

For once it wasn't foggy or damp.

As the butler showed us into the first-floor drawing room, I saw Lady Ashwin already had callers—the vicious Lady Castleley and the twittery Lady Beatty.

We curtsied and nodded and greeted each other before sitting down in a drawing room where every surface was covered in photographs, miniature paintings, and porcelain statuettes. The Princess of Wales would have felt at home here, since this was the style she had popularized. Blackford House wasn't decorated that way, and I certainly wouldn't introduce it to my new home.

The topic of the weather was dispensed with, sunshine having lasted too long to allow for more than a few words, before Lady Castleley turned to me and said, "How is your business doing? It's something quaint, I believe."

"It's doing very well, thank you." *Witch.*

Lady Castleley and Lady Beatty exchanged smug looks as Lady Ashwin hurriedly turned the conversation to a ball held the previous week. They'd made their point. I was in trade. It would have been bad enough if my grandfather had been in trade. That I was in trade was completely unacceptable. Nothing short of prostitution could make me less eligible to marry a duke.

Conversation started and died several times. I was trying to think of some way to pay Lady Castleley back for her taunt. Lady Westover took one look at me, knew what I was thinking, and kept a stern eye on me.

We were all making moves to leave when two more women were announced, the Duchess of Duleign and her daughter, the Viscountess Tidminster, who'd just returned from her honeymoon. I'd met them both before. The duchess was stiffly formal and didn't bother me. The younger woman gave me a look of loathing as she gave me the scantest curtsy of acknowledgment.

If my life had to be lived among people like this, I wasn't totally sure I wanted to marry Blackford. Then I thought, perhaps that was their aim. To convince me I wasn't worthy.

Blackford thought I was, and his was the only opinion that mattered.

As we were leaving the room, Lady Castleley shifted her position so she was next to me. "You're a very lucky woman. So many eligible ladies could have become his duchess. No one can understand how you bewitched a sensible man like Blackford."

She kept her voice lowered so I was the only one to hear her cruel words. Giving me a smile as she left me speechless, she walked away.

My hands curled into fists. I was about to make a

rude reply, not caring who heard me when Lady Westover took my arm. With Lady Phyllida behind me nudging me out, we left before I could say anything.

Once we were on the pavement, I demanded, "Did you hear what she said?"

"Of course not. She knows how to egg you on so you look foolish while she appears innocent. In a few days, you'll be the Duchess of Blackford and all her complaints, if she dares make any, will sound like sour grapes," Lady Westover said. "Now, Miss Whittington's next, do you think?"

I hoped for a better reception.

At our second call of the afternoon, in Miss Whittington's blue satin-and-damask-covered drawing room, I found myself introduced to yet another aristocrat I hadn't met.

Miss Whittington introduced her to Lady Westover, Lady Phyllida, and myself as "my aunt, Lady Derwaller."

After a round of curtsies, I said, "I've heard your name recently in connection with the Europeans in Egypt."

We all sat down and the plain, middle-aged lady, her sleeves a season out of date, said, "My husband, Sir Antony Derwaller, was first secretary to the British Residency for the past five years."

I gave a silent cheer. Here was a perfect opportunity to learn a little more about this new investigation.

CHAPTER FIVE

"And do you come back to London every summer to avoid the heat in Cairo?" Perhaps not the best way to begin questioning Lady Derwaller, but I'd not expected this opportunity. If I could begin by ruling out one possibility for Hathaway's accomplice, we'd be that much ahead.

"Yes, but now we've come back for good." She gave me a bright smile.

"Your husband will be in a position in the Foreign Office?"

"No. He'll no longer have anything to do with the government." She didn't seem upset about her husband no longer having a position or a salary. "We're free of living with insects and heat and sand and diplomats."

"Oh?"

She didn't reply, taking a sip of her tea, and joined in enthusiastically when her niece started to talk about the play they had seen the night before.

Only later, as we were leaving, did I manage to speak directly to her again. "How long has it been since you returned to London, Lady Derwaller?"

"We arrived four weeks ago. Ship across the

Mediterranean, train across France, and then boat across the Channel. I won't miss making that trip twice a year. Our daughter was seasick throughout both sailings. Thank goodness the Channel crossing is a short one."

Miss Whittington smiled before she said, "My cousin is a terrible sailor. She became ill once punting in Cambridge."

"Your daughter was with you in Cairo?" Lady Westover asked. I silently thanked her curiosity.

"Both of our children came out for the last month. Our son took leave from his job and our daughter is getting married shortly, but they both came out to help pack up the house."

"I didn't know your daughter is about to be wed. Best wishes to her," Lady Phyllida exclaimed.

"Yes. The wedding is next week, and immediately after, Sir Antony and I leave London. We're looking forward to our new life together so much that you'd think we were going to be the newlyweds." She smiled warmly as she thought about her future.

The conversation veered off to other subjects, but I knew Sir Antony could have been Miss Munroe's attacker. He was in London at the right time. He was also in Cairo at the right time to have participated in the theft and then acted as Mr. Munroe's murderer.

Was theft and murder making Lady Derwaller's dreams come true? "Where are you traveling to?" I asked.

"Home."

Before I could ask where that was, a woman called her from another room and she left our company.

* * *

Before I needed to dress for the very grand dinner at the Robson-McLains that evening, I traveled back to Bloomsbury to see Miss Munroe once more. I hoped my news would remind her of something Mr. Burke had said.

She was coming from the other direction as I reached the large townhouse on Queen Square where she was staying.

"I've been visiting the British Museum. What a splendid place," she said, ushering me inside. "Mrs. Allen, would it be all right if Miss Fenchurch and I talked in the drawing room again?"

"Of course. I'll bring in some tea." The broad, middle-aged Mrs. Allen smiled and disappeared down the hall.

I'd had enough tea that afternoon to float away.

We went into the comfortable drawing room and this time sat together on a sofa facing the cold fireplace. Behind us, the window facing the square was open, letting in a cooling breeze that fluttered the lace curtains.

"Have you heard something?" Miss Munroe asked as she pulled off her short gloves.

"Possibly. There is a Lord Burke in County Armagh in Ireland. An old man, possibly old enough to be Grayson Burke's grandfather."

"Excellent. We must contact—" She looked ready to

jump up from the sofa.

"Wait. There was a fire at his castle recently. Both he and his son, who is reported to have been mad, were killed along with two or three other people."

She settled down. "Oh. How dreadful." After she sat silently for a moment, she said, "But there must be a new Lord Burke. We must inquire of him for any knowledge of Grayson and his whereabouts."

"He's unavailable at the present time. He's reported to be traveling outside the country." I didn't mention the unidentified fifth body.

"So that path is blocked." She sighed. "We must think of another way to reach Grayson Burke. Perhaps other family members?"

"Possibly. The Archivist Society and I will make inquiries and we'll get back to you. Is there anything else you can tell me about Grayson Burke? Anything else you remember?"

Mrs. Allen bustled in with the tea tray. When she acted as if she would linger, Miss Munroe thanked her very firmly and the woman left.

Once she'd poured the tea, Miss Munroe shook her head. "I can't think of anything else of use. I have the feeling he didn't like his family. I don't think he'd be in touch with all of them, but there may be someone in the family he'd be in contact with."

Taking my hand, she added, "Please find him. I can't avoid a sense of doom. Whoever killed my uncle and Mr. Hathaway and now wants to kill me knows Gray—Mr. Burke is looking for him, and that makes this unknown man a grave danger to him. You must save him."

"You've been attacked. Don't you want me to save *you*?" I found her attitude to be melodramatic.

"Of course I do," she snapped, "but at least I'm aware of the danger."

I didn't understand her attitude. "Don't you think Mr. Burke is intelligent enough to know the killer is still at large?"

"He doesn't know about someone redirecting the crates containing Mr. Hathaway's Egyptian statues to be picked up in London. And that must be important." Miss Munroe was adamant.

"Has he been in contact with Lord Salisbury? You told me you sent him word about the change in destination of those statues."

"I did. When I arrived in London the other day, his secretary again assured me they have not been in contact with Mr. Burke."

"But you said you and Mr. Burke already examined Mr. Hathaway's statues while on board the ship?"

"The *Minotaur.* Of course. And we didn't find any trace of the gold."

"Then why should they be important?" I didn't see any reason why these cheap statues should be a vital clue. They'd already been verified not to contain the gold.

"I don't know why they're important." She looked at me, a puzzled look written across her face. "I only know the statues are the only things that are missing. The only things someone, I suspect the murderer, has shown any interest in."

"He's also shown an interest in you," I pointed out. I made my voice brutally cold. ""Let's look at this another way. What do you have or know that makes you the target of a killer?"

She looked at me with big, pitiful eyes. "I don't know. I wish I did. I'm scared."

She had told us about something earlier that day that someone might be determined to retrieve. "You mentioned decoding a letter. A stolen letter. And you mentioned there were others."

She brushed the idea aside with one hand. "The one we decoded was the easiest. A ship's name and a cabin number. The rest were longer and we couldn't figure out the key. They're still unintelligible. They're of no use."

"May I take them? I know someone who has had some experience decoding messages." Blackford knew so many clever people that one of them must know how to decode messages. I hoped.

"Go ahead. I've had no luck. And if I no longer have them, perhaps no one will try to kill me." She gave me a wry smile as she set down her teacup.

She went up to her room, returning in a few minutes with a small packet of folded notes tied together with string. I slipped them into my handbag.

"My uncle protected these from his killer. I hope they'll tell you who that person is," Miss Munroe said.

"I hope so, too." Without leading to any more deaths. Especially since I had them now.

The coded notes and I made it back to Sir Broderick's, my home since the previous winter after Emma married and Aunt Phyllida left to nurse Lady Westover. I had faltered, trying to work all day at the bookshop and take care of my home in my off hours. Sir Broderick saw the toll it was taking on me and invited me to move into his spacious house. I agreed immediately.

I admit I spent the entire trip to Sir Broderick's looking over my shoulder so much that anyone around me should have been suspicious. While I dressed for the dinner party we were to attend that night, I hid the coded notes in my room under the letters Blackford had sent me when he'd been in America the previous winter.

The notes should be safe there for the time being.

When he came to pick me up, Blackford kept staring at my new blue gown.

"Is there something wrong with my attire?" I finally asked. Better to find out now if I was wearing a style he couldn't stand.

"No. It's rather breathtaking. You're rather breathtaking. I'm afraid I'll have to fight a duel to keep you." Then he gave me a smile that made me think of sin.

Before that moment, I hadn't noticed how hot the evening had become.

I didn't have a chance to reply since Mrs. Hardwick chose that instant to wheel Sir Broderick into the hall. They were followed by Sir Broderick's ward, Jacob. They "oohed" and "aahed" over my appearance.

They also made clear they were taking their roles as chaperones very seriously. Sir Broderick asked where we were going and what time they should expect my return. This was something he would do if we were sneaking around the East End while working on an investigation, but in a less formal tone of voice.

Blackford made the whole business farcical by answering him gravely, as if I were eighteen and we were still courting. We'd be married in less than eight days' time and I had turned thirty. I rolled my eyes and nudged him toward the door.

Instead of the Wellington coach of which he was so proud, Blackford brought his ducal carriage, which was much easier to get into while wearing an evening dress. It was also much more comfortable for the two of us to sit very close together.

As soon as we had boarded and were on our way, I said, "I have been working on the investigation. And yes, I convinced Miss Munroe to allow the Archivist Society to join in the hunt for Mr. Burke. I can't do it alone."

His dark eyes bore into mine. "You've been working on it this close to the wedding?"

"I've assured her the Archivist Society will take over when we marry. But we may need your help using your ties to the Foreign Office."

"Go on." He sounded as if I was trying his patience.

"From what I learned from Lady Westover and Aunt Phyllida, Grayson Burke may be related to the Lord Burke who recently died when his castle burned. I haven't had any luck tracing Mr. Burke so far, but help in getting in touch with the new Lord Burke would be useful. And apparently the chief of police for the king of Egypt had been in the British army with the missing man. If we could get in touch with this police chief, he might be able to tell us how to reach this Burke fellow. Or someone in the British delegation might have an address."

"Khedive."

I looked at Blackford in confusion. "I'm sorry?"

"Khedive. Not king. And his chief of police, the inspector-general, is always a former British army officer. It's thought this makes it easier to train the local police."

"Does it?" I found myself skeptical. The police hadn't made any progress in finding the gold, according to Miss Munroe.

"So they say." Blackford pulled me close and kissed me.

It was a most satisfying kiss.

"Much better," he said, nuzzling my neck before I could speak again. "I didn't think you'd ever stop talking so I could kiss you properly."

I stretched my neck to kiss him full on the lips, wrapping my arms around his shoulders. "Is that proper enough?"

"Or improper." He grinned. "What's this police chief's name?"

I stayed where I was, draped over his chest. "She only knows him as Colonel Gregory."

"I'll put in a request tomorrow for someone at the

British Residency to let us know where Colonel Gregory is and how to reach him. Also if someone has a forwarding address for a Grayson Burke. Will that satisfy you?"

"Yes, Blackford. Thank you." I gave him a hug and a kiss. "There's also the matter of deciphering the coded notes Mr. Munroe stole from Mr. Hathaway. I think the notes hold clues to the identity of the mastermind behind the theft. Since Miss Munroe's uncle was charged with finding the treasure, finding this man may tell us, and Miss Munroe, who killed her uncle."

He looked annoyed. "Anything else?"

"No, Blackford," I said in my sweetest voice.

"Georgia, when are you going to call me Gordon?"

"About the time our third child is born?"

He kissed my forehead. "Very well. Perhaps you can call me Ranleigh?"

"I try calling you Ranleigh, but I keep thinking of you as Blackford. It makes you sound more like a medieval knight. Part of the king's inner council."

He grinned. "I suppose I should be flattered."

"Oh, my passion for medieval knights is very flattering." If only he knew how risqué my dreams of knights in shining armor were. "Blackford, are you certain we can't spend the next year in the Americas or the colonies?"

He leaned his forehead against mine. "Lady Castleley again?" I could hear the chuckle in his voice.

"Yes." I'd admitted the problems I'd had with this woman to Blackford more than once. He'd been sympathetic, but he'd left me to solve my problems on my own.

"Once we're married, she won't bother you anymore. I promise." Then he showered kisses on my face and neck, making me forget my fears of Lady Castleley.

"And there's the matter of the redecorating," I blurted out.

"What?" He looked like I had started speaking in tongues.

"Lady Westover said everyone's going to expect invitations when we return from our honeymoon to see how I've redecorated Blackford House. But it isn't mine. It's yours, and you might like the way it's decorated now."

He pulled me closer and spoke into my hair. "It will be ours. The house hasn't been redecorated since my mother's time, and she died many years ago. I've always thought the style was gloomy, since it was last redone in the early days of Victoria's widowhood. Maybe that was what was expected then."

"I've never decorated a home before. First it was my parents' house, and then Phyllida saw to the flat, and now I'm at Sir Broderick's. I wouldn't know where to start."

"Start by asking Lady Westover, and Lady Phyllida, and Emma, and Mrs. Hardwick. Figure out what you like, call in the decorators, and give them their orders. Simple."

That was simple? "You don't mind?"

He laughed. "Why should I mind? Just make sure we have adequate accommodations at night." Then he tilted me backward as he nuzzled the base of my neck.

That was most satisfactory until I realized I no longer felt the carriage moving. I glanced out the window and said, "Oh, dear. We're here."

Blackford helped me repair my hairdo and neckline and then handed me out of the carriage. He escorted me up the short walk to the Robson-McLains' door. There the butler led us to the drawing room where everyone was awaiting their pairing to go into dinner.

Lord Herbert Robson-McLain came over to greet us immediately. Blackford had told me that Lord Herbert, the second son of a duke, had been a good friend during his early years in London. They still enjoyed shooting together. I'd been warned we'd travel to Lord Herbert's family seat in the Highlands for "a spot of shooting" in September. "Blackford. Miss Fenchurch. I'm so glad you could make it tonight. You must be busy so close to the wedding."

"I hope you'll be joining us on our happy day," I said. I'd already received confirmation that he and his wife would attend, but it was the only thing I could think of to say.

"Agatha and I wouldn't miss it. Ah, the Hales are here. And Agatha is signaling me that it's time to line up to go into dinner. If you'll excuse me?"

When he walked off, Blackford squeezed my hand. I headed toward the back of the line, where all of us commoners went, while Blackford headed toward the front. I glanced over to see him take the arm of Lady Agatha. As the highest-ranking male present, he was escorting the hostess into dinner.

All these dinners were similar. Blackford and I weren't seated near each other. I was congratulated on my upcoming nuptials, and then I practiced showing an interest in things I had little knowledge of. Some of my dinner companions were fascinating and some were dull. All of them were people I had rarely, if ever, met before.

After eight or ten or twelve courses, I adjourned with the other ladies to the drawing room.

I looked around, making mental notes of the things I liked, including wallpaper with floral stripes running vertically, and didn't like, such as velvety sofa cushions that grabbed the skirt of my gown and wouldn't let go. Blackford said I was to redecorate Blackford House. I might as well start listing the things I liked or didn't.

That night, unlike so many others since we announced our engagement, Blackford came up to me as soon as the men rejoined us. "Come with me," he said, bending down to murmur in my ear.

I tried to hide my surprise. Normally, Blackford acted like every other man present, polite to the point of dullness. This was a secretive command. He held out a hand and I took it to help me rise from the sofa, shoving the clingy cushion down with my other gloved hand. We walked out without either of us excusing ourselves to our hostess.

"What is it?" I whispered as we hurried down the

hallway.

Blackford, not the butler, opened a door for us, and I walked into a paneled library. Under the light of the single lamp burning in the room, a man about Blackford's age was standing by a bookcase reading a book. He turned to face us, his dark hair as straight as Blackford's, his blue eyes catching the light.

"Miss Fenchurch, may I present Lord Burke?"

CHAPTER SIX

"How do you do, my lord?" I said as I curtsied to the tall, stern-looking man. "Are you any relation to Grayson Burke, recently of Cairo?"

He gave Blackford a weak smile and in that moment I knew his identity. I instantly saw why Miss Munroe thought he was handsome. He had a strong jaw, a well-proportioned nose, and eyes that twinkled with barely disguised mirth. "You were right. She doesn't beat around the bush."

Before I could say anything, he turned and faced me. "Yes, I am Matthew Walford Grayson Burke, fifth Lord Burke of County Armagh."

"I thought the fifth Lord Burke's name was James."

"My older brother died of typhoid in South America. The family and our solicitors received word of his death a week before the fire." He had a pleasant baritone and an easy manner about him. I could see his attraction for Miss Munroe.

"There was a report of a fifth body found in the ashes."

"Two of the grooms, as well as my father, grandfather, and my father's valet who doubled as his night jailer, died in the fire."

"My sympathies, my lord, on all your losses." I glanced at Blackford and continued. "How did you learn about my connection with detection and the Archivist Society?"

"Blackford mentioned you when I met him on a case last year. He spoke very highly of you."

That explained how Miss Munroe heard my name. "There is a young lady you met in Cairo, Miss Eugenie Munroe, who's very worried for your safety."

"That's unfortunate. I don't want her to worry about me. I've left the service of the crown and plan to live very quietly." He gave me a dazzling smile, but his eyes lost their gaiety.

"She has information for you about Mr. Hathaway's belongings that she thinks is vital. She sees this discovery as pointing to a danger to you."

He glanced toward Blackford for help. Blackford, I was pleased to say, kept his face neutral and his voice silent. Then glaring at me, Burke said, "Really, Miss Fenchurch, it doesn't matter any longer. I have my duties as a peer and as a landowner. I'm sure the crown will find someone else to look into the stolen gold and the death of Mr. Munroe."

He folded his arms. "My castle is nothing but a shell, roofless and windowless. There's no point in rebuilding it, not that I'd want to. But I must build a new, grand house. I need to focus all my energies on this project and protecting my legacy."

I wondered if Miss Munroe knew she'd given her

heart to a selfish prig. "The least you could do is speak to Miss Munroe. Assure her of your safety and tell her what you know about this continuing investigation."

"I can't do that."

"Why not? What aren't you telling me?"

The two men exchanged looks. I suspected I would be lied to.

"I had dreamed for years of studying medicine. I hoped for a reward for successfully completing an investigation to finance my studies. Now, I have other duties that take precedent. Responsibilities to my relatives and an entire village because of the fire. However, I'm afraid Miss Munroe would find me a failure for not pursuing my dreams."

"You don't know that—"

He held up a hand. "She was most insistent that, after working for years with the hope of attending medical school, I should use the reward for recovering the gold to finance my education. However, I have no time to spend chasing after the Egyptian gold, and so I am no danger to anyone."

"Reward?" Blackford and I said in unison. Miss Munroe hadn't mentioned a reward.

"Ten percent of the value of the gold for returning it to the British government. A fortune. While I could still use the money, I won't have the time to pursue gold or medical studies."

"Why not explain your situation to Miss Munroe and let her make up her own mind? You've already decided your course. There's nothing her disapproval can do to change that." I didn't add that it would only be good manners.

"I have no desire to see her again or to explain myself. Now if you'll excuse me?" With a nod to Blackford, he walked around me and out the door.

I turned to Blackford. "What is he hiding?"

Blackford stared at the empty doorway. "I understand about needing to get your feet under you when you take on a title and estates, particularly when you haven't been trained for it or expected it. And losing so many family members in such a short period of time must be difficult. But yes, Georgia, that doesn't explain avoiding a short conversation with a young woman of your acquaintance. Especially one who has been counting on your help in solving the murder of her uncle."

"What should I do?" I knew what I wanted to do.

"Let me make some inquiries tomorrow. We'll discuss it tomorrow night."

"And in the meantime..." I marched back toward the drawing room. Blackford followed, grumbling disapproval.

When we reached him, Lord Burke was saying his good-byes to our hostess. I waited until he finished and had started toward the door. "My lord, I have another question for you."

"I'm sorry. I'm afraid I have another—" Burke looked from me to Blackford, who was now blocking his path. He gave a polite, quiet snort. "Very well."

We stepped to the side of the hallway. "You were

certain Mr. Hathaway was behind the theft, and then he was murdered. Who do you think his accomplice was?"

He stared at me. "You believe the accomplice killed him and kept the gold for himself?"

"Yes."

Burke considered this for a minute. "Hathaway wasn't a sociable man. His accomplice was probably someone who could help him carry out this audacious theft. That would be either Colonel Gregory, the inspector-general of the Egyptian police, or Lord Barber, the British controller-general of the Egyptian treasury. There is also the secretary to the British mission who was assigned the job of Mr. Hathaway's vice chair of the tax code committee, Sir Antony Derwaller. In addition, there is Lord Barber's second-in-command, Lord Cecil Isle, a lazy young aristocrat, and Lord Cromer's private secretary, Mr. Damien Reed. Reed was our assistant in all things practical. Pay records, shipping, obtaining things not easily obtained. But Reed left Egypt as soon as the Queen's Birthday celebrations were over, since he had been named the secretary of the Royal Antiquities Society here in London."

"Anyone else?"

Burke lowered his voice. "Mustafa Fahir, the Egyptian finance minister, but I can't see him aiding the British, and Lord Cromer, head of the British Residency, although he's a nonstarter like Fahir."

"Why?" I'd seen the least likely person be guilty before.

"They already have power, they don't need the

money, and the risk for either man would be far greater than the reward."

"Who would your money be on?" Blackford asked him.

"Gregory, but that's because I don't like him."

Before Burke could say another word, I said, "Did you know an attempt has been made on Miss Munroe's life here in London?"

His head snapped around to stare into my face. After an instant, he blinked and said, "No. How would I have known? Is she all right?"

"For the moment."

I could see his exhale release the stiffness in his shoulders. "Now, may I go? I really do have another appointment."

"One more thing. What was Mr. Hathaway's Christian name?"

"Andrew."

Blackford stepped out of his way and with a curt nod, Burke fled with long strides, grabbing his hat, gloves, and umbrella from the butler on the way.

* * *

I wasn't about to wait until Blackford tracked down all the men Burke had listed through the Foreign Office. I'd been an Archivist Society member long before I met him, and I refused to give up my brain and my talent for marriage, even a marriage I'd long desired.

Fortunately, Blackford knew that. Unfortunately, he didn't yet realize how often this would put us at odds.

I understood how much of a problem this could

become, and it worried me.

In the morning, I packed trunks full of my belongings that would go to Blackford House to await our return from the honeymoon. I must confess they were heavy, as most of my belongings from before our engagement were books. I felt sorry for the removal men who had to carry the trunks down to their wagon for transport.

Then I went to Fenchurch's Books to look up the Royal Antiquities Society and their secretary, Damien Reed. As soon as I walked in, the smell of old paper and older bindings in the shop filled my nose. I breathed deeply with the sensation of coming home.

"How are you, Georgia? Are you ready for the wedding?" Frances Atterby said, dispelling my peaceful mood.

"Not quite. I came in to look up something."

She watched over my shoulder as I read up on the Royal Antiquities Society. They had an address near the British Museum. "What do you need them for? Valuating something?"

I kept reading. "No. It's the new secretary I need to see. Damien Reed. He was in Cairo when a large shipment of gold was stolen."

"You don't have time for a case now. You're getting married." Frances sounded like she was speaking to a misbehaving grandchild.

"Don't worry. The wedding will be on time, and if this isn't finished, the Archivist Society will carry on the investigation." As I shut the volume, I felt something brush against my ankles.

Frances bent over and picked up Dickens. "I think he misses having you around, Georgia."

"Not as much as I miss seeing him daily. Miss all of you." I moved to scratch him between the ears, and he swiped at my bare hand. He connected with his claws out.

I jumped back and cried out, only to see Dickens' eyes close in bliss as Frances cuddled him.

"That I didn't miss."

"Perhaps he feels abandoned. Animals can take strange fancies." She scratched behind his ears and he purred.

"No. I'm his favorite scratching post. Some things don't change."

Pulling on my gloves to protect my throbbing fingers, I took an omnibus to the Royal Antiquities Society. I was shown into Mr. Reed's office, a large, dusty space on the top floor of the large, musty building. Glass-fronted cabinets lining the walls contained bits of friezes and pottery that looked as if they might disintegrate into the sands of time. The man behind the desk stood to greet me, and I saw he was tall and slender and dressed in a well-tailored dark suit.

He fit the general shape of Miss Munroe's attacker.

I curtsied and said, "Mr. Reed?"

"Yes, Miss—Fenchurch?" he said, looking at my calling card. "How can I help you?"

"I understand you were in Cairo until recently. You must have met Miss Eugenie Munroe and her uncle, Mr.

Bradley Munroe."

"Yes. Nice people. Very nice people. Munroe was a diligent colleague. You do know Mr. Munroe was murdered?" he added with a frown.

"And Miss Munroe was attacked here in London."

He looked concerned. "Is she all right?"

"Yes. What can you tell me about the theft?"

He gestured and I took a seat. "I was working in the British Residency when someone came in and told us about the gold payment disappearing. By that evening, there were several stories, but the main facts seemed to be that the handoff seemed normal, but when the team from the Caisse de la Dette Publique opened the casket, it was full of iron nails, not gold coins."

"Who could have done that?" I tried to sound amazed.

"The Egyptians, obviously. They like getting European money, but they don't like paying their debts."

That was probably true of everyone. "There are thoughts that an Englishman planned it."

"Blaming the English is practically a sport down there." He started to rise, pulling down his frayed cuffs. "Since I can't help you, would you like a tour of our museum? It's small, but quite good."

"In a moment." I waved him back into his chair. "Did you travel with your family to Cairo?"

"I'm not married, Miss Fenchurch."

"So there's no wife who would have been a friend to Miss Munroe." I gave a sigh as if this blocked what I wanted to ask him. "Were the Munroes sociable people?"

He looked confused by my question. "I suppose."

"How did you find the social life of those employed in the Residency?"

"The younger single men played a great deal of cards. The families entertained each other."

"I'm sure there weren't many single English women in Cairo."

He chuckled. "Now there you'd be wrong. A lot of English women came out in the winter to escape the snow and see the antiquities. But except for dances, we never saw them. They tended to be from the titled families and hung around with their own kind. They had no time for a mere private secretary, and the tasks were more in line with a head clerk position."

I widened my eyes. "Have you come back to England with hopes of starting your own family?"

He gave me a hard stare. "What brings you to ask me these strange questions, Miss Fenchurch?"

I gave him the first story I could think of. I couldn't ask him why he came back to London and whether he aided in the theft. "Miss Munroe has mentioned you favorably on more than one occasion. As her friend, I wanted to discover your—plans."

He laughed. Poor Miss Munroe, if she'd ever had any thoughts about this man. "She's a lovely young lady, with emphasis on the young. I would like in due course to start my own family, but I'm in no hurry, and I'd choose a woman closer to my own age."

I forced a smile on my face. "No wonder you were in

such a hurry to leave Cairo."

He looked offended. "I wasn't in a hurry. It was the requirement of my new post here at the Royal Antiquities Society that I be at my desk by the first of June. I feel myself quite lucky to obtain this prestigious position."

"Undoubtedly."

"And I had Lord Cromer's approval to leave a few days early."

"Of course."

"Now, would you like a tour?"

"I'd love one." I could use the time to ask the questions I suspected he had tried to deflect.

We looked over the displays in the cases on that floor before we went to the main floor. He pointed out the important features of ancient statues and friezes, which were too large to fit into cabinets. There were a few people looking at the exhibits, singly and in small groups, as we walked around. "Did you have much to do with Sir Antony Derwaller? I believe he's interested in antiquities."

"Yes, he is. He and I and Colonel Gregory and some others in the European community used to go out on nice weekends and do a little excavating. We did so for three or four years. Lord Barber used to meet us at the end of the trip to see what we had found."

"Why not go with you?"

"He doesn't have the stamina. Too many good meals."

"Did you make any good finds?"

That chuckle again. I was growing suspicious of his laughter. "Some broken pottery. Some beads. Nothing of any scientific or monetary value."

"Monetary value?" Another possibility to investigate.

"Some of the items coming out of the tombs, gold and gems, have a monetary value as well as scientific value. Some museums and collectors will pay a great deal for the best artifacts coming out of the digs."

He hurried on to show me a few more exhibits before he asked, "Why do you think Miss Munroe was attacked? Surely it was street thugs."

"I doubt it. She had Mr. Hathaway's coded letters."

"Had?" His voice nearly squeaked.

"Yes. They have since been handed off to someone to break the code." Well, I hadn't done it yet, but I didn't want to be attacked if someone thought I still had them. "It must be lonesome being in London, away from all your friends in Cairo, after you'd spent weekends for three or four years together in the desert."

"Oh, no. I've seen practically everyone I knew in Cairo in just the last week."

"Even Colonel Gregory?" No one seemed to have seen him.

"We ran into each other and had a drink at my club three days ago."

"And Lord Barber? Sir Antony Derwaller? Lord Cecil Isle? Everyone?"

"Yes." He chuckled. "These things do happen, seeing everyone here in London that I saw every day in Cairo.

As Cromer's private secretary and head clerk, I was often called on to straighten out paperwork and shipments and pay records. If anyone needs help, they still come to me. Old habits die hard."

"Why did Lord Barber come to see you?"

"Oh, a shipment—"

The explosion deafened me. I shut my eyes and hunched my shoulders before I peeked out through my eyelashes. Mr. Reed had a surprised look on his face as he glanced down at the dark stain soaking his suit jacket. He set his hand on the spot before he lifted it and looked in wonder at the red dampening his fingers. Then he collapsed.

I screamed. As I knelt to see if I could help Mr. Reed, a second explosion tore at my ears. Chips of marble from the statue behind me sprayed down on us.

There was no sign of breath or pulse. Whoever had wanted Mr. Reed dead had good aim.

As people fled in panic toward the lobby, screaming and sobbing, I heard the sound of a single pair of footsteps running away in the opposite direction and then the sound of an outside door opening. I rose and rushed to the door where daylight spilled into the room, but when I looked outside, all I saw was an empty alley.

The shooter was gone.

CHAPTER SEVEN

I sat in the guard's chair as the police photographed Damien Reed's body and searched the main floor of the building. Finally, Inspector Grantham came over and said, "You were with the deceased when he was shot? Were you questioning him for the Archivist Society?"

I raised my eyebrows at him. He was being quite brusque. "Good morning, Inspector." Edward Grantham was Lady Westover's grandson. We'd been involved in the same investigations for years and had a great deal of respect for each other.

He nodded. "Good morning, Miss Fenchurch. Now, were you here as part of an Archivist Society inquiry?"

"Yes. Mr. Reed had only been in London a month. Before that, he was in Cairo working for the British government when there was a huge theft of gold from the Egyptian government. He worked with people who may have been involved."

"Did you see the shooter?"

"No. By the time I got off the floor and reached the open door leading outside, there was no one in the alley. But I'm sure it was someone he knew in Cairo."

His voice softened. "I'll have someone get you a cab,

Georgia. Can't have you walking the streets covered in blood."

I looked down to realize I had Reed's blood on my skirt.

I rode home in a hansom cab. I didn't care about the cost. I was shaking and I needed the safety of Sir Broderick's drawing room, and a hot cup of tea, and a new skirt, before the trembling would stop.

Mrs. Hardwick took one look at me and had tea brought before I asked for it. She added plenty of sugar in mine and sent me upstairs to change before she allowed Sir Broderick to begin his questioning. "Did you see anything of the shooter?"

"There were several other people looking at the exhibits. Any one of them could have been the shooter, and I didn't pay attention to any of them. And when I ran to the door I thought the shooter had escaped through, there was no one in the alley."

"What were you talking about before the shots were fired?"

"He said he'd seen everyone from the British Residency here in London because he had taken care of their paperwork for shipping things and straightening out pay records. I'd just asked him why Lord Barber had come to see him when he was shot."

"Perhaps he knew how the gold traveled to England," Sir Broderick said, staring deep into his teacup.

"And now that it was here, Mr. Reed was no longer needed." I shivered despite the warmth of the summer day.

"You need to be careful, Georgia. If these killings have all been by the same person, he's already killed two in England and who knows how many in Cairo."

I still had an hour before I had to make afternoon calls with Lady Westover and Aunt Phyllida. "I need to warn Miss Munroe to be careful."

"You shouldn't be going anywhere. Not without an escort."

"But—"

"I can just hear Blackford now if we let anything happen to you."

"Please don't tell Blackford."

"Georgia."

"I'll tell him myself tonight. I promise." If I had to.

Promising to pay heed to Sir Broderick's insistence that I be careful, I hurried to Queen Square. When I reached the house where she was staying, I met Eugenie Munroe opening the front door as I was about to ring the bell. "Miss Fenchurch." She looked as surprised as I felt. "I was on my way out."

"I need to talk to you."

"Walk with me, then. I'm on my way to a meeting, and you might find it interesting."

"Does this meeting have anything to do with your uncle or the stolen gold?" I'd certainly find that interesting.

"No, although I think he'd approve."

"Did your uncle have anything to do with Mr. Reed?"

"Nothing more than the usual. If you needed

something while in Cairo, or you needed to send something home, you spoke to Mr. Reed. He arranged to send home my uncle's effects for me."

"Mr. Reed is dead."

She came to a sudden stop on the pavement, forcing a man to step around us. "The poor man just arrived in London. What happened?"

"He was shot while at work at the Royal Antiquities Society."

"Do they know who—?"

I shook my head. "No. Did your uncle suspect Mr. Reed of involvement in the theft?"

She glanced at me as she resumed walking. "No, but I did."

"Why?"

"It was the way he made things appear and disappear outside of normal procedures. Paperwork that carried seals for special diplomatic handling that shouldn't have. At least I suspected some of the shipments shouldn't have been marked private."

Another line of inquiry. "What do you mean?"

"There are a lot of valuable items coming out of the tombs. In some cases, more than one person is claiming them. And Cairo is at a crossroads. Artifacts, jewelry, artwork from Africa and Asia arrive in the markets and are sold. Some of this is stolen elsewhere and sold there at low prices. If anyone started asking questions, a lot of Englishmen in Cairo might be embarrassed." She raised her eyebrows.

"He must have made a lot of friends that way, if he

could ship things back to England without anyone being the wiser."

"Oh, yes," she said with a grim expression, "everyone loved Mr. Reed. You should ask Lord Barber."

"Why?"

"Lady Barber found a little onyx figurine of Bastet. I'm not sure what the problem was, but she couldn't send it home. Or perhaps it would have cost too much to send it back to London. Anyway, Lord Barber spoke to Mr. Reed and the next thing anyone knew, Lady Barber was thrilled that the little onyx cat had arrived at their London home." She looked at me with raised eyebrows. "Everyone loved Mr. Reed."

"It sounds like you didn't." And here I'd told the man she had developed feelings for him. Had he realized how unlikely my story was?

She dismissed him with a shrug. "I didn't dislike him. I just didn't trust him. Oh, here we are."

"Here" was an impressive house north of Oxford Street. Two young women walked into the house as we approached, each carrying a large bundle.

When we reached the door, Eugenie rang the bell, and when the door opened, a middle-aged woman greeted her. "Miss Munroe, I'm so glad you decided to return. And I see you've brought a friend."

"Yes. Mrs. Halford, this is Miss Fenchurch."

"Welcome, Miss Fenchurch. We'll set you both to stuffing envelopes in the drawing room, shall we?"

She led the way and I lingered behind Eugenie, wondering what I had been invited into. Then I saw the stacks of flyers I would be folding and putting into envelopes. The lettering was bold and well printed on plain paper. The images were a bit smudged, cheapening the effect of the suffragist message.

Mrs. Halford said, "Have a seat and we'll see how many of these we can do before the meeting."

"Meeting?" I asked.

"Are you a suffragist, Miss Fenchurch?"

"I'm in favor of votes for women."

"Good, because we're a local chapter of the NUWSS, the National Union of Women's Suffrage Societies." She introduced me to a half-dozen women busily folding flyers and sliding them into envelopes. "Tell us a little about yourself," she added while I sat down and took off my gloves.

"I own Fenchurch's Books just off Charing Cross Road."

"A businesswoman. How wonderful," one of the women said. "Are you married?"

"No, I'm single."

"But she's engaged," Eugenie Munroe said, adding after a moment's pause, "and she's a part of the Archivist Society."

This provoked some gasps. I could have choked Miss Munroe. I hated being valued for my membership in the Archivist Society. All the members tried to be reticent about our part in that organization. It made carrying out our investigations easier.

"We've heard of the society and the good work it does in the press," Mrs. Halford said. "Is it satisfying work? It's certainly not an ordinary woman's role."

"Yes, it is satisfying, but we try not to advertise our participation in the society." My cheeks were heated by this time.

"You must be glad of the Married Women's Property Act, seeing as you have property and are getting married," an older woman said.

"I am, but that's been the law my entire adult life."

"You don't know how lucky you are," the woman replied, a bitter tone in her voice.

I wondered what her story was. "Now that women can vote in local elections on an equal footing with men, I would think the day will soon be here when we can vote in national elections, too," I said with confidence.

"Gaining the vote in local elections was the product of years and years of work. We're committed to many more years of labor to gain full suffrage," Mrs. Halford said.

I continued stuffing envelopes, but I begged off when it came time for the meeting, pleading a prior engagement. Then I told Eugenie, "Thank you for bringing me today. I'll be in touch soon."

"Please," she said quietly, glancing around to make sure no one could overhear, "next time don't come to tell me someone else was murdered."

"I wanted to warn you to be careful." I decided she deserved to know Burke's secret. I was willing to tell her since Burke wasn't, and it didn't seem fair. "I do have some other news for you. It appears Mr. Burke has inherited the title from his grandfather. His grandfather, his father, and his older brother have all died."

"Oh." She looked shocked. "That's good news for Mr. Burke, but he must be upset about the loss of his entire family. At least you're not telling me Mr. Burke was murdered like poor Mr. Reed."

She sounded indifferent to the threat the theft and murders could mean to her. "You need to be careful," I warned her. "With Mr. Hathaway and now Mr. Reed killed, there may be another attack on you soon."

She looked up, straightened her shoulders, and with a sniff said, "I'm certain I'll be perfectly safe. I'm an unimportant person."

Nothing like a client who didn't take advice. Then I thought of what Sir Broderick would say if he heard me speak about someone else not taking advice. With a guilty itch at the back of my neck, I said, "I wanted to keep you informed of what I've learned."

"Do you know where Mr. Burke—Lord Burke is?"

She seemed determined to get in touch with him. I doubted it was only because of the investigation. "I've made inquiries."

"When you've learned Grayson Burke's address, I hope you'll come to me immediately so I can speak to him and put my mind at rest."

"You still fear for his safety here in London due to what happened in Egypt? He hasn't been attacked. You have. Shouldn't you worry for your own life?" I couldn't help but find her focus troublesome. She should be frightened for herself.

"I'm aware I should take care of my safety. Mr.

Burke doesn't know the danger that followed us from Cairo."

Since I wouldn't learn anything else from her, I walked back to Sir Broderick's to dress for afternoon calls. I decided the measure of how much my life had changed was that I no longer found it odd to dress for, or make, afternoon calls, even after seeing someone I was questioning shot dead in front of me.

When I came downstairs, I discovered I wouldn't be leaving for Lady Westover's quite as soon as I'd planned. Inspector Grantham of Scotland Yard was waiting for me in the drawing room. Sir Broderick looked up when Humphries opened the door for me and said, "At last. The inspector has some questions for you."

"Have you filled him in on the theft of the Egyptian gold and our investigation into Bradley Munroe's death?" I asked.

"I have, and I just finished telling him about the death of Andrew Hathaway, everyone's first choice for thief."

"Quite an investigation for the Archivist Society to take on. Theft and murder more than a thousand miles from London. And now you were the closest to a shooting victim," the inspector remarked.

The thought of it chilled me, but I kept up a calm front. "I was speaking to Damien Reed because he was chief clerk at the British Residency and private secretary to Lord Cromer. He was the man to see if you needed to ship anything between Egypt and England or help to straighten out a pay record. I've been told he could get anything transported, and sometimes used unorthodox means to do it."

"Such as this stolen gold?" the inspector asked.

"He'd have been the best person to arrange moving it to England." What Miss Munroe said had convinced me.

"And once he was no longer needed—" Sir Broderick broke in.

"Just like Mr. Hathaway," I added.

Grantham nodded. "So you believe there were at least three people involved in the theft, and the unknown person is killing off his accomplices so he doesn't have to share the wealth."

"Exactly."

"We've been looking at his position at the Royal Antiquities Society and his life in London to explain his death," the inspector said, shaking his head. "It's left us with nothing. Now I see why. Could the shooter have been anyone from the British Residency?"

"Of course he could, but I didn't see the shooter. I was faced away from him. He shot past me to hit Reed."

Sir Broderick jerked upright in his wheeled chair. His expression told me how much he disliked this detail.

"You were lucky." Grantham's expression was grim.

"Or he's a good shot. You might want to find out if anyone now in London, formerly of Cairo, is proficient with a pistol," I suggested. I refused to be forced out of this investigation by others' fears for me.

"It couldn't have been a rifle shot from outside?"

"The alley door wasn't opened until after the

shooting was finished." I pictured myself running to the now-open door. "I don't know how he disappeared so fast. He must be speedy."

The inspector told me to greet his grandmother for him and left to continue his investigation into Reed's death. I gave Sir Broderick a cheerful smile and headed for Mayfair.

When I arrived at Lady Westover's house, I was shown into the drawing room where she waited. "We need to have a serious talk, Georgia."

My heart tipped over. After Mr. Reed's death, my first thought was she or Aunt Phyllida was ill. "What's wrong?"

"You'll be leaving on your honeymoon in a few days and you still don't have a lady's maid."

Relief slid out of me in a whoosh of breath. A subject that wasn't full of carnage and funerals.

Lady Westover didn't appear to notice. "Not only will you make life more difficult for your traveling party, but you will diminish the duke's standing among his peers."

"You're joking." My lack of a lady's maid would hurt Blackford's reputation?

"I am not. You have to look at this from the point of view of his class. A duchess without a lady's maid at best shows poverty and at worst is a scandal."

"Then we need to find one that I am willing to hire. I do have experience in hiring staff."

"You do, my dear. However—"

I shook my head at Lady Westover. "No. I've read

the letters of recommendation of at least a dozen lady's maids I wouldn't hire. They all sounded like thieves or troublemakers. And I've interviewed three women on your recommendation. They may sound respectable and hardworking, but they are all domineering. I'm going to have a terrible time learning to give orders to servants. I don't want to deal with servants who want to give orders to me."

"Anyone applying for this position is going to look you up and know you are a middle-class bookshop owner who is about to rise to the top of the peerage. They know you're going to need help. And so do I." She set her cup and saucer on the tea tray. "We've found another candidate."

I decided to try logic. "What is different about this woman from the ones you wanted me to interview before?"

Lady Westover pressed her lips together and looked away.

I didn't want to hurt her feelings. She'd been too helpful to me and to the Archivist Society for too long. And I thanked heaven every day that she'd introduced me to Blackford. "I know you're trying to help and you have my best interests at heart, but the women you've suggested before were all wrong for me. Not for the job. For me."

"For pity's sake, Amelia, tell her about this one," Aunt Phyllida said as she entered the room. "If you don't, I will."

"She needs to find a lady's maid. And I'm trying not

to prejudice her against this one." Lady Westover's nose rose a fraction more into the air.

For once, the candidate sounded promising, if only because I thought the possibilities couldn't get any worse. I glanced at Aunt Phyllida.

"The truth is, this one has never been a lady's maid. Not really. She was a housemaid in the Duke of Duleign's household and dressed the daughter of the family. When the girl got married, she chose a more experienced lady's maid."

"You might as well tell her the rest of it," Lady Westover said, glaring at Phyllida.

This was starting to get interesting. Aunt Phyllida was putting the girl forward while Lady Westover was against the idea. They normally agreed on everything.

"She's a fast learner," Phyllida said in a timid tone.

"I'm sure all of the women I've interviewed are fast learners."

"Not at safecracking," Lady Westover said, disapproval ringing from every syllable.

"Really?" Now I was intrigued.

"You're not interviewing her for a part in the Archivist Society. This is the woman who needs to help you dress and do your hairstyle and repair tears and pack for trips." Lady Westover shook her head. "Georgia, I'm sure the girl deserves a chance. But if neither of you know what you are doing, you are the one who will suffer the brunt of society's disapproval."

"I disagree," Aunt Phyllida said. "The duchess's lady's maid is Bunker, and there is no one better. I wrote her without telling either of you to get her opinion on Lucy. She said she taught her over the course of a year and a half while the girl took care of the duchess's only daughter."

"Then why didn't the daughter take her with her?" There had to be more to that story.

"Lucy is lively. The daughter wanted someone more—seemly."

"She would have to be lively to learn how to break into a safe." Lady Westover sounded completely fed up.

"I'll interview her." If nothing else, the experience would be diverting.

"Oh, good. Would now be all right?"

I stared at Aunt Phyllida. "Now?" I felt cornered.

"Now?" Lady Westover sounded outraged.

"Today is her afternoon off. She's Callow's cousin."

"Callow?"

"My maid," Lady Westover said. "At least she comes from a good family."

I knew Lady Westover's maid was sensible and meticulous, even if I had forgotten her name. She could also be described as lively. Or perhaps outspoken.

"I guess you'd better tell her to come up. If she can drag herself away from Callow."

Lady Phyllida walked over and rang the bell.

The footman who responded sent Lucy up immediately. She knocked and then walked in, a girl of twenty or so with light brown hair and eyes. She gave the room a curtsy and then took a step or two forward so the footman could shut the door.

"You sent for me, milady?" she asked Lady Phyllida.

"Yes, this is Miss Fenchurch, soon to be the Duchess of Blackford, who is in need of a lady's maid."

She looked down. "Yes, ma'am."

"Tell me about the safecracking."

Her gaze flew to my face. "You know about that?"

"No, I don't, but apparently, Lady Westover and Lady Phyllida do. So, please, tell me all about it."

"Well, miss, I have very good hearing. The butler and the first footman had a disagreement over just how good my hearing is. The butler knows the combination to the silver safe, but the footman doesn't. They decided to have a wager on whether I could open the safe by using my hearing."

I glanced at Lady Westover. Even she sounded fascinated by this explanation.

"The footman showed me how to listen to the lock tumblers using a water glass to increase the sound," Lucy told us. "You put the glass against the front of—"

"I know how it's done. Go on, please."

"When I tried it, I had the butler and the first footman watching me at the beginning. Then word got out around the house and several other servants came by to see if I could do it. It took a while, I suppose, because when I finished, I discovered I was being watched by the duke's heir, who's the Earl of Wallace, and a friend of his."

She blushed. "They thought it was great fun that I succeeded, but the duchess and her daughter, Lady Arabella, were unhappy with me wasting my time that way."

"Now that we know you have this gift, I hope you wouldn't put it to use unless the duke or I ask you to."

"Oh, no, milady—miss. I wouldn't have done it before, except it seemed harmless."

I raised my eyebrows. "And seemed like a lark."

"Yes, miss." She sounded more subdued, as if she realized this interview wasn't going well.

Actually, I was getting her measure and was impressed. Safecracking wasn't easy.

I'd tried to learn from a member of the Archivist Society and never managed to open any but the simplest locks. As a soon-to-be duchess, I couldn't admit I'd attempted this. Lady Castleley might find out.

We went through the normal skills needed for a lady's maid. She had the foresight to bring along a sample of her stitch work. Both Lady Westover and Lady Phyllida had seen Lady Arabella at one or two occasions and were impressed with her hairstyle and how immaculate her gown was. I hadn't thought much of Lady Arabella and hadn't noticed how she was dressed.

All I'd noticed was the hatred simmering in her eyes whenever she looked at me.

Questions still lingered in my mind. "Why didn't Lady Arabella take you along when she was married?"

"She wanted someone older, with more experience."

"Was she unhappy with how you had served her?"

Her eyes widened. "Oh, no, miss. I always tried my very best and she seemed satisfied with my work.

Bunker supervised me on Her Grace's orders and they were both satisfied. Lady Arabella said I was just too young and lively for someone in her new position."

"Who did she marry?" Aunt Phyllida asked.

"Walter Isle, Viscount Tidminster."

"Isle?" I asked. Things were definitely looking up.

"It's the family name of the Marquess of Lasherham." Lady Westover sounded as if I were a particularly slow student. When it came to aristocratic families, I suppose I was.

"Is Walter Isle any relation to Lord Cecil Isle?" I asked.

Both ladies looked amazed. It was the first time I'd shown any interest in all these tangled relationships.

"Cecil is his younger brother," Lucy said. She looked uncomfortable as she tugged on her sleeves.

"Lucy, why does the mention of Lord Cecil Isle make you uneasy?"

"Oh, miss, I really don't want to say."

"Why? If he tried anything you didn't welcome—?"

"Oh, no, miss. That's not the problem. I've never met him."

Now she was starting to sound silly. "Then what is the problem?"

"It's not my secret to tell."

"Something Lady Arabella said in front of you?" Aunt Phyllida guessed. Her expression told me to listen carefully, as she could be surprisingly insightful.

"Yes, milady."

"Was he forward with her?" Lady Westover

demanded, rather than asked.

"Oh, no, milady. It was just a bit of flirting, I'm sure."

The girl was definitely wary of answering us. She looked like she wanted to run out of the room. Her need for a new position was the only thing keeping her with us.

And that was what gave me the clue. "This secret is why Lady Arabella didn't employ you after she married."

Lucy lowered her head and nodded.

I glanced over to see both ladies were looking at me. "Your discretion is to your credit, and I want to hire you as my lady's maid, but I'm worried about what this secret is that you won't reveal."

She stayed resolutely mute.

Drat it. Lucy was the first applicant for the position of lady's maid that I would consider hiring, even if time was running out. And something told me I needed to know what she was hiding. "If Lady Arabella wouldn't hire you because of this secret, why should I? Did you promise never to repeat what she said?"

When she stayed silent, Phyllida said in a kindly voice, "You need to answer her. It's important."

Lucy looked at her, and Phyllida nodded.

"I wasn't asked to promise." Lucy looked defiantly into my eyes. "I don't want to say because it's something she and her husband's brother planned to do after the wedding. Something you couldn't possibly do because the Duke of Blackford doesn't have any brothers."

CHAPTER EIGHT

My eyes widened at Lucy's implication. Lady Westover's brows rose. Aunt Phyllida shook her head and gave a tiny groan.

Into the silence, Lady Westover said, "Well, it's one way to make sure the line continues. If one brother fails, the other brother may succeed." I thought her attitude was—what? Pragmatic? Perhaps more than a little too understanding for my taste.

"How do you know they plan this?" I asked.

"She told me. I gasped, and she read on my face what I thought of her idea. I'm a good Christian. The Bible tells us that's wrong."

"And why do you know the Duke of Blackford doesn't have any brothers?" This girl knew far too much about the duke.

"Before your engagement was announced, Lady Arabella considered the Duke of Blackford the best catch of the season. She set her cap for him, and she would prattle off all the things she learned about him. After your engagement was announced, she accepted Lord Tidminster and they married almost immediately by special license. But before they did and she left, she would repeat everything she heard about you."

Oh, dear. "And what do you think of me from what you learned?"

"When she mentioned your shop, I went on my next day off to see it. It's well run. Your employees seem happy. You're a successful businesswoman, and I think the duke must be very proud of you, him being a success in business, too."

I gave her a smile. "Lucy, can you start on the morning of the second?"

Her eyes and mouth rounded. "Yes, miss. Thank you. Thank you very much." Then she looked down and bit her lip.

"Something is bothering you."

"Well, not exactly bothering me, but it was something else Lady Arabella said. Something she heard. Someone told her you're an investigator. You chase purse snatchers and baby snatchers and find out if the servants stole the jewelry their mistress lost."

I looked at Lady Westover and Lady Phyllida. "You might as well be honest with the girl. She's been honest with you," Lady Westover said in a businesslike tone. Phyllida nodded her head.

"I'm a member of the Archivist Society. We're a group of ordinary citizens who have suffered losses from crimes that Scotland Yard couldn't solve. Including murders. Especially murders. We've banded together to help others gain justice for their loved ones after Scotland Yard has given up on finding the criminal," I told her. "And I hope to continue in some fashion once

I'm married."

"In secret, you mean?" Her voice dropped to almost a whisper.

"Yes, I'd like to keep my role secret. So please be discreet about this."

"Oh, yes, miss. I think that is exciting. I'll be proud to keep your secret." Her eyes were even wider than before.

As I wrote down Sir Broderick's address, I said, "We might as well start by having you get me ready for my wedding. First thing on the second. And if you need to see Blackford House, where we'll live after the honeymoon, I'll write you a note of introduction to the housekeeper. For the honeymoon, I'll be taking most of my wardrobe with me from Sir Broderick's house. We'll be traveling for six weeks and then going to Blackford Castle for a week or two before returning to London."

She nodded. It was the normal pattern for aristocratic honeymoons. Only the bride would be out of the ordinary.

Once the interview was finished, Lucy went back downstairs to tell her good news to her cousin. Lady Westover, Aunt Phyllida, and I made two social calls. Both ladies we called on were elderly and all I learned was I never wanted to have rheumatism, gout, or pneumonia.

* * *

Blackford and I were to attend a ball that night, after Sir Broderick questioned us both in a ceremonial manner and then indicated he found the ball acceptable for me to attend.

I muttered something to the effect that I wasn't his ward. Women in their thirties did not have guardians. He ignored me. Blackford and Mrs. Hardwick had trouble hiding their smiles.

Once in the ducal coach, Blackford told me, "I made some inquiries for you about Lord Burke, Colonel Gregory, and the situation with the Egyptian gold. On the surface, everything appears to be as we were told."

"On the surface?" How much had we heard was a lie?

"The gold was stolen during the spring transfer. That was on the first of May. No sign of it was found despite a widespread treasure hunt across the city. Then on 24 May, the Queen's Birthday was celebrated with parades and fireworks and a ball at the Residency. The next day, Europeans began to desert Cairo in large numbers for the summer season."

I nodded. I'd been told all this.

"There were several British citizens who, due to their positions, were expected to stay until the first of July or later. These included Mr. Hathaway, chair of the committee to reform Egyptian tax codes, who had a report to finish. There was also Colonel Gregory, inspector-general of the Egyptian police force, Lord Barber, British controller-general to the Egyptian treasury, Sir Antony Derwaller, first secretary to the British Residency—well, the list goes on and on. To a man, everyone who had anything to do with treasury or finance or law enforcement raced back to England."

"Trying to save their positions?"

"That or escaping blame by the Egyptians or going into hiding with a great deal of stolen gold."

I felt my eyes widen. "Lord Burke could be hiding with the stolen gold and trying to avoid Miss Munroe."

Blackford was grim. "When you're talking about that much money, there usually is no desire to share."

"Do they know where any of these officials went, besides Lord Burke?"

"We know Hathaway was murdered. Strangled within minutes of leaving the ship in Southampton. The police report is useless. A few of the assistants came back and turned in their notice to the Foreign Office, expressing a wish never to see any place hot or foreign again. There are always some who can't stand the years of discomfort to earn advancement. Gregory and Barber, who had both earned their high positions and were both closely involved in the transfer, have disappeared."

"Don't their families know where they are?"

"Gregory is single and his family said they only hear from him at Christmas, if then. Lord and Lady Barber were scheduled to take the waters at Bad Brueckenau, but he never showed up. She took the waters with friends for a few weeks and recently returned to London. Attempts to reach him have failed."

A shocking thought sprang full blown in my mind. "I hope he hasn't met the same fate as Mr. Hathaway or Mr. Munroe."

"No more bodies have been found." Blackford was always practical. "At least not English ones. You can never be certain about the local population's fate when England's interests don't coincide with theirs."

I glared at Blackford. "Our empire builders sound like terrible people."

"A lot of those we send out to the colonies are not nice people. They wouldn't get anything done if they were nice." Blackford didn't sound too worried about this.

In a small voice as I again pictured the horror, I said, "There's someone awful involved in this business here in London. Mr. Reed was shot in front of me today."

"What? Georgia, they could have been shooting at you. You need to drop this investigation immediately. Leave it to the police."

A shiver ran through my body, but I put determination in my tone. "The police have no leads in Reed's murder and aren't looking into the theft of the gold. I have to persevere. You could do me a favor, though. Do you know anyone good at deciphering a code?"

"I might. Why do you need to decipher something?"

"A series of letters were in Hathaway's possession when he was in Cairo. They were stolen by Mr. Munroe before his death and passed on to his niece. She gave them to me, believing them to be a clue to the identity of the others who, along with Hathaway, stole the gold. All the messages are in code."

Light from a passing streetlight showed grim planes on Blackford's face. "And possessing them puts you in danger. I'll find someone for you."

"On an afternoon visit, I also met the wife of Sir Antony Derwaller, the first secretary to the British Residency in Cairo. One of the men Burke mentioned. She said they weren't returning to Cairo, but she wouldn't say anything about what they plan to do next. Only that he doesn't have a new appointment at the Foreign Office and they're leaving London soon. She seemed very happy about her new freedom."

"I wonder how many others are in London now," Blackford said in a distracted-sounding voice as he stared out the coach window, "and not returning to Cairo. We need photographs of all the principal suspects. The Foreign Office should be able to provide those."

We arrived at the ball, ending our discussion.

Every gas lamp and candle in the house was ablaze with light. Jewels sparkled, debutantes giggled, and the men were all in their best black coats and starched white collars and shirtfronts. Some of them wore sashes with diplomatic or military honors. Blackford was the handsomest man there, and I was glad he could dance with me more than once.

A certain freedom was given to those about to be married.

But after two dances, one of them with the wife of a friend while the friend danced with me, Blackford went off to talk business with a couple of lords I had met in passing. I was alone, watching the dancing from the side of the room, when I bumped into someone. Turning to apologize, I found it was Lady Ashwin.

"Lady Ashwin, I'm so sorry—"

"No, no, Miss Fenchurch, my fault—"

"I hope I haven't damaged your gown. It's lovely."

"No, I'm fine. Miss Fenchurch, have you met my sister-in-law, Lady Barber?"

"No, I haven't. How do you do?" Lady Barber had returned to London fresh from a German spa. Lord Barber had been to see Mr. Reed before his death and definitely had been, and might still be, in England. How involved in the theft was he? Trying not to show how interested I was, I curtsied as I said, "How was your travel back from Cairo?"

"How on earth did you know that?" Lady Barber said, eyeing me suspiciously. Her mousy brown hair was liberally streaked with gray, so her curls in the debutante style, ringing her face and drawing the eye to her weak chin, made her look older. The jeweled bib that covered her chest in gaudy diamonds, rubies, and emeralds called even more attention to her thick neck. I hoped Lady Ashwin, impeccably dressed in understated glamour, would give her some advice.

"I've met Miss Munroe, who mentioned you. She's trying to get in touch with Mr. Burke."

"What a small world. They were both in Cairo with us. Not from the leading families, of course, but it's such a small community one gets to know everyone. And you say Miss Munroe is trying to get in touch with Mr. Burke? Not the done thing when I was young." Her voice dripped snobbery.

I tried not to show my instant dislike for her

attitude. "I believe she wants to learn how the investigation into her uncle's murder is coming along."

"Oh. That." Lady Barber rolled her eyes heavenward. "She must leave *that* to the police. Of course, with those Egyptian policemen, I doubt they'll ever make any progress. She must learn to bear her sorrows with more fortitude and not impose them on all and sundry."

With an outlook like that, I doubted Lady Barber would take Lady Ashwin's fashion advice, no matter how accurate.

I tried again. "Someone mentioned that you and Lord Barber were taking the waters at Bad Brueckenau. That must have been enjoyable."

A haughty sniff. "Lord Barber changed his mind at the last minute and came straight back to London. I, on the other hand, needed the break. I have a delicate constitution."

She hid her *delicate constitution* behind a formidable front. "Then it must be nice to get a break from the summer in Cairo. Rest up in Germany and England before you have to go back." Not too graceful, but I hoped it would lead the conversation into the right direction.

"What makes you say that?" she snapped.

"It's well known how hot it is in the summer along the Nile. Aren't you returning in the fall?" I asked as innocently as I could manage.

"As a matter of fact, no. And for that I am truly grateful."

The Detecting Duchess 109

"Another government posting?"

"Never." Her nose went into the air and led her path away from me.

"I'm so sorry," I said with a deprecating smile to Lady Ashwin.

"Don't be. She's quite pleased that her husband has come into some money and they can stay in England, unfettered by any need for employment." She gave me an apologetic smile and followed after her sister-in-law.

I watched her go, knowing another on my list of possible attackers must be in London.

"Violet is such a difficult color to pull off, particularly for anyone over twenty."

My gown was violet. I closed my eyes, praying for patience with the woman whose voice had carried from somewhere behind me. When I opened them, I found several people at the ball trying not to stare.

My cheeks were hot. My face was probably bright red and clashing with my dress. I hurried forward, not stopping until I reached the nearest door to the flower-draped veranda. As I went outside, I was sure I could hear feminine laughter.

I was so embarrassed I hadn't turned to see who my attacker was, and I wasn't certain of the voice. Lady Castleley? Lady Tidminster? One of any number of young ladies who didn't think it fair that a woman of thirty without breeding or connections should be engaged to the most eligible bachelor in London? An engagement they had wanted to be theirs.

I paced the flagstones, trying to get my temper

under control. Couples strolling under the stars glanced my way and then turned their heads. I suspected they were just giving the angry woman some privacy. Or avoiding the madwoman.

I liked my gown. Blackford said he liked my gown.

Or was he only saying so?

The door opened from the ballroom, and I held my breath, hoping it wasn't Lady Castleley.

Lady Ashwin stepped out, looked around, and then headed toward me. "It's a lovely evening."

I took a deep breath. Well, deep for wearing a tight corset. "Yes. Yes, it is."

"A word of unsolicited advice, Miss Fenchurch. You seem like a bright woman, a kind woman, a woman of sense and proportion. Don't bow down to Lady Castleley and her ilk." She lowered her voice so none of the strolling couples could hear us.

"I have no intention of bowing down to her," I said through clenched teeth.

"That's what you're doing. If they can have you quaking in your dancing slippers now, you'll never be able to claim your standing as a duchess later on. You're going to have to face them now, before the wedding, if you're to have any peace in London after the wedding." She gave me a smile that seemed genuine in the torchlight, and then turned and walked back inside.

It took me a minute to rein in my temper. When I was certain tears would no longer overflow my eyes and my cheeks were cool, I went back inside.

Lady Castleley was holding court with several other

people of both genders at the edge of the dance floor. Now was not the time to stand up to her. I walked away, relief warring with my desire to end this feud now.

I was relieved to see Blackford returning to the ballroom. When he reached me, he said, "Lord Burke is in one of the parlors waiting for us. Apparently he's had a change of heart and wants to give us more information on the theft."

He took my arm and escorted me to the parlor. Burke was standing by the cold fireplace next to a young thin-faced blonde woman. He gave us a bow when we walked in. The woman looked me over as she curtsied. "Lovely gown, Miss Fenchurch," Burke said.

"Thank you," I answered with a graceful curtsy. Inside, I was waltzing. Someone liked it who wasn't obligated to defend my choices.

Blackford gave the couple a nod and said, "Will you introduce us to your friend, Burke?"

"Of course. Miss Fenchurch, Your Grace, this is Miss Sylvia Prescott, daughter of Lord Prescott. Miss Prescott is the sister of an old friend of mine."

Goodness, another aristocratic debutante clashed in my mind with *What is she doing here if we're to discuss the case?*

"I want to help," Burke said. "I owe Eugenie and her uncle that much. The trouble is I can't see any way forward."

I was relieved at his change in attitude, but I was puzzled by the young woman's presence. "I'm afraid you're going to be bored by our discussion, which will wander around in circles," I said to her.

"Oh, not at all," she assured me as she latched on to Burke's arm like a leech. "Lord Burke is a fascinating conversationalist and I'm sure you and His Grace are equally diverting."

"I doubt that."

I spoke an instant before Grayson Burke said, "Sylvia finds talk of a missing treasure to be exciting, like an adventure tale. She wants to listen to us."

I glanced at Blackford who gave the vaguest hint of a shrug.

If they didn't mind, who was I to say anything? I plunged into the topic. "There must be only so many people who could have stolen the gold. Then if you eliminate all those not in England at the time to kill Mr. Hathaway—"

"It's not that simple," Burke corrected me. "It could have been anybody."

"What do you mean, the gold could have been taken by anyone? How many people were involved in the actual transfer?" This was not what I wanted to hear. The theft had been on another continent several weeks ago. Since then, five people that I knew of had died in connection with the theft. Two of them here in England.

And Eugenie Munroe had nearly died after I failed to protect my new client.

"The gold is handed from the Egyptians to the Caisse de la Dette Publique, the body that receives the money to pay back the Egyptian government debt. There are six representatives, one each from Britain,

France, Germany, Italy, Austria, and Russia, who then see that the various debt holders are repaid on schedule. All six know every detail of the ceremony, as do those few clerks in their employ."

"How many were in Britain when Mr. Hathaway was murdered?" I wanted to find the flaw in Burke's reasoning.

"The British representative would have been the only one. The rest of the representatives are home, enjoying a vacation in cooler weather than they'd find in Cairo this time of year. The clerks have also left."

"Are any of the clerks English?"

Burke nodded. "Yes. One. Paul Lemington. A nice young man from Bristol." He looked at Blackford. "It would pay to check up on him, if only to rule him out."

"Who is the British representative to the group accepting the payment?" I asked.

"Sir Ralph Wyatt."

"The economist and mathematician?" Blackford asked, standing a little taller.

Burke nodded.

"You know him?" I asked.

Blackford glanced at me. "He's invited to our wedding."

I nearly choked. "Then I certainly hope he's not a murderer. Is he capable of strangling Miss Munroe or bashing in Mr. Hathaway's head?"

"Physically, I suppose, but I don't think he's our killer."

Blackford turned toward Burke, but I moved

directly in front of the duke. "Why not?"

"He's a friend of mine," Blackford assured me.

"Do you have any other reason?" I did not want a murderer at my wedding.

Blackford glared at me. "Georgia. There is no reason to believe he's a killer. He has high standing in political and academic circles. He doesn't lack for invitations to the finest houses in Britain. And he's a nice, jolly sort of middle-aged man."

I limited my response to "We'll see."

"Don't forget Hathaway's British second-in-command on the tax reform committee, Sir Antony Derwaller," Burke said. "He'd know every detail of the ceremony and the layout of the Egyptian treasury building, too. He was in the perfect position to plan and carry out the theft."

I looked at Blackford. "The list of possible killers seems to keep growing."

"What form was the stolen gold in? It wouldn't be easy for the thief to spend it in London, would it?" Miss Prescott asked, not sounding half as dim as I'd thought.

"It was in special gold coins minted in Cairo by the Egyptian government for the purpose of international transfers and for international collectors. Lovely distinctive things. And no, they would be difficult to spend in London if you had them and wanted to change them into pounds sterling," Blackford told her.

A clever young woman, I decided. And one definitely focused on the gold in this investigation, rather than the murders. "What would your next step be, Miss Prescott?"

She gave me a vapid smile. "I don't know. It was just a thought that popped into my head. You're probably way ahead of me already."

"No, I'm not." But it was an idea that I could put the Archivist Society on to follow up.

CHAPTER NINE

Blackford and I thanked Burke and Miss Prescott and went back to the dancing. The rest of the ball was more fun. We waltzed together once more. I felt safe and loved in his embrace.

His friends asked me to dance and so my dance card, at least for the end of the evening, was as full as the leading debutante's.

In fact, I didn't give Lord Burke, Miss Munroe, or Egypt another thought until we arrived back at Sir Broderick's house. He and Mrs. Hardwick had waited up for us. Again. They were taking their chaperoning duties seriously. Too seriously.

"Well, that ruins any thoughts I had of ravishing you," Blackford murmured in my ear.

I grinned.

I was certain Mrs. Hardwick couldn't have heard Blackford's comment. But with one glance she said, "Oh, my. You're blushing."

Sir Broderick cleared his throat. "Blackford, your house rang here about an hour ago. Apparently, an agent for a foreign power wants to speak to you as soon as possible."

Frowning, Blackford asked, "Do you mind if I use your study for a phone call?"

"Not at all," I answered before Sir Broderick had a chance. "May I listen in? I'm afraid it has something to do with this investigation."

"Have there been developments?" Sir Broderick asked.

Blackford gave me a hard stare. "Not everything I'm working on concerns Miss Munroe." He bowed and left the room.

I sat down and smiled at Sir Broderick, organizing my thoughts, when he said, "You realize this may not have anything to do with your investigation. Blackford is a chief negotiator for the crown and government on—delicate matters."

"I realize that."

"Then you realize there may be times when you cannot listen in on his private conversations."

My cheeks heated. I was so focused on my investigation that I never considered what else might be going on in Blackford's life. A fault I'd have to curb if we were to have a successful marriage. "Let me give you my report and see what you can make of it."

We had finished discussing my small amount of news when Blackford returned to the parlor. "Have you heard of a Pierre Aveneil?"

"No. Please don't tell me he's a good friend of Mr. Hathaway working to protect his reputation." It was the only thing this investigation seemed to lack.

"He's a French investigator hired by French banking

interests. The Foreign Office told him to contact me. My queries about the primary suspects in the theft have been noted and make certain parties think I know more about the missing Egyptian gold than I do."

"How many people are looking for the treasure?" I asked. It was late, I was tired, and I was getting exasperated as the number of suspects kept climbing.

But then, one million British pounds sterling worth of gold coins tends to bring out the avarice in everyone.

"Anyone would want to claim the gold. The more people we can eliminate from consideration in the theft, the sooner we can solve this mystery and concentrate on our wedding." Blackford appeared completely unruffled. Another characteristic I wished I could learn from him.

"I hope you aren't speaking to Mr. Aveneil tonight." It was too late to conduct business.

"I sent him a message promising him some time tomorrow. He'll have to be satisfied with that." He said good night to Sir Broderick and Mrs. Hardwick, and I walked him to the door.

He turned to face me before he left. "I'll try to find out the current location of everyone Burke mentioned and where they were when Hathaway was murdered. And get copies of their photographs. Is that good enough?"

His kiss, the sweeter for being stolen while no one was in the front hall, nearly made me forget his question. "Yes. Does this include your friend Sir Ralph Wyatt?"

He grinned. "I thought we'd start with him. Shall I come by for you in the morning?"

"Is he in London?"

"No. Oxford. I thought we'd take the train down. And bring the letters you want deciphered."

"You know someone who can do this?"

"I know several someones who can decipher any code anyone could dream up. And they're all in Oxford." His smile reached his eyes.

Of course Blackford knew people who could break a code. He was a diplomat. I was a fool to be even mildly surprised.

Tomorrow sounded wonderful. An escape for the day, from London and everyone's interest in our marriage plans. Just Blackford and me. "Come by for breakfast and then we'll leave from here."

* * *

The next morning after breakfast, Blackford and I rode in his carriage to Paddington Station. The roads were slick with rain and traffic was more clogged than usual. When we finally arrived, a footman saw us inside the terminal while holding an umbrella over us. The huge roof of the station covered us as we climbed into a first-class carriage on the train to Oxford. The plush seats and swept floor were at odds with my experience with rail travel without Blackford by my side.

Once we were out of the city, the views would have been of green fields if it had been possible to see through the rain-streaked windows. At least the windows stayed shut, blocking out the smoke from the engine.

We read in companionable silence for the short journey to Oxford. Blackford quickly procured a small coach outside the station that took us to his old college.

We waited in the covered entrance by the porter's lodge, watching rain strike the cobblestones in the street on the town side of our dry haven. Young men in short capes dashed madly through the muddy quad inside the college. A scout in a black suit and bowler hat stuck to the gravel paths as he went to tell Sir Ralph Wyatt that we had arrived.

A man in a longer academic gown hurried toward us a few minutes later, his umbrella dripping a circle around his steps. Once under the portico, he lowered his umbrella to reveal a round face and a thinning fringe of hair. "Ah, Blackford, I received your telegram. And this must be the lovely Miss Fenchurch."

After his bow and my curtsy, he took both of my hands in his and gazed into my eyes. He was about my height, with a soft, pale look that I put down to living a quiet academic life. "I am so looking forward to attending your wedding, my dear. Blackford was one of my best students."

"The best," Blackford quietly corrected him.

"Certainly the most successful. Can we agree to that?" he asked with a chuckle.

"Agreed," Blackford said, returning a smile.

I was sure he was physically the wrong shape to be the man who had attacked Eugenie Munroe near my shop. I was equally sure I would like this jovial man.

"We need your help. We've become involved in the Egyptian gold theft," Blackford told him in a low tone.

"Oh, dear. Well, we can't talk here. And I'm afraid, Miss Fenchurch, rules preclude your entrance into the college. Would the chapel be all right? It should be empty this time of day."

"Most appropriate," Blackford said, and with our umbrellas raised, we walked along the path to the college chapel. I held up my skirt, showing off my ankles while trying to protect my hem from ruin.

It was chilly and dim inside the chapel. The stained-glass windows looked dull with the rain, but the wood carvings in the screen and the altar showed skilled medieval workmanship.

After a short tour, we took seats in a single pew with Sir Ralph in the center. "Now, what would you like to know?" he asked.

"How much detail of the workings of the Egyptian treasury was known to the members of the Caisse?" Blackford asked.

"In some matters, quite a bit. We were all experts in reading balance sheets and budgets and we knew the strengths and weaknesses of the Egyptian economy. And of course, we talked to one another, so if I wasn't aware of some problem within the treasury, someone would be sure to point it out to me."

"And the ceremony handing over the payment?"

"It was always done the same way. And before you ask, nothing was done any differently this last time than any other time. Well, except for the young man having a bloodied nose. The captain of the guards ordered another guard into his place and sent the man with the injury out of the room. If you blinked, you would have missed the incident."

"Were they late in arriving with the gold?" I asked.

Sir Ralph turned to me. "Not in the least. Which was surprising. The injured guard must have taken a moment to recover from whatever accident befell him."

"The bloody nose was obvious?"

"Oh, yes. I could see it the moment he walked in pushing the cart."

"Did the cart seem hard to push? Did it seem to be weighted down?"

"Not any more than usual. That much gold weighs a great deal." He gave me a smile that said he was happy to talk to us, but the theft and the gold had made no impression on him.

"I understand one clerk at the Caisse is British. Paul Lemington," Blackford said.

"Yes. Nice chap. Took a first at Cambridge a year ago and came out to work and see a little of the world. Get a bit of experience."

"Where is he now?"

"Home in Bristol, I'd imagine. His father is something big in shipping. Paul was just working with us for the one year before he took his place in the family business."

"I'd appreciate it if you'd give us his address."

"Of course." He looked from Blackford to me and then back to him. "What has caused you to get involved in Egyptian matters?"

"It became British matters when Andrew Hathaway was murdered in Southampton and then Miss Eugenie Munroe was attacked outside Miss Fenchurch's bookshop. And now Damien Reed has been murdered." Blackford gave his old tutor a grim look.

"Oh, dear. On top of Bradley Munroe's murder. This is troubling. Most troubling." His voice faded as he appeared to slip into deep thought.

My saying "Why?" jerked him out of his thoughts.

"Why is it troubling?" He gave me a quizzical look.

"I understand why the murders are troubling. I don't see why all these attacks are happening now."

He nodded, then gave me a smile. "I can only speculate based on gossip and details I noticed."

"Please feel free to speculate," I told him.

"At least we're raising this above the level of gossip. One gets so much of that in academia. I would talk to Sir Antony Derwaller."

"And what would I ask him?"

"What did he and Bradley Munroe argue about the day before Munroe died? And why did he and Hathaway snap at each other every time they had to speak to one another?"

"Sir Antony and Hathaway didn't get along?"

"I once overheard Sir Antony say he looked forward to attending Hathaway's funeral and Hathaway replied that Sir Antony's funeral would occur sooner if he had to listen to Sir Antony whine one more minute. Then he called him a fossil and stormed out of the room, nearly knocking me over."

"Who stormed out of the room? Hathaway?"

"Yes. I had thought it might be his favorite way to leave a room," Sir Ralph said with a chuckle. "He reminded me of so many undergraduates."

"Did his mood get worse after the theft?"

"No. Hathaway's mood improved afterward. He kept saying, 'Now everybody has something to worry about besides ledgers and heat and sand.'"

"And Sir Antony?"

"He was disgusted with the treasure hunt going on all over Cairo. Caused a lot of damage, a lot of chaos, a lot of bad feelings, particularly with the locals."

"And Sir Antony's argument with Mr. Munroe the day before he died. Do you have any idea what that was about?"

"No. There were raised voices, but no one could make out what they were saying."

"Where was this?"

"Down the street a short distance from Shepheard's Hotel. There was so much street noise, no one could have made out a word they said."

"Did you try?" Blackford asked in a dry tone.

"Me, dear boy? Certainly not." Sir Ralph smiled. "I knew it was impossible."

"So you think Sir Antony was behind the theft?" I asked. He seemed to be leading us that way.

"No. I'm sure he wasn't, but I can't give you a reason beyond my hunch."

"Who would you bet on, if you were a betting man?"

Blackford asked.

"Young Lord Cecil. He's a slippery one. Someone I wouldn't trust. Again, I have no reason beyond watching him play cards. He cheats."

I was surprised. Cheating went against the standards of a young gentleman. Standards he would have learned as the son of a marquess. "Has anyone accused him of that?"

"No. Because of his father. You don't accuse someone like that of cheating. I do know most of the young men would play for extremely low stakes or drop out any time Lord Cecil showed up for a game. However, it was fun to watch him play Mr. Hathaway. He also cheated."

Fascinating. "How are you so certain, Sir Ralph?"

He gave me a smile. "My academic specialty is statistics and probability. It's something you might say I've been trained to spot."

I glanced at the duke as I pulled out the stack of coded notes from my handbag. When he nodded, I turned to Sir Ralph. "Blackford tells me you're good at deciphering codes."

"Ciphers and codes are two different things. Setting that aside for the moment, do you have a puzzle you want me to work on?"

I handed the stack of notes to Sir Ralph. "Mr. Munroe had these in his possession when he was murdered. He managed to slip them to his niece before he succumbed to his injuries, and she has given them to me."

He slipped off the string and studied the first note. "No one has been able to decode these?"

"No."

He silently read over a few notes. "What a delightful puzzle. Thank you, my dear. How soon do you want the answer to what they say?"

"As quickly as possible. I don't want anyone else getting hurt."

He stared into my eyes. "You mean, getting killed."

I stared back. "Yes."

"I have them now. I certainly don't want that." With a smile, he added, "Leave them with me. I'll contact Blackford the moment I have an answer."

He turned then to Blackford. "Any word on those stolen antiquities?"

"Only rumors. We haven't been able to pin anything down."

I looked from Sir Ralph to Blackford. "What stolen antiquities?"

"Never mind, Georgia," Blackford grumbled.

"Are they Egyptian?"

"Some of them," Sir Ralph said the same moment Blackford said, "Foreign Office business. Please don't ask."

Being cut off from Blackford's investigations hurt, but I guessed I'd have to get used to it. This wouldn't be the last time.

The rain let up enough for us to go to a respectable hotel for lunch with Sir Ralph. Having not attended Oxford, I was enthralled with the mathematician's well-told tales of student high jinks and academic foibles.

Once we were on the train back to London, Blackford looked around our empty compartment and said, "Do you believe me now when I say Sir Ralph isn't the killer?"

"Yes. He's delightful. I think it's time to get the Archivist Society fully involved."

"What line of inquiry will they follow?"

"We'll try to find out why officials in Cairo are resigning from the Foreign Office. They couldn't all have benefitted from the theft. If we can start eliminating some of our suspects that way, it will have to help. And check the numismatic shops for anyone trading in Egyptian gold coins."

"Be careful, my duchess." He kissed the inside of my wrist. "We have a wedding very soon."

"You be careful, too. Stolen antiquities from Egypt can be dangerous."

"No one's been killed over them yet." He began an assault on the side of my neck and my ear that made me forget for a moment that we were on a moving train.

My pulse sped and I leaned into him, the immovable wooden armrest digging into my side. I sighed in frustration. Horse-drawn carriages were much better than trains for courting.

* * *

I returned to Sir Broderick's in time for Mrs. Hardwick to join me for the final fitting for my wedding gown. The dressmaker Evelyenne greeted us with assurances that I would love everything I put on. At least Mrs. Hardwick was excited by the prospect of seeing my fashion secrets before they would be revealed in the coming days.

Lady Westover, with Lady Phyllida and Emma in tow, showed up a few minutes after we arrived, and I felt like a dressmaker's dummy as I put on my going-away gown for their inspection. It was a soft blue, with lace at the collar and cuffs and a darker blue pleated inset in the bodice. Lady Westover, who sat in front of the others, suggested a change to the collar.

The more I thought about it, the more I thought she was right. Evelyenne agreed with good grace.

Then I tried on the violet afternoon gown, which was my favorite. No lace, but a deep purple striped front that ran from neck to hem. Everyone oohed and aahed at it except Lady Westover, who thought I should have chosen a color closer to my eyes.

Finally, I tried on my wedding gown. Lady Westover said, and we all agreed, that it needed taking in a little at the waist.

"You've been working too hard on your investigation," Phyllida said.

"You shouldn't be working on an investigation. The wedding is practically here," Lady Westover said. It sounded more like an order.

"What investigation?" Emma asked.

"I didn't want to bother you because of your—" I gazed at her protruding stomach.

"You sound like Sumner. I'm going mad with boredom. Oh, let me at least do some research."

"Emma, you'll upset yourself and the baby," Lady Westover said.

Emma shot me a look that said *She is so old-fashioned*.

I bit my lip to keep from smiling and then mouthed "Later."

Evelyenne spread out my train. It was an extension of the skirt that spread out six feet behind me. All of the hem, both skirt and train, was embroidered with silver thread. The embroidery was repeated at the waist and wrists and high collar.

The ladies again oohed and aahed as they moved forward for a closer look. I felt like I could have been replaced by a stand to hang the dress on.

Emma walked around it and said, "Look at all those tiny buttons. Do you have a lady's maid yet?"

"I will. She starts the morning of my wedding day."

"I'll come and show her how to do your hair. Otherwise, it's liable to turn into a rat's nest while the vicar is speaking. Where's your veil?"

Evelyenne produced it and Emma set it on my head so she could see what hairstyle she'd need to employ.

"Oh, you're going to be a beautiful bride," Aunt Phyllida said and burst into tears. "Both my babies married."

Emma gave her a hug. I patted her shoulder, unwilling to mess up the gown. I'd only known Phyllida a little more than ten years and Emma a little less, but I guessed we must have felt like daughters to her. All along, I had thought she only felt that way about Emma.

The lump in my throat must have been from my heart swelling up in love for Aunt Phyllida and Emma. And the tears that threatened to overflow my eyes? I must have been tired.

With help from Evelyenne and her assistant, I quickly climbed out of the gown and back into my own afternoon dress. It felt much looser, but I decided that was because it was familiar. It was mine.

Emma came in while I was changing. "You have something for me to research, don't you?"

I nodded. "It's a possibility, but one I hadn't thought of until it was pointed out to me. Check the numismatic shops for anyone bringing in those distinctive Egyptian gold coins to sell for pounds sterling. If the thief has need of money, selling a few of the coins would raise funds. And see if you can get the seller's name and address."

She favored me with her brilliant smile. "I'll start tomorrow."

We left the modiste's shop and stood on the pavement, chattering about the dresses and the wedding. At least the morning rain had stopped, and people were crowding the streets again. We must have been taking up too much of the pavement, because someone shoved me hard in the back. I fell against Lady Westover.

The lady was frail. I stopped myself from going over while I tried to keep her from falling. Emma leaped forward and supported her from the other side.

It was only when I was sure Lady Westover

wouldn't tumble over that I realized the man had stolen my handbag.

CHAPTER TEN

I glanced around. There he was, several yards away, a tall, well-dressed man in a cape carrying my bag in one hand, blending into the pedestrian traffic. The only man wearing a cape in our warm weather.

"Stop! Thief!" I ran after him, relieved that at least I no longer carried the coded notes in my bag. I couldn't lose them. They were vital clues. I hoped.

People on the pavement stared at me and then looked around in confusion. I rushed past them, dodging in and out, keeping my eye on my assailant.

As if he knew I was gaining on him, the caped man tossed my handbag aside on the pavement as he strode off on long legs.

I hurried forward to pick it up. When I opened it, rather than finding the contents gone, something had been added. On top of what was already there, the man had left a note.

Ignoring people walking past, I unfolded the message and read, STOP YOUR HUNT FOR THE GOLD OR YOU WILL BE THE NEXT TO DIE.

Emma caught up to me and looked over my shoulder. "Good grief. How many people know you're working on this case? Even I hadn't heard until today."

"We've started looking at several possible suspects, but I don't know what most of them look like. That man could have been one of them, and I wouldn't know. I didn't even get a close look at his face." I stomped my foot in frustration, despite the raised brow I received from Lady Westover as the older women walked over to join us.

"Do you know who he was?" Phyllida asked.

"No."

"There was no damage done. Forget about him and get on with your wedding," Lady Westover told me.

It wouldn't be easy. Had the second shot been meant for me at the Royal Antiquities Society or did the killer fire only to frighten me to stop pursuit? Either way, I was sure Eugenie Munroe was still in danger.

Mrs. Hardwick took me firmly by the arm as she signaled for a hansom cab. "I'm taking you home where you will be safe."

"A good idea," Phyllida agreed.

"You look pale," Emma told me.

It was clear I wasn't going to have any say in the matter. The whole ride back Mrs. Hardwick continued to chatter, but my mind was on the who and the why of this threat. Why threaten me with gunshots one day, and the next slip a note into my handbag? The attacks on me were like they'd been done by two different individuals. Unless the second shot was simply meant to slow down any efforts to identify the killer.

Sir Broderick thought our return was a good idea

when we reached his house and Mrs. Hardwick immediately launched into her story. "Show me the note," he told me.

I pulled it out of my handbag and handed it to him. He studied the handwriting and the notepaper before he said, "There's nothing distinctive here."

"I believe it was the same man who tried to strangle and stab Miss Munroe. He was dressed the same and he seemed to be about the same size and strength. I think he's our killer. We need to find him."

Sir Broderick smacked the armrests of his wheeled chair and said, "Listen to yourself. The wedding will be here before you know it. You shouldn't go anywhere alone. Let the Archivist Society handle this case."

"This is my last case before I get married. Probably my last case, ever, if Emma's situation is anything to go by. I want to see it through before I have to give up playing a role in anything more difficult than putting on a dinner party."

"You have no idea how difficult that will be," Mrs. Hardwick murmured. Her expression was grimmer than Sir Broderick's, probably because she'd seen the warning delivered.

"Stay in until Blackford comes to take you to tonight's ball—"

"Dinner party." I said it like a spoiled debutante, bored with all the attention of being popular.

He sighed. "Take this seriously, Georgia. Whoever this man is, he's dangerous."

"Not for me. He just keeps brushing me aside while

other people are killed, or almost killed in Miss Munroe's case. He's not taking me seriously." How dare he not take me seriously. That made me still angrier.

"Well, take this seriously. Your lady's maid is in the kitchen."

I stared at Sir Broderick. I didn't have a—oh, wait. Yes, I did. "Lucy?"

"Yes. Miss Lucy Kebten. I've been told she arrived in tears because she's been sacked and Lady Westover wasn't home. Apparently, she has nowhere to go, so I told them to put her in the servants' hall until you returned."

I turned on my heel and marched downstairs. Probably not what a duchess would do, but I wasn't a duchess yet. "Lucy? What is going on?"

She set down her mug of tea and looked at me with reddened eyes. "This morning, the Duchess of Duleign said she would pay me in lieu of working out my notice. I was to pack up and leave the house immediately."

"Had you done something to make her angry?"

"No. I told the other maids I had turned in my notice, and one of the maids asked Her Grace if she could have my position and my pay. The maid was quite persistent in it. Her Grace said if I was going to sow discord in her house, I could leave immediately."

"Oh, well, it's probably for the best." I needed practice having a lady's maid. And I needed help packing. "Let me ask Mrs. Hardwick where we should put you until the wedding."

"There really is nowhere," Mrs. Hardwick said,

entering the room. "We're full to the rafters."

"Do we have a trundle we can put in my room?" I asked.

"Oh, miss, I couldn't do that," Lucy said.

"We have no choice until the wedding," I told her.

"Yes. I can get a trundle bed if that's what you want," Mrs. Hardwick said. "Show Lucy up to your room so she can put her things there. And I'm glad you're here, Lucy. At least if you're with her, she won't get hurt."

Lucy gulped down her tea and rose to follow me upstairs. I had to get her settled and then dress for the dinner party.

I was gloomy because I had to get ready to go out for the evening rather than do what I wanted to do. What I needed to do. Warn Miss Munroe that a dangerous man was growing bolder. And I was angry that I had grown so shallow that I cared what others thought of my gowns and my appearance. That I wasted so much time over something so petty when people were being attacked, and murdered, in front of me.

But if Lucy could tame my hair for this party the way Emma could, it would be worth having her as a lady's maid earlier than expected.

Sir Broderick had made certain he filled Blackford in on the afternoon's events before I came downstairs, dressed for the evening.

Blackford's dark eyes were pools of fury. "Hand the investigation off to people who will be more careful. I don't want to postpone the wedding while you're in hospital."

"If he'd wanted to hurt me, he could have done it easily this afternoon in front of the ladies. I was in a group and it wasn't any protection. All he wanted to do was warn me away from looking for him, which tells us one of the people we are looking at killed Mr. Munroe and now probably has the gold."

"Which is a good reason for others to now work on this search. He threatened you, Georgia. He knows who you are. He knows where to find you."

"While you consider the note a warning, I think of it as a challenge." The killer was aware of me. Now I had to find him.

"There's nothing I can say, is there?" Blackford looked hurt, and I hated to think I was the one disappointing him.

I put my arm through his. "Let's go to dinner and forget this."

* * *

We had a lovely time at dinner, never saying a word about Egyptian gold, but once I was home Blackford and Sir Broderick sat together to discuss the security arrangements for the house.

After breakfast the next morning, I slipped the folding knife Blackford had given me into my handbag and left for the bookshop before anyone thought to stop me.

Anyone except Lucy. I told her to stay home and continue on my packing. She looked hurt, but she followed my orders.

I felt safe with the weapon's weight in my bag. Once I arrived at the bookshop, I began with a search for Lord Barber's address in the listings for peers.

"Good morning, Georgia," Grace Yates, my bookshop manager, said. "You're here early."

"So are you."

"I'm expecting a shipment of periodicals and red cloth-cover editions of popular fiction, and they always deliver early. Plus, there's a new gothic novel from Mrs. Hepplewhite due out. The shop will be busy."

We both grinned, knowing inexpensive red cloth-covered volumes and cheap periodicals were the purchases of choice for our voracious readers. And also knowing that the famous novelist Mrs. Hepplewhite was in truth brawny, scarred John Sumner, former soldier and bodyguard, and now Emma's husband.

A bang on the back door told us the delivery had arrived. Grace hurried off and I went back to my work.

Dickens decided to help by jumping up on the shelf and sitting on the page I wanted to read. Trying to shift him only made him relax his body over the entire volume until moving him became like moving a thirty-pound sack of porridge.

I finally drove the cat away by the simple expedient of making a fuss over him. Dickens gave me an unfathomable stare, rose, and stalked off. I was then able to discover the address of Lord Barber's house in Mayfair. I headed there, hoping to find out what I could about his movements and his second-in-command, Lord Cecil Isle.

I was in luck. As I reached the large townhouse, wedged between two even more massive homes, I spotted a woman with a shopping basket coming out of the servants' door. I walked up to her. "Is Lord Cecil visiting here?"

"Who?" She looked at me suspiciously.

"Lord Cecil Isle. He was second-in-command under Lord Barber at the Egyptian treasury and I understand the two are good friends. I've been sent with a message for him, with the expectation that I put it directly into his hand." My gown was from before I became Blackford's fiancée. I could be someone's companion or a middle-class family friend, wearing slightly out-of-date fashions.

The woman looked down her nose at me as if I worked for a courtesan. "No. He's not staying here. It's just milord and milady."

"Oh, dear. You don't think someone in the house, the butler or someone, would have a location in London where I can find him or leave this message?" I tried to look hopeful and innocent.

"Butler? We're not so grand a household as that, no matter what milady thinks. Ask the housekeeper, Mrs. Smith. If he's been here to dinner, she'll have his address for the invitation."

"Oh, thank you. I'll just knock on the downstairs door?"

"Where else?" The woman looked at me suspiciously again.

"Indeed." With a smile, I walked to the door and

knocked. When I glanced back, the woman was a distance down the street.

The door was opened by a young girl. "Mrs. Smith, please."

She hurried off, leaving me on the doorstep with the door ajar. I heard, "Well, tell her we don't want any. What do you mean, you don't think she's selling anything? I don't know where she got my name, now do I."

The owner of the voice, who turned out to be a big-boned woman in a plain gray dress, opened the door and said, "Whatever you're selling, we're not buying."

"I understand from your housemaid that you might have Lord Cecil Isle's London address from when he ate dinner here."

"And if I do?" She glared at me.

The role I had chosen would consider herself at least the equal of the housekeeper and probably a step or two above. I glared back and said, "I have an invitation I'm to deliver into his hand, if possible. At his address, if he's out."

Suspicion covered her face. "How do you know so much about our dinner parties?"

"I don't. The sender of the invitation does."

After a moment, she said, "You'd better come in, then." She left the door open and walked away.

I stepped into the kitchen and shut the door behind me, only to find the young girl who'd answered the door staring at me. I gave her a smile and looked down the hallway where the housekeeper had disappeared.

"I imagine this room is lovely and warm in the winter," I said.

"Dunno. Just came here in the spring," the girl replied.

"Just in time to get things ready for his lordship's arrival." I faced the girl, who leaned on her broom.

"Didn't know his lordship was coming back until the day before he arrived with all sorts of trunks from Egypt. Her ladyship didn't come back for a long time after that."

"That must've lessened your work, only having his lordship at home."

"And then he would leave for a day or two at a time, a couple times a week. Confused Mrs. Smith something fierce, but it was easier on the rest of us. Then her ladyship came home and we've all been powerful busy since then."

I heard the housekeeper coming toward us. "Well, you've certainly made this room shipshape," I said, still facing the girl.

"It won't be shipshape until she finishes her sweeping," the housekeeper said. "Here's his address." She handed me a black leather notebook with a series of names and addresses inscribed.

"Thank you very much." I glanced down the names but didn't find any others mentioned in this investigation. I quickly copied down the information I needed and handed the notebook back.

The woman opened the door and stared at me.

"Good-bye." I gave her a smile and left. At least I had

an approximate date for Lord Barber's return. We might be able to narrow down his involvement in the theft by when he returned. He certainly would have been available to attack Miss Munroe near my bookshop.

And what did "all sorts of trunks" mean? Did he have the gold hidden in his household effects?

I knew roughly where Lord Cecil Isle was living, because the St. George Club was a large building on Pall Mall. I took an omnibus in that direction and arrived in a short time at the front steps.

I was greeted, as well as stopped, by the porter on duty immediately inside the open door. "I have a message for one of your residents. Lord Cecil Isle. I'd like to put it into his hand if at all possible."

"If you give it to me, Miss, I'll make sure he gets it as soon as he comes down."

"He is staying here? He did make it back from Cairo?"

"He's been here four weeks now." He scrunched up his forehead. "Maybe five. No, it must be less than that…"

"And you have no way to call him?" I broke into his train of thought.

"He could be anywhere in the building, it being too early for most of our gentlemen to go out. And we can't be running all over the building looking for them." He gave me a superior sort of smile, as if I wouldn't know these things.

Perhaps playing to his superiority might help. "Oh, no. I couldn't impose on your time that way. But could you describe him to me? I will feel foolish if he calls at the house and I don't have any idea who he is. My mistress is very particular in that way."

"Well, Lord Cecil's tallish, and thin, and has fair hair that's fine like a baby's."

"And blue eyes?" I was aware of someone fitting that description stopping when he heard the porter's words and then walking toward the door with his face averted.

"Yes, a pale sort of blue. Why, there he is. My lord. This lady has a message—"

Lord Cecil looked at us and burst through the doorway. He ran down the still-empty pavement of Pall Mall. I dashed after him until, a block later, my lungs were bursting from lack of air. Dratted corset. How I wished my corset would allow me to chase after suspects. I stopped, gasping, and looked around. Lord Cecil Isle had disappeared.

It was probably just as well. I didn't know what I would have done if he'd stopped and asked for the message.

There were too many suspects, and one innocent young woman who knew more than she should. Maybe I thought that because of the undeciphered letters.

I traveled to Mrs. Allen's house on Queen Square. The maid answered the door and I asked for Miss Munroe. After a short wait on the step, enjoying the warm fresh air, Mrs. Allen came to the door.

"I'm afraid Eugenie's gone out. She's attending a meeting."

In my mind, she was bound and gagged and in terrible danger. "Do you know where this meeting is? It's important I get in touch with her."

"There's some women's group she's become a part of that is meeting today. She should be back by teatime."

As soon as Mrs. Allen mentioned the "women's group," I knew where Eugenie Munroe had gone. I thanked Mrs. Allen and walked the several blocks to Mrs. Halford's house.

When I rang the bell, a maid answered.

"Is Miss Munroe visiting?" I asked, hoping she'd made it here.

"They're in the drawing room," she said, opening the door wider and stepping back.

Eugenie, Mrs. Halford, and two other ladies were busy addressing envelopes and licking stamps when I walked in. "Miss Munroe, could I have a moment of your time?"

"Sit down and join us, Miss Fenchurch," she said with a smile.

"Not today, I'm afraid. My mission is rather urgent, if you don't mind." I didn't want to insult them, but I didn't have time to lick stamps today.

She rose and as we walked into the hall, Mrs. Halford joined us. "Do you know anything about the man who asked about the two of you after our last meeting?" She sounded suspicious, as if we weren't quite the young, middle-class women she thought we were.

"What man?" Eugenie and I said in unison. From her

expression, I was certain we shared the same fear.

"He said his name was Mr. Smith. I'm not sure I believed him. He didn't look like he'd ever used that name before."

"What do you mean?" I asked.

"When I asked his name, he appeared to think for a moment before he spoke. Then he seemed very proud of himself. I'm sure it wasn't his real name."

"What did you tell him?"

"Only that our business was none of his and wished him a good day. He knew your name, Miss Munroe, but not yours. I'm afraid I mentioned you were Miss Fenchurch," Mrs. Halford said.

"What did he look like?"

"He was a big man. Tall. He wore a cape, which I found a little odd in this weather. Perhaps he feared it would rain."

Eugenie glanced at me. "Or he was accustomed to the warmer temperatures of Cairo."

"Was he fair-haired with pale blue eyes?"

Mrs. Halford shook her head, staring at me as if I were not as upstanding as I should be. Then she walked away.

So it wasn't Lord Cecil Isle. "Be cautious everywhere you go. You're being followed," I warned Miss Munroe.

"So are you," she replied.

"I'm afraid this isn't the first time." But if Blackford heard about this, it would be the last.

Why was this thief or treasure hunter or whatever he was interested in me? Had I learned something that I didn't recognize the significance of?

"Miss Munroe, I just had Lord Cecil Isle run away from me when I called on him at his club. Was he in any difficulties that you know of?"

She looked puzzled. "None."

"What about the other men your uncle dealt with concerning the robbery?"

She wrung her hands as she paced across the hallway and back. "I would have said they were all models of rectitude until my uncle was murdered. Since then, I'm not sure about any of them. I don't know anything detrimental. That's the whole problem. I don't know anything specific. I have nothing but fears and suspicions."

She stopped and looked at me. "Have the letters been decoded?"

"Not yet. The cryptographer is working hard on them, but he said it would take a little while."

She held me with her gaze, her arms folded across her chest. "I'll feel much safer when we can read the letters and know who our enemies are. I want to know that Mr. Burke is safe and I want to know who killed my uncle."

CHAPTER ELEVEN

I had just reached Sir Broderick's front door on my return when I heard, "Excuse me. I am looking for Miss Fenchurch," in a heavy French accent.

I turned to find a middle-aged man with dark hair and beard alighting from a hansom cab. "I am Miss Fenchurch."

Once he was out of the cab, I could see he was not tall enough to be Miss Munroe's attacker or the man who had stolen my handbag and left me the note. I found it a good sign that he wasn't wearing a cape.

I loosened my grip on the clasp of my bag. I wouldn't need to get out my knife.

Unaware of how close he had come to being skewered, he paid the driver and then faced me as he removed his high silk hat. "I am Monsieur Pierre Aveneil, investigator for the French government."

I nodded, not moving from the top step where I could quickly summon help from the house. I wasn't sufficiently worried to pull out my knife, but I suspected he could be the most dangerous type of all. A man after a missing treasure.

"I believe we are investigating the same crime." I'm

sure he meant his smile to be ingratiating. I found it annoying.

"And what crime is that?"

He raised his eyebrows at my response. "The theft of a fortune in gold from the Caisse de la Dette Publique."

I was right. He was a treasure hunter.

"You're wrong, then. I'm investigating the murder of Bradley Munroe, who was investigating the theft of gold during a transfer from the Egyptians to the Caisse."

He looked around him at the carriages rumbling past, their horses trotting with a steady clop as their shoes hit the cobblestones. A maid carrying her shopping basket hurried down the pavement. Then he gave me a level stare. "Perhaps we could discuss this somewhere other than on the street?"

"Please come in." I rang the bell and Humphries answered immediately. "I'm going to speak to M. Aveneil in the drawing room. Could you let Sir Broderick know and send up a pot of tea?"

"Yes, miss."

I led M. Aveneil to the drawing room and asked him to take a seat. "Do you have any favorites for the role of thief and killer?"

"It must be an Englishman." He spoke with the certainty of someone who didn't care for Englishmen.

"Why?"

"It stands to reason. It cannot be a Frenchman." His superior tone immediately annoyed me.

"Because there weren't any Frenchmen in Britain

when Mr. Hathaway was murdered on the Southampton docks? Please." I didn't try to hide my scoffing tone.

"I agree with Bradley Munroe that Andrew Hathaway was involved. I suspect Hathaway killed Munroe because of what he knew or thought he knew. I believe Hathaway was killed by his accomplice. And that accomplice could only be an Englishman."

"Why?"

"Hathaway had nothing to do with anyone else."

An outsider, a Frenchman, who held the same opinion as the Englishmen I'd talked to. Interesting. Aloud I said, "How did you get involved? Were you in Cairo at that time?"

"My government sent me there immediately after we received word of the theft." He gave me a deprecating smile. "It is not only British bankers who will lose money if the gold is not recovered."

He would have another view of these people, not clouded by Eugenie's love for her uncle or Burke's hatred of Colonel Gregory. "You've met all of these people. What did you think of Mr. Hathaway?"

"He was very fond of himself. As a result, he didn't seem to have any friends. Certainly not anyone of another nationality. He thought of us as not worthy of his time." He gave a hiss that showed his view of that opinion.

"And Munroe?"

"A nice, polite diplomat. A gentleman, even if he did not carry that title in your country. But far too transparent a man to investigate something as complex as the theft of a large shipment of gold."

My question was whether this led to his death, but I decided to ask, "Did you work with Mr. Munroe on this investigation?"

"Yes, and he told me he believed from the start that M. Hathaway was in the perfect position to plan this audacious theft. I discovered he was right about M. Hathaway."

His rhythmic French accent held me spellbound. "Then the day M. Munroe died, he told me he had some new suspicions. Suspicions he would be able to prove shortly. He said he had proof that would soon point to one particular person acting in concert with M. Hathaway."

"Who was this person?"

"He did not say. Only that he would not tell his niece as a way of keeping her safe."

I shook my head. "It hasn't. The day she came to see me, she was attacked at midday on the street in front of my shop." And I still felt guilty for not doing something quicker. For not acting sooner to protect her.

"Who was this person who attacked her?"

"I don't know. She didn't see him as he grabbed her from behind and choked and stabbed her. I only saw him from the back. He was wearing a cape and a top hat, hiding his features. Did Munroe say what form this proof of the accomplice consisted of?"

Had Munroe told the Frenchman about the coded notes?

The tea arrived a moment before Sir Broderick. I

introduced the two men and set about pouring. Sir Broderick and M. Aveneil went through the usual pleasantries while I handed around cups of hot tea.

Once that was done, Sir Broderick changed his tone to a more businesslike one. "What have you learned in your investigation so far?"

"I've spoken to the French representative to the Caisse, who was at the Egyptian treasury that day. The cart was not noticeably late in arriving in the grand salon, but one of the soldiers pulling the wagon had a bloodied nose and a stunned expression. He was immediately pulled out of the room and did not reappear during the ceremony."

"The gold delivery arrived on time," I said as the thought occurred to me, "but did you check to see whether they left on time? They might have left early."

The Frenchman frowned. "No. I didn't. Did the English investigators?"

"I'm going to find out." It might tell me how good an investigator Grayson Burke really was. "Now, you didn't tell me what form this proof Mr. Munroe possessed might be in."

"Proof?" Sir Broderick asked, looking at me.

"Mr. Munroe told M. Aveneil that he would soon have proof of the identity of Hathaway's accomplice in this theft," I explained.

"Munroe did not tell me the nature of the proof. And he did not tell anyone else, to my knowledge. He only said he expected it to tell him the identity of Hathaway's accomplice," Aveneil replied.

The coded notes. That had to be the answer. An answer I didn't plan to share with M. Aveneil.

"What else have you learned?" Sir Broderick asked.

"I tracked down the five continental representatives to the Caisse. None of them are in England, nor have they been in months. Having met M. Hathaway, I considered this a formality. I found it doubtful that he would work with anyone other than an Englishman."

"You met Mr. Hathaway, where we did not. Do you think his preference for Englishmen was for our aristocrats or for any Englishman, regardless of rank?" The more we knew about Hathaway, the easier it might be to find his accomplice.

"He preferred those in power or with title or rank. He was respectful, even if he didn't like Lord Barber, who, as the British controller-general of the Egyptian treasury, was his immediate superior."

"It was that obvious that he didn't like him?" Sir Broderick asked.

"I'm not sure," Aveneil told him. "I do know it was clear to all that Hathaway and Lady Barber couldn't stand each other."

Having met her, I thought Hathaway was wise to keep his distance from Lady Barber.

Aveneil continued. "Hathaway nearly bowed down to the sirdar, or commander, of the Egyptian army, who is a British general. The inspector-general of the Egyptian police is a British colonel, Colonel Gregory, and the two of them were at least cordial. And Hathaway was deferential to the consul-general, Lord Cromer."

"How about Mr. Munroe? Did Mr. Hathaway get along with him?" Sir Broderick asked.

"He showed him contempt."

"Could that be because Mr. Munroe was investigating him in connection with the theft?" I asked.

"Possibly, but after a particularly rude encounter, M. Munroe told me M. Hathaway had always treated him like that and to pay no attention."

"Who do you think was Hathaway's accomplice?" Sir Broderick asked.

"I do not know. Who do you suspect?"

I decided on honesty. "I don't know. We're looking at several people, all of whom were in Cairo, and then England, at about the right times. So far we haven't been able to eliminate any of them."

"Who are you investigating while you are in London?" Sir Broderick asked.

"Sir Antony Derwaller. As first secretary, he had access to practically everything. A handy position, don't you agree? And Damien Reed, who handled all the logistics for the Residency—"

I interrupted him. "Damien Reed is dead."

"What?" Aveneil's head swiveled to stare at me.

"He was shot and killed right in front of me while he was giving me a tour of the Royal Antiquities Society museum. I didn't see the shooter, and the police have no leads." Stated baldly, it had more power than if I'd been dramatic.

"I am sorry, mademoiselle. Does anyone know why he was killed?"

"I suspect it had something to do with the theft and the other killings. He was the expert in shipping goods between Egypt and England. That would be a handy skill for anyone wanting to move a quantity of gold in secret."

"Your suspicion is a wise one." His words sounded strange in his heavy accent. "I am also looking at Lord Burke. He says he did some things, but did he really?"

"You doubt his word?"

"I spoke to the doctor who was called when M. Munroe was attacked. He said M. Burke interfered with his treatment of M. Munroe. He didn't cause the man's death, M. Munroe was already too badly injured, but he was a problem."

"He was trained by a British army doctor," I told him.

"The doctor told me he said that, but it was the doctor's opinion that M. Burke was trained as an orderly, not a medical practitioner."

"Why would he interfere?" I knew how Miss Munroe felt about Lord Burke, and I didn't believe she would favor a man who'd hurt her beloved uncle.

"The reward. The finder's fee was at least 100,000 pounds in your English money for alerting the authorities to the location of the gold and the identity of the thief. Burke needed the money. As a traveling investigator for the crown, he wasn't paid well. Munroe was also after the reward."

"Mr. Munroe also wanted the finder's fee?"

"Of course. That reward would be the difference

between a comfortable retirement and a cold and meager one with his brother, the vicar."

Sir Broderick glanced at me, his face expressionless, but I could tell he was seriously considering M. Aveneil's words.

"Keep in mind M. Burke is now an impoverished aristocrat and he is still in need of money. He is still a threat."

I didn't like M. Aveneil's warning tone. "Are you also after the reward?" I asked. I probably sounded rude, but it needed to be asked.

"Of course. Aren't you?"

I shook my head. "I began my inquiry as a missing persons case. With any luck, I may find a murderer, too."

M. Aveneil rose and I followed. "Then please, don't get in the way of those of us who want to find the treasure and claim the reward," he told me in his pronounced accent.

Sir Broderick followed us to the door where we said good-bye to the Frenchman. Once I had shut the door, Sir Broderick said, "I wonder how many others in this business are after the reward. It is quite the incentive."

"What he said could be true of Lord Burke. And if true, is Miss Munroe searching for him because she loves him and is worried for his safety, or because she suspects he killed her uncle?" This gave me a whole new way to look at my client.

What I didn't need at that moment was more suspicions. "I have Emma doing research for me, but I need help from Jacob and Adam Fogarty, too."

"I thought you might. I've invited them for high tea. Neither one can resist that." Sir Broderick gave me a smile. I was reminded once again how well he knew me and knew our Archivist Society business.

They both arrived soon after, Jacob from the office where he was reading law, and former Sergeant Adam Fogarty of the Metropolitan Police from wherever he'd been talking to currently serving constables.

We sat down to a cold but filling meal, refreshing on a warm day, and once we were finished, Mrs. Hardwick left us to talk business in the drawing room.

"I've found four of our Egyptian murder suspects in London. Any one of them could have attacked Miss Munroe near my bookshop three days ago," I said after we were all seated.

"I think they'd appreciate the background to this investigation and what we know about these suspects," Sir Broderick suggested as I leaped into the heart of the case. "And here are photographs of the men that Blackford dropped off this morning."

Blackford? I turned toward Sir Broderick, my mouth open in surprise.

Sir Broderick said, "You were out, my dear. Blackford was most disappointed."

I was disappointed, too. Grumbling a little, I told them about the theft of the gold and the murders. Then I began to list the suspects for Hathaway's murder and the attack on Miss Munroe, pulling out the labeled photograph as I mentioned each one.

"Sir Antony Derwaller, first secretary to the British

mission to Cairo," I began. "He came back to England with his wife and two grown children and is currently living in London. He's leaving London shortly, doesn't have an obvious source of funds, and was in a position to orchestrate the theft. I have a way to obtain his address."

"Okay, Georgia gets Sir Antony," Jacob said.

"Lord Barber, British liaison to the Egyptian treasury office and currently residing in his Mayfair townhouse with Lady Barber. Again, he's resigned his post, no apparent source of money, and was well positioned for planning the theft."

They nodded and I continued. "Lord Cecil Isle, Lord Barber's assistant, is living in the St. George Club on Pall Mall. Well placed for the theft and reportedly no longer employed. He's the second son of a marquess, so he has an expensive style of living. He ran when he found me asking for him in the lobby of the club. He's tall and thin and very fast," I added in annoyance.

"I'd better take the runner," Jacob said with a grin as he glanced at Adam Fogarty and me.

"And then there is Mr. Burke, now Lord Burke. He recently inherited an Irish title when his grandfather died in a castle fire. The younger Burke was sent by our government to Egypt to investigate the theft after the gold was stolen, but he could have been present to murder all of the victims and is thought to be keen to get the reward. A 100,000-pound reward."

Adam Fogarty whistled.

Jacob said, "Who wouldn't want it?"

Fogarty asked, "What do we want to learn about them?"

"Where they were the morning Mr. Hathaway was murdered in Southampton. Since they've all quit their jobs, where their money is coming from. Are they in hiding, and if so, from whom."

Jacob nodded.

"There's a fifth suspect, Colonel Gregory, formerly the head of the Egyptian police. We don't know whether he is in London and whether he's involved, although Mr. Reed mentioned he had seen him perhaps a week ago."

"Shall I see if the Met knows anything about whether he's in town?" Fogarty asked.

"Please. He is or was the head of the Egyptian police. His title is inspector-general."

"Oh, some section of the Met will be interested in an important person like him." Fogarty gave a satisfied smile and leaned back in his chair.

"We'd better get to work."

All three men stared at me. "Georgia, you have a concert and party tonight," Sir Broderick said. "Lord Cecil Isle will no doubt be off in some gambling hole, and the men Fogarty needs to speak to about Colonel Gregory have gone home for the day. We'll start in the morning."

No one else seemed to find any urgency in this case, but I had a wedding very soon and I wanted to find the killer and the treasure before I said, "I do."

Humphries showed Emma in and Jacob and Fogarty rose to their feet while Sir Broderick gave her a nod. She bobbed a curtsy and then sat next to me. "Georgia, I found a coin dealer who bought eight Egyptian gold coins, 'beautiful things,' he said, from a man a few days ago, and then 'another blonde young woman,' as the clerk described her, came in this morning asking the same questions I did."

"Did you learn the man's name and address? Did you learn the woman's name?" This could be a huge break in the case.

She pulled out her notepad. "He said his name was Bradley Munroe. This is his address." Adam Fogarty copied down the information. "The woman identified herself as Cynthia Finch."

"Did she say why she was interested in Egyptian gold coins?" Sir Broderick asked.

"No, but after she left, there were only seven gold coins. The clerk's upset. The coin is quite valuable. He's reported the theft to the police."

"Someone's trying to steal stolen coins?" Jacob asked. "That's brazen."

"And the person who supposedly sold them to the dealer," I pointed out, "died in Cairo over a month ago. We need to find out who really lives at the address he gave."

"If it's anyone beside a ghost," Fogarty said with a smile. "And if any of the gold resides there, I'll be surprised. After giving a false name, I can't believe the thief would be foolish enough to give his correct address."

CHAPTER TWELVE

I had no idea how the investigation would go when I arrived at the breakfast table the next morning after a late night at a concert and party afterward. Then I learned Mrs. Hardwick had other plans for me. "You need to take Lucy to Blackford House and let her see her new working conditions."

"But I have—"

"Responsibilities other than to the current investigation," Sir Broderick said. "I spoke to Blackford last night. They will expect you and Lucy at Blackford House first thing this morning."

After breakfast, I went to my room to find Lucy busy with the packing. "Are you ready to see where you'll be working?" I asked.

"Oh, yes, miss."

We both put on gloves and hats. I noticed then that the skirt on her dreary gray frock was an inch or two short, showing her polished boots, although the collar and cuffs were new and well sewn.

"Have you tried letting out the hem on your skirt?" I asked. "I know it's none of my business…"

"I'm sorry. I know I don't look good enough for a

lady's maid for a duchess. But this is my best dress. I've grown since I got it when I joined Her Grace's household."

"If I bought you some fabric, could you make up a dress to wear when you go out with me?"

"Oh, yes, miss. I'll have it ready by your wedding day."

She certainly was eager. "That's only three days from now. In that case, we'd better buy some after we go to Blackford House," I told her. "Let's go find a hansom cab."

We walked to the corner and Lucy, with a shrill whistle and a wave, hailed a cab in a moment. "Well done," I said as I climbed in.

She followed me up and I gave the driver the address.

Lucy gave me a smile. "It was a skill I needed to develop with Lady Arabella. She never liked to wait for a cab. She was afraid someone she knew would pass and see she was out without a male escort."

"It's a handy skill." One I might one day need.

We arrived at Blackford House in a few minutes, and Lucy hopped out and looked around. "There's Hyde Park." Her mouth hung open.

"Indeed," I said, paying the cabbie. I hoped she'd grow used to her surroundings quickly.

We went up to the door and rang the bell. Stevens answered the door. "You've been expected, Miss Fenchurch."

"Lucy, this is Mr. Stevens, the butler. This is Lucy

Kebten, who's going to be my lady's maid. Your tour is going to have to include her accommodation."

"How do you do, sir?" She bobbed a curtsy.

He nodded. "Hello, Kebten. Well, shall we start with the duchess's room?"

Lucy swallowed a giggle. I guessed she'd never been called Kebten before. I suppose I should call her that, but calling her by her Christian name fit her better.

We went up one flight and Stevens opened the first door to the right at the top of the stairs.

I walked in and gasped. It was a huge room, well outfitted. I had expected this and had never asked before now to see what would become my room. However, everything—the flocked wallpaper, the bed hangings, the draperies, the seat cushions, even the lamp shades—was red. With my auburn hair, I looked terrible surrounded by red.

Lucy walked over and pushed the draperies open. "The view of the gardens is lovely. And it's nice and quiet back here."

I was grateful for that.

Stevens walked over and opened a door. "This connecting room is the boudoir."

I walked over and peered in past him. There was room for all my clothes, with a dressing table and massive wardrobes. There were red draperies at the window that matched those in the bedroom, and the same flocked red wallpaper.

Nothing the decorators couldn't fix in a hurry. It would be my first act as duchess.

Lucy slid past me while I was still trying to recover from the sea of red around me and looked at one of the wardrobes. "Good," she said. "You have a three-sided full-length mirror." She then demonstrated how to move the wardrobe doors to be able to see yourself from three sides without turning.

"Georgia?"

I turned at hearing Blackford's voice. He stood in an open doorway on the opposite side of the bedroom. It had to be the door to his room. The risqué sight made my heart beat a little faster, and I gave him a huge smile.

"What do you think?"

"You know how you said I could redecorate?"

He nodded.

"I want to start here. The red has to go."

"What color do you want?"

"Pale lavender. Pale yellow. Well, one or the other."

"Stevens or Mrs. Turner should be able to help you get that done before we return from our honeymoon. In the meantime, I want to show you something."

I followed him into his bedroom, trying not to stare at the furnishings or the dark blue colors. I wouldn't even face toward the bed. It felt like bad luck to gaze upon such a tempting location.

He opened a door at about the same position as the one in the duchess's room that led into the boudoir. This opened up into a white tiled area with a bathtub and a mahogany water closet and a pedestal sink, all with water taps piped in.

"The sink and tub have hot water come out of the

spigot," he told me. "Very hot water, heated by gas. The most modern accommodations I could find."

"Could I use it sometimes?" I asked in an awed voice. I had never seen such luxury.

"We're going to be married in a few days. Then you can use it all the time. Anytime you want." He stood there, looking as proud as if he'd built it himself.

He was very clever. I wasn't sure he hadn't. "It's beautiful. When did you have it installed?"

"Just recently."

"I'm so glad you did. But I must get back to Lucy and Stevens." I pointed behind me, where they were standing in the doorway between the bedrooms, pointedly studying the rug.

"May I meet Lucy? She's your new lady's maid?"

"Of course." I walked to where the servants waited. "Lucy Kebten, I'd like you to meet the Duke of Blackford. My fiancé."

She gave a deep, graceful curtsy. "Your Grace."

"Hello, Miss Kebten. I hope you'll be happy living in our household. I'm sure Stevens and Mrs. Turner will show you around."

"Thank you, Your Grace."

I turned to Stevens. "After we see Lucy's room and go downstairs, I'd like to meet Mrs. Turner. And find out who I should talk to about redecorating these rooms."

"Of course, miss."

Blackford went with us while we climbed up to the attic where Lucy would have a small room, plainly furnished, to herself. "Is it all right?" I asked her.

"All right? I've never had a room to myself before. It's a palace."

Blackford looked slightly surprised. "Good," he mumbled and headed for the stairs.

We followed him down to the ground floor, where Stevens led us to a small room facing the back not far from where I knew Blackford's study was. He opened the door to a cheery white and yellow sitting room with a small desk. The two windows, covered with white lace curtains, stood open to any small breeze that came in from the gardens.

A stocky, middle-aged woman in a light gray gown with white collar and cuffs stood in the middle of the room on the thick Turkish carpet. She gave us a deep curtsy when she saw us.

"Mrs. Turner?" I asked.

"Yes."

"Even though we haven't met, I believe I'm going to be relying on you a great deal, starting with the wedding breakfast and in getting the duchess's rooms redecorated while we're on our honeymoon." I walked over to her and held out my hand.

She looked a little surprised, but she reached out and shook it. "Whatever I can do to help. The wedding breakfast is taken care of already."

"I love this room," I said, looking around.

"It's the duchess's morning room. Of course, you'll want to put your own touches to it."

"I suspect my books will end up in here. Since this room is yellow, I would like to do the duchess's rooms upstairs in lavender."

She smiled. "Lavender is a pretty color."

I smiled back. I thought we'd get along fine. "This is my lady's maid, Lucy Kebten. She's new with me, and I'll be new to being a duchess, so we'll both be learning and asking for your advice."

"If I can help in any way, I'll be glad to."

After making plans for redecorating the duchess's rooms, we headed toward the front door. Blackford mentioned our plans for that night as an excuse to keep me close for a moment. I approved of his technique. I only wished I could have thought of an equally good excuse.

Then Lucy and I stopped at a fabric store on the way to Sir Broderick's. Lucy picked out a dark blue muslin with a tiny white overall pattern and dark blue thread. I couldn't wait to see how her gown would turn out. It would give me a good idea as to how well she would dress me.

From the way she held the brown paper parcel, I knew she was pleased with the fabric.

Once we alighted at Sir Broderick's, I sent Lucy inside to begin on her new frock. I had decided to gather as much information about as many suspects as possible in the hopes something would turn up to point the way in the investigation.

I made my first stop Miss Whittington's comfortable but narrow house, where I had called a few days before with Lady Westover and Lady Phyllida. I was again shown into the first-floor drawing room by the maid and stood there, admiring the porcelain miniatures, when a young lady in a dark green day gown came in.

"You wanted to see my cousin?"

"Yes," I told her, "I'm Georgia Fenchurch. I met her a few days ago."

"And what does this concern?" Despite her light brown hair and china doll complexion, she sounded as if there was real steel in her backbone.

"I need her aunt's address."

"Mother's address?" Her surprise sounded genuine.

Within the blink of an eye I realized this was the Derwaller daughter. "You're getting married next week, aren't you? Best wishes."

"Thank you. Yes, I'm Deborah Derwaller. Why do you need Mother's address?"

"Actually it's your father I need to speak to." And how could I explain that without raising more questions?

"Father? Why?"

"Gold was stolen from the Egyptian government and a Mr. Munroe was chosen by Lord Cromer to look into the matter. Within a week or two, he was murdered. His niece, who had been in Cairo with him, has asked me to investigate. Your father worked with everyone involved. I'm hoping he can shed some light on this tragedy."

"He had nothing to do with Mr. Munroe's death."

"Even so, he knew these men. His insights on his colleagues may help us catch a killer and let a young woman see justice done." And it was possible he was the killer, I silently added.

"How did you come to be involved in police work?" Her question sounded as if it came from a mind that never stopped inquiring.

"Mr. Munroe was killed in a foreign country, but those suspected are all now in England. Out of sight of the Egyptian authorities but not eligible to be investigated by Scotland Yard. I belong to an organization that helps grieving family members learn how their loved ones died when the circumstances are beyond the scope of our police and quite often who, if anyone, caused the death."

She stared at me out of big brown eyes. "Truly?"

"Truly."

"Good for you. I wish you luck." She walked over to a desk in the corner of the room and pulled out pen and ink. In a minute, I was escorted out of the house with the information I needed.

I hoped the other Derwallers were as forthcoming.

Perhaps they might have been, but when I rang the bell, no one answered. No maids, no footmen, no Derwallers. I looked around the street, hoping for inspiration, when a maid came out of the basement door at the next house.

"Excuse me," I called out, "do you know if the Derwallers will be home soon?"

"There's no Derwallers there. The family is the Pearsons, and they're in Russia. He's a diplomat and the government sent him there. Can you imagine?"

I wasn't sure if she meant our government sent people to Russia, or her next-door neighbors were going on a fabulous adventure, but she sounded amazed.

"No, she means the renters," said a voice through the open window from inside the kitchen next door. "They've only actually been here for an occasional day now and then since they moved in. She'll have to keep trying."

When the maid moved to repeat it, I told her, "I heard. Thank you," and went on my way.

Where were the Derwallers? Hiding out with their stolen loot? Hiding out from the law?

Frustrated, I headed back to Sir Broderick's in time to find Jacob coming up the pavement from the opposite direction with a dirt-smeared, bloodied, and torn Lord Cecil Isle walking unwillingly next to him. Jacob kept a firm grip on the man's arm with one hand while the other held fast to his shoulder.

Fortunately, Jacob looked to be in better shape. His jacket sleeve was half-torn off and I suspected he'd display a black eye for my wedding, but he appeared satisfied with his efforts.

I hurried ahead and rang the bell, summoning Humphries so that Jacob could march the young lord straight into the hall.

"Good heavens, look at you," Mrs. Hardwick said, her tone somewhere between horror and annoyance as she walked into the hall. "Jacob, go right upstairs and get cleaned up. And you, young man, come down to the kitchen with me while we make you look respectable. And don't drip blood on my carpet. How badly are you hurt? I don't know why…" Her voice could still be heard as she herded him downstairs, but the words were indistinct.

"I'd better go with her," I said, following her down the stairs. "It's Lord Cecil Isle. We don't want to lose him again."

By the time Mrs. Hardwick and I had cleaned up his cuts and bruises, Lord Cecil no longer looked like a whipped dog. "What happened to you?" I asked. "And don't even try to tell me Jacob did this to you."

He considered this before he shook his head and looked down again.

"Well?" I put insistence in my tone.

"Jacob saved my life. He jumped in and helped me fight off the thugs who were trying to kill me."

"Well, good for Jacob. Now why would anyone try to kill you?"

He looked up at me with a roguish grin, as if this attack had been an adventure. "I owe a gambling den a lot of money."

I shook my head. "If you owe them money, they don't want you dead. They wouldn't get paid back. They only planned to give you a beating. It looks like they succeeded."

He lowered his face, but I spotted a sly smile on his swollen lips. "I tried to pay off my debt by telling them I know where to find the gold stolen from the Egyptian treasury."

Could he be the murderer we were searching for? He didn't look violent. He just looked pathetic. "So what happened? It doesn't appear to have worked." I kept my voice hard.

"I told them it was hidden in Lord Barber's office. They broke in but couldn't open his brand-new combination safe." The grin slid off his face. "The bobbies arrived in less than five minutes and they had to scarper."

"Did you call the police?"

"No. Lady Barber did. She went out and got them. Lord Barber probably stayed in his bed, hiding."

"Why do you think that?"

"Where else would he have been? I slipped in behind the thieves, hoping if they found the gold I could find a way to claim the reward, and I didn't see his lordship." He shrugged and then grimaced. "Once things went badly for them, the thugs came looking for me. I didn't get out of London fast enough."

"Why would you tell them Lord Barber has the gold?"

"Stands to reason. Lady Barber always wants more. More money. More status. More jewelry. I think Lord Barber took the gold just to keep her happy. And why else did he get that brand-new combination safe in his study?"

CHAPTER THIRTEEN

"He couldn't have carried off the theft by himself." I wouldn't believe that.

"No, he had Hathaway and the Egyptian guard pull off the theft. Then he sailed on the same ship back to England with Hathaway." Lord Cecil Isle had an answer for everything.

"The *Minotaur*?"

"Yes, and met Hathaway on the dock after they landed in Southampton. He took the gold and came back to London. He's hidden it somewhere."

"Not his office, from the look of you," I scoffed, hoping to prick his pride to get him to reveal more. "Did Barber and Hathaway meet on the docks in Southampton?"

"Yes. And I suspect it had to do with the theft."

"How do you know?"

"Their ship was delayed by a storm in the Atlantic. I crossed the Mediterranean and reached England ahead of them. I went to follow Barber and find out what he did with the gold. And the first thing I saw was him on the docks talking to Andrew Hathaway."

"Where had Hathaway hidden the gold? If he stole

it, he had to get it back to London."

"I don't think he did. I think Lord Barber worked out the shipment with Damien Reed and has the treasure neatly tucked away somewhere. I'd bet on that safe."

Something else bothered me. "Then why did he attack Miss Munroe?"

"Who? Oh, the fair Eugenie. When did this happen?"

"Four days ago, near Charing Cross Road, in broad daylight."

He shook his head, and then winced. "I don't know. Four days ago, right after breakfast, a man banged on Lord Barber's front door demanding to see his lordship. Barber shot out the back door still pulling on his coat and hat. I lost him in the gardens. I thought he'd gone for the gold, but when he returned to the house after dark, he didn't seem to be carrying anything heavy."

"Why were you following him?"

He stared into my eyes. His voice turned hard. "It stands to reason Lord Barber has the gold. Hathaway wanted a share and now he's dead. I wanted a share to keep quiet about it. I still want my share. Or the reward. You have no idea what it's like working for a man like him. Vain, incompetent, selfish prig. And I'm the son of a marquess. I'm used to better treatment than to be someone's lackey."

I instantly pledged to raise my children to be less arrogant than this man was. I ignored his boast and said, "Who was the man at the door who frightened Lord Barber?"

"I have no idea."

Another task for Blackford. There weren't many financial secrets that escaped his notice, and I was willing to bet Lord Barber's morning caller was there about money. Or gold.

I had a few more questions for Lord Cecil. "Do you know where Lord Barber was when Mr. Munroe was murdered? It happened shortly after the party at Mustafa Fahir's."

His expression scornful, the young man said, "He could have been anywhere. He could have been killing Mr. Munroe."

The investigation was suffering from not being able to recognize the principal suspects. We had photographs now, but they were of the men's faces only. If they added or removed a beard, they would have worn the perfect disguise. "What does Lord Barber look like?"

"He's fat. Tubby. Disgusting. As big around as he is tall."

"Oh, he's short, is he?"

"He's your height."

The man who attacked Eugenie Munroe was taller than me and no more than average weight, from what I could make out of the man under the cape and top hat. The same description I would give of the man who took my purse and left me the threatening note.

But if Lord Cecil's theories were to be believed, Lord Barber killed Mr. Munroe and Mr. Hathaway.

Who better to be Lord Barber's accomplice than his

second-in-command, Lord Cecil Isle? And he was the right size to be Eugenie's attacker and the man who threatened me. "Where were you when Mr. Munroe was killed?"

"I suspect in the British Residency playing cards with some of the other officials."

"You weren't at the party at Mustafa Fahir's?"

"Assistants aren't important enough." His tone sounded scoffing. "We just do all the work."

He could have slipped away from the card game early and killed Mr. Munroe before the dinner party broke up. "You played cards at the Residency often?"

"Nearly every night Lord Cromer didn't have us playing charades and entertaining guests. Just penny bets. The others didn't have the stomach for serious gambling, but it passed the time in that sandpit."

"When did you return from Cairo?"

He smirked. "The day after Lord Barber left."

"Why then?"

"To follow him to England and find the gold, of course. I know he planned the whole robbery. He told me to stay for five more weeks and finish things up in the treasury. If he wanted anything taken care of, he should have seen to it himself. I wasn't paid to do his job and mine, too."

His expression turned hard. "Especially when it meant he could hide the gold, change it into our currency, whatever he wanted, before I could prove he was the thief and claim the reward."

"What route did you take back to England?"

"A ship across the Mediterranean, then a fast train across France and a boat across the Channel."

Allowing him to arrive at Southampton before the *Minotaur* docked. "What did you do after you saw Lord Barber and Mr. Hathaway talking?"

"I followed Lord Barber the whole way back to London. I was determined to have it out with him and learn what he'd done with the gold. It took me days to get in touch with him because he kept dodging me. He had the servants say he wasn't at home. When I caught up to him, he told me about Hathaway's death. He also swore he had no idea where the gold was."

"You didn't see him kill Hathaway."

"No, but it stands to reason. They only spoke for a minute and then his lordship," his tone dripped with sarcasm, "started toward the railway station. I had to hurry away to stay hidden."

"And you want the reward for finding the gold?"

"The reward, a share, anything I can get. I'm not rich, Miss Fenchurch. I can use gold as well as the next man." I thought he meant his smile to be ingratiating, but I thought it was sly.

"You're the son of a marquess. You should be better off than almost anyone around you."

"You've been badly misinformed, Miss Fenchurch. My older brother gets the title, the house, and all the perks and bills that go with that position. There's nothing left for me except a taste for the lifestyle I glimpsed as a child. I need the gold."

For once he appeared deadly serious, and I believed

him. "You're welcome to the reward if Lord Barber has the gold, but I don't think he does." I deliberately sighed. "I'm trying to find out who killed Mr. Munroe, and it wasn't for the gold."

"I thought the old man had identified the thief when he spoke to Lord Barber. I know he had a long talk with Barber the day before he was killed."

This was new, and I hoped true. "Who did Munroe name as the thief?"

"His lordship told me to mind my own business."

I hoped "his lordship" would tell Blackford.

Lord Cecil Isle left, looking his debonair, stylish self again despite bruises coming out on his face and dirt and rips to his clothes. I didn't feel sorry for him in the slightest.

As soon as he was out the door, I found Jacob, who was with Sir Broderick in the study. "Why would Lord Barber have a combination safe in his study? A brand-new safe he had installed only a few weeks ago since he returned to London and quit his position in the Foreign Office."

"I've had some of the Archivist Society members looking into the income and wealth of various suspects in the treasury theft. Lord Barber can't afford to resign," Sir Broderick said. "None of them can. Yet they have."

"Do you think the gold is in the safe?" Jacob asked.

"He was in a good position to plan the theft," I answered, "but I doubt he's Miss Munroe's attacker."

"There's no reason to suspect the same person did both," Sir Broderick said.

He was right. I'd been assuming too much. The mastermind of the theft didn't have to be Miss Munroe's attacker. "So how do we find out what's in there? Lord Cecil and his burglars didn't do very well."

Jacob grinned. "They tried at night. What if we were to go in during the day?"

"You need a safecracker," Sir Broderick said.

"Lucy," I replied. "My new lady's maid has very keen hearing. She opened the silver safe at the Duke of Duleign's."

When I saw their shocked looks, I said, "The butler and the footman had a bet."

"Would she be willing to try? And keep her mouth closed afterward?" Sir Broderick asked.

"She seems like a young lady who's up for anything."

"What shall we use? The gas leak ploy?" Jacob asked.

We'd had good luck with that before, but in houses with few residents. "There's Lord and Lady Barber plus a number of servants to get out of the way."

"Ask Blackford to get the Barbers out of the way for an afternoon."

"I'd have to tell him why," I told Jacob, "and he would refuse and tell me not to get my new lady's maid involved in safecracking for the Archivist Society. He may not admit to fearing a scandal, but he doesn't want me to take too many risks."

"What club does Lord Barber belong to?" Sir Broderick asked, digging through some papers. "Ah, here it is. Blackford belongs to that one. Have Blackford invite Barber to meet him there, and ask Blackford to question him for us."

"That he would do. And there's that big matinee recital tomorrow in aid of some good cause that every lady wants to be seen at and rub shoulders with royalty. Aunt Phyllida does a lot of the work for that committee. She'd know if Lady Barber has bought a ticket."

"Then if we can put Blackford to work tomorrow, we should be able to fix their gas lines. If the servants can't check with their employers, they'll listen to us." Jacob sounded so confident, I was certain he could carry out his part.

Now if Lucy could do hers.

A moment later, Humphries found me. "Lady Phyllida is here for your shopping expedition, miss."

The look on my face told them I had forgotten. "Show Lady Phyllida to the drawing room and tell her I'll be with her presently."

I ran upstairs. As Lucy helped straighten my outfit and repin my hat, I asked her, "Would you be interested in opening another safe the way you opened the last one? It would be for the Archivist Society, and you could never tell anyone."

"Will it be as easy as the silver safe?"

"I don't know. And if you can't open it, no one will be angry."

"I'll try to do it. When will you want me to do this?"

"Tomorrow afternoon."

I went downstairs and joined Phyllida. We traveled

by hired coach to Regent Street, the sunshine seeming to sprout shoppers on every inch of pavement. When we climbed down from the coach, Aunt Phyllida looked around and asked, "What are we looking for?"

"Hats, gloves, stockings, handkerchiefs. All those things I will need on the honeymoon that I can never have too many of." I gave her what I hoped was a smile.

"And then we'll go and have lunch." Phyllida sounded so eager that I couldn't refuse, no matter how hopeless I found the investigation and how much I was worrying about Miss Munroe's safety.

I rushed through buying stockings and handkerchiefs and lucked out on finding a light blue hat that was perfect for the outfit I had in mind. When we reached the glover, Phyllida entered first and then I walked in, blinking in the dark interior after the bright summer sunlight.

"Miss Fenchurch."

I heard the man's voice a moment before I could see his face as he walked toward me. "Lord Burke. How lovely to see you. Aunt Phyllida, this is Lord Burke. Lord Burke, my aunt, Lady Phyllida Monthalf."

We went through a round of bows and curtsies before a young man and woman joined us. A young woman that I'd met before, a simpering blonde to use one of Blackford's favorite descriptions, latched on to Lord Burke's arm and eyed us carefully. "Miss Fenchurch," Miss Sylvia Prescott said.

"How lovely to see you again, Miss Prescott." I wanted to add, were you the young woman who stole an

Egyptian coin from the dealer? There weren't many young women in this investigation, and checking the numismatic shops had been her idea.

"Let me introduce you," Burke said as he tried to detach Miss Prescott from his arm. "Lady Phyllida Monthalf, Miss Fenchurch, may I present Miss Sylvia Prescott and her brother Mr. Simon Prescott, children of Lord Prescott."

Another round of bows and curtsies, followed by comments about the weather, followed by good wishes on my upcoming marriage. Already I was bored, and Burke was one of the suspects in my current investigation. Mercifully, a clerk approached Miss Prescott with the gloves she had asked for, and another clerk came over to help me.

While Aunt Phyllida and I waited for the clerk to check the stock in the back, we wandered into an alcove to examine men's leather goods. I had delayed buying a wedding present for Blackford and needed inspiration. Across the shop, I heard Burke speak to his friends and then the bell jingled over the door.

Ten seconds later, I heard Miss Prescott whispering, "I don't care if he's penniless, he has a title. I would be Lady Burke. That makes up for all sorts of deficiencies."

Her brother murmured, "How would you pay for all the fripperies you so love?"

"If he should happen to find the gold, he'll be able to buy me anything I want. Gold and a title? Every woman will be after him. I need to get in there first." Her voice was just a hiss, but it carried nicely in the small shop.

"What if he misses out on all that nice gold?"

"I'll have to make sure he doesn't. Or make sure we find it first."

"I have no hope of finding the gold. You know I'm lazy. You need to find a rich husband, dear sister, who can afford us both." His voice was a purr, but I could hear every word.

"See to your own marriage. I want a title that will protect me from shopkeepers wanting to be paid. But first I'm going to visit every numismatic shop in London until I find the man with the rest of the gold coins. Can you imagine the offers I'd get with a dowry the size of the reward? Are you going to come with me?"

"So far you've had better luck with those shopkeepers than I would, dear sister. You keep up the hunt, and when you find the thief, let me know."

By now my temper was flaring and my face was so hot I must have been beet red. Phyllida raised her eyebrows and handed me a leather portfolio to examine. "Do you think Lady Westover would like this?"

It was a masculine-looking portfolio. After a second, I said in a carrying voice, "Do you mean for her to give to her grandson, Inspector Grantham of Scotland Yard?"

I heard some activity on the other side of the shop and then Miss Prescott said, "Oh, I don't know. I guess I'm not in the mood for shopping today. Simon? Let's go find Lord Burke." With a rustle of petticoats and the jingle of the shop doorbell, they left.

Lady Phyllida gave a little giggle. "Do you know, I just picked that up for a diversion. You looked so angry.

I didn't notice what it was."

I hoped Burke was smart enough to avoid Miss Prescott's clutches. Not that I thought he was worth Miss Munroe's attention, but he was certainly better than his friends.

It left me wondering what sort of crime made the Prescott siblings nervous at the mention of Scotland Yard. I suspected the gold coin stolen from the coin dealer. Perhaps this wasn't the first time they'd stolen valuables out of shops.

That, and Sylvia's comment left me suspecting that the Prescotts planned to hunt for the gold on their own. The field of treasure hunters seemed to grow by the day.

CHAPTER FOURTEEN

"What do you think those two are up to?" Aunt Phyllida asked near the end of our luncheon in the Cavendish Hotel dining room.

I set aside my linen serviette, ready to leave and avoid any thoughts on the Prescott siblings or more comments on my wedding from Aunt Phyllida. "I wonder what Lady Westover would make of these ferns. They look wilted."

"They are, rather. I imagine she would have a talk with the manager." She smiled at me. "Those Prescott children. They are up to something and I suspect it's rather dangerous. You saw how they left when you mentioned Scotland Yard."

"I think she wanted to chase after Lord Burke. Which explains why he's avoiding Miss Munroe."

"Who's Miss Munroe?"

I told her.

"She sounds a good deal more wholesome than Miss Prescott. And rather daring, too. I'd like to meet her."

"Perhaps you will." I was noncommittal, because I really needed to get on with my day. I tried to catch the eye of the waiter to sign the check. Blackford had put me on his account here and suggested it as a treat for Aunt Phyllida, Emma, or anyone else I wanted to take to luncheon.

This hotel had a fabulous restaurant, both in food and in service.

Blackford took good care of me. I wished I could pay back his kindness. A little voice inside said, *You'll have to be the best duchess you are able.*

"Oh, I'm so happy that both you and Emma will be well married." I'd lost count of how many times Aunt Phyllida had said that. She'd nearly worn me out with her enthusiasm.

"How are all the last-minute preparations going for the concert tomorrow?" I asked for a diversion. And for information.

"Wonderful. We're almost ready. You have your ticket, don't you?"

"Of course. Tell me, is Lady Barber going?"

"Let's see. As I recall, Lady Barber is Lady Ashwin's recently returned sister-in-law. Yes, they're both coming tomorrow."

"Splendid. I'm looking forward to seeing them there." Although I planned to be somewhere else.

* * *

I had just returned to Lucy and my neglected packing, knowing how far behind I was, when Blackford arrived at Sir Broderick's. I hurried to the door to greet him. "I'm sorry. I thought you said you'd be here later. I've been so busy packing I haven't dressed for the party yet. I'll hurry—"

He remained in the front hall. Odd, since he normally went to greet Sir Broderick first thing. "No need. I'm not here for tonight's ball. Did you meet with M. Aveneil? Your name and this address were on a note in his pocket." I could see concern etched in the lines appearing at the corners of his eyes.

A note in his pocket? "Yes. Sir Broderick and I met with him yesterday. We—"

"He's dead. Murdered."

"What? Oh, dear." My tea boiled in my stomach and I blinked away tears of shock and outrage. "He told us he suspected Lord Barber and Lord Burke. Do you think one of them...?"

Blackford held me, making me feel safe as he talked with his lips against my ear. "I want you to be careful with this investigation. Someone feels threatened and he's striking out at anyone who might prove a danger."

"Then why kill other people and only leave me a note?" Not that I minded being left alive, but it was insulting. Someone didn't think I was much of a threat.

"I don't know, but I'm grateful." He pulled me tighter against his chest. "I want you to take more precautions."

"I'm always careful," I said, snuggling into his embrace. "What happened to him?"

"He had his throat slit. I've spoken to Inspector Grantham. He said it was a particularly brutal killing."

I gasped. I wished I could escape the image in my mind.

"He was found on the banks of the Regent's Canal in

Camden Town, close to the rail lines. Nothing was stolen from the body. He had his money and his watch."

"Do they have any leads?" I rested my head against Blackford's shoulder and wished Scotland Yard had someone in mind. I wanted this nightmare to end.

"None that Grantham mentioned to me. He seemed particularly interested in Aveneil's interest in the stolen gold."

"I wonder who he was following?"

Blackford answered my question with one of his own. "Why was he interested in Burke?"

I pulled away and took a step or two into the hall, rubbing my hands over my arms. Now that I suspected Miss Munroe's unspoken fear was the possibility Burke was behind the murders, I hoped Burke wasn't the killer. "Mr. Munroe stood in his way of collecting the reward. M. Aveneil said it is worth about 100,000 pounds."

Blackford nodded with a grim expression. "And he needs the money now more than ever, since he's inherited the title and a burned-down Irish castle."

"But he would still have the rents from the farms. And people expect aristocrats to be slow in paying their bills. He should still be in a good position."

"He would be if the castle hadn't burned down. He needs to repair it or build a new one if he wants to continue to collect the rents from the farms. The Irish expect their landowners to live at the castle, the family home, from time to time. To show they're in charge."

In a dry voice, he continued. "Otherwise, they feel

free to rebel and not pay rent. And Burke isn't stupid. He knows what the Irish are like. He knows what he has to do to keep his position and keep the rent money coming in."

"The reward is enough to rebuild a castle?" Castle building was far outside my experience.

"Not only rebuild it, but improve it." Blackford gave me a wry smile. "Tenants in the north aren't much different than those in Ireland. Less rebellious, but equally demanding of our time. We'll be expected to make an appearance shortly after the wedding. They'll want to get a good look at you."

The fiery fear rose up inside me again. "Do you think they'll approve?"

"Just be yourself, friendly and polite, and they'll approve."

I knew the expectation as well as Blackford did. "As soon as the new heir is on the way, I'll be accepted."

He gave one jerky nod. "I'm afraid that's how they look at things."

Blackford left, promising to return at the appointed time and warning me not to leave the house. I wouldn't have listened to him, but I didn't have enough time to get ready and do any investigating.

I was also left with the task of telling Sir Broderick about M. Aveneil. I headed up to his study.

His response was one I expected. After I dressed and saw him in the drawing room later, he repeated his earlier worries. "I wish you'd stay in tonight. I'm worried about this killer, especially since he's already left you a note under strange circumstances and attacked Miss Munroe in public." He shook his head. "By the way, you look particularly fetching in that gown."

When Blackford arrived, he said the same thing, but in a more gratifying way and for my ears only. I must have blushed, because both Mrs. Hardwick and Sir Broderick came out into the hall at that moment and both of them raised their eyebrows.

We went out to the ducal carriage and climbed inside. Once we started off, I said, "You know the identity of every aristocrat who has money trouble. Please, Blackford, is Lord Barber one of them?"

"Why would you ask that?"

"I think aristocrats would have far fewer problems if they had to work every day like their servants instead of doing nothing."

Blackford smiled at me, just as he did every time I expressed what he called my radical views. "Being a man of leisure is the whole point."

"Well, I am very glad you're not like that." He knew I knew how hard he worked.

"I'm not, but I've found balls and dinner parties are good places to meet with financiers and other aristocrats with the goal of gaining their agreement or their partnership. You'll soon find society events are good places to learn things for Archivist Society cases."

"How bad are Lord Barber's financial problems?"

His expression was unreadable. "Georgia, why do you think Barber has money woes?"

"A few days ago, a man apparently called at his

house in the morning and Lord Barber ran out the back door, pulling on his coat and hat."

"Interesting."

Blackford was beginning to annoy me. "Yes, it is. What is going on?"

"Lord Barber's financial situation has nothing to do with your investigation." His tone was stuffy.

"That's true." I had to admit he was right, even if his staid tone annoyed me. "May I ask Lord Barber what Mr. Munroe told him the day before Munroe was murdered?"

"Can you limit it to that and not ask about him dashing out his back door?"

"Yes."

"Well, then, we'll just have to ask him, won't we?"

"Yes, thank you." I smiled at him, glad he'd said "we" so we wouldn't argue.

"I'll arrange it, but you must also promise not to ask where he went the day he ran out his back door."

"You know already, don't you?" That explained his tone. He couldn't, or wouldn't, tell me Lord Barber's secrets. He'd given his word, and his word was unbreakable.

"Yes." His tone held a note of finality. I knew I'd get nothing further from him.

I hoped he was learning which times he'd get nothing further from me.

The silence between us was stiff with edginess. Trying to dispel the tension, I said, "I realize you have secrets you need to keep to yourself. Business secrets.

Other people's secrets. Just remind me, when I get too inquisitive, that what you are keeping from me has nothing to do with any concerns of mine."

He smiled. "They're not secrets. They're confidences, and I must keep them. I'm not trying to exclude you from my life or my concerns."

We arrived at the ball and he helped me down. The skirt to this ball gown, a very deep blue that shimmered in lamplight, was wider than most and was liable to trip me up. That would be horrible, since the overabundance of fabric in the skirt was balanced with too little in the bodice. I feared springing out and causing a scandal.

The tiny puff sleeves above my long gloves, also in a very deep blue, would hardly be a help if disaster occurred.

Once more, I prayed the very well-paid modiste Evelyenne knew what she was doing.

We left our cloaks and headed toward the ballroom. As our names were called out and we entered, the entire room seemed to pause for an instant. I gave a quick glance down to make certain everything was still in place.

Blackford and I danced the first waltz together before he led me aside to introduce me to acquaintances of his. The first one, an elderly judge, went well, but I nearly choked when I heard the name of the second, a tall, thin, middle-aged man with a full head of gray hair.

"How do you do, Lord Castleley?" I gave him a deep curtsy. He wore the same arrogant expression that his wife did when she looked at me. Apparently, he had learned I was in trade.

His nod to me was perfunctory as he said, "Miss Fenchurch."

Blackford gave him a dark stare that told me he noticed the slight, and his voice was cold when he said, "Where is your wife tonight, Castleley?"

Please! Not here.

"She's somewhere around. Oh, she's over there talking to her cousin, Lord Cecil Isle, and his brother's wife, Lady Tidminster."

I looked over my shoulder to see the terrible Lady Castleley in close conversation with the money-grubbing Lord Cecil Isle and the angry Lady Arabella. He seemed to be enjoying what they were saying. Perhaps they were telling him all the ways they had made fun of me. "I didn't know she was related to Lord Cecil Isle."

"Yes. Are you acquainted with him?" Lord Castleley sounded amazed that I should know anyone in society.

"He called at our house this afternoon." Well, that was one way of putting it.

"Lord Cecil is the second son of the Marquess of Lasherham," Castleley said, talking directly to Blackford and ignoring me. "You'd think with all the opportunities that boy has had, since he won't inherit, he'd try to make good at some position."

"How many has he held?" Blackford asked, his voice dry, as if he were agreeing with Lord Castleley. I suspected he was after information without being obvious about it.

"Three, and nothing has lasted more than a year. His

father is fed up, I can tell you."

I could read between the lines. Isle wanted an income that didn't require effort and a life of ease that was handed to him. Unfortunately, he was born second. His brother, Lord Tidminster, was the only one who would inherit.

When Blackford went off to conduct business, I decided to try to do the same. Perhaps I could find Lady Barber or Lady Derwaller. As it was, there wasn't a single person associated with the British presence in Egypt to be found in the ballroom with the exception of Lord Cecil.

I spoke to several people I had met at dinner parties or Blackford had made a special point of introducing me to and tried to enjoy the party, but without Blackford or anyone associated with my investigation, I found it dull.

After a time spent watching happy couples dance past, a whirl of shining fabrics and sparkling jewels, I glanced over and saw Blackford coming toward me with a man I recognized from his photograph as Lord Barber. He didn't quite come up to Blackford's chin.

At last! I hoped he'd tell us everything Mr. Munroe told him or asked him the day before he was murdered. I also wouldn't mind finding out the source of income that allowed him to stay in England and not work for Her Majesty's government anymore, but I'd have to tread carefully or Blackford would stop me.

I wanted to eliminate Lord Barber as a suspect. I wanted the chance to eliminate anyone as a suspect. And I wanted Blackford to keep Lord Barber out of the way the next afternoon.

I started toward Blackford, focused only on him, when the commanding tone of Lady Castleley sounded directly behind my left ear. "Quite daring tonight, aren't you, Miss Fenchurch."

Not stopping to consider the wisdom of my words, I turned and faced her. "I don't have time for your nonsense now. There are two peers who wish to speak to me. When we finish, I'll return and you can be rude then."

I turned away and walked the few steps toward Blackford, only realizing once I reached him that Lady Castleley and the two women with her had been absolutely silent. And one of those women was Lady Arabella, who supposedly had set her cap last spring for Blackford.

One of the women to my left, I wasn't sure who, murmured, "Well done."

Blackford raised his brows.

I gave him a smile and turned to the short, pudgy man next to him, the top of his head devoid of any gray hair. "Lord Barber," I said with a curtsy.

"Miss Fenchurch," he replied with a bow.

"We'll talk in the library. It's vacant for the moment," Blackford said.

We walked off, past lovely portraits hung on the hall walls, and shut ourselves in the library. "I've been told you had a long talk with Mr. Bradley Munroe the day before he died. His niece has asked me to discover anything I can about his death."

"Our talk would have no bearing on his death," Lord Barber immediately said, a horrified look on his face as he leaned away from me.

"I'm sure it doesn't, except to tell us what Mr. Munroe was working on and what he was thinking. I'm sure your information will be valuable. And his niece would be most appreciative." I hoped I hadn't poured on the honey so thick that he would be suspicious.

As it was, he seemed mollified. "Miss Munroe is a nice girl. I don't know that anything we discussed might help her."

"Did Mr. Munroe come to see you, or had you needed to meet with him?"

"He came to see me. I had no need to visit with him."

I inclined my head. "Did he state a reason for seeking you out?"

"He did. He wanted to know if I trusted my second-in-command, Lord Cecil."

"Did you trust Lord Cecil?" Munroe must have had his doubts about the young man.

"I did at the time. His father is a marquess. His is an old and well-respected family." Lord Barber sounded like that was the best sort of proof.

"And now?"

"My good wife tells me she saw him when she went for the constable the night our house was overrun by burglars. Horrible, brutal men."

I wondered exactly what they'd done.

"He also left Cairo before he was due to leave and then turned in his notice from London." From his tone, I could tell he saw one event as troubling as the other. "And he'd taken a great deal of interest in our statue of Aphrodite."

"Oh?" Where was this leading?

"I bought the statue shortly before we returned from Cairo. It was quite large and made of porcelain. I was afraid it would never survive the sea journey, but we were lucky."

"And Lord Cecil was interested in it. Did he want to buy it?" Blackford asked.

"Cecil? Never. The man doesn't have any money, although I understand there's a great deal of money in his family. No, this was the only statue that was broken during the robbery. Not just knocked over, but deliberately ruined as well. Destroyed. An arm snapped off. All that lovely value gone. I could have sold it for a fortune."

Did Lord Barber value the statue for its beauty or its value? "Was anything else broken?"

"No, they never had a chance. The constables arrived at that moment and the burglars ran. Although it did appear that they had targeted my Aphrodite."

Was this where Lord Cecil thought Lord Barber had hidden the gold? Or had the statue been knocked over while the intruders were trying to open the safe? No wonder the men he owed money to were angry with him. They'd left emptyhanded, and Lord Cecil put the gamblers in danger from the authorities.

Lord Barber turned his pudgy face toward me, his eyes sunk between thick cheekbones and broad forehead. "I think Cecil believed I was smuggling gold in the statue. But Aphrodite was much too fragile to hide anything inside."

I smiled at him. "Why would he think you'd smuggle anything?"

He smiled back. "Why, indeed?"

There was something in his smile that told me the man had returned from Egypt with enough smuggled loot not to have to return. And it was in his safe.

CHAPTER FIFTEEN

"What else did you discuss?" Blackford asked, a little too quickly. What did he know that he didn't want me to find out?

"Munroe asked my views on who stole the gold. I told him I believed Mr. Hathaway was involved."

"Did you have any evidence?" I asked.

"He was holding furtive conversations." He nodded ponderously, as if this explained everything.

"With whom?" Would this man ever come to the point?

"The inspector-general of the police, among others."

"Perhaps he was sharing what he knew with the authorities."

"Then why did the police never get any further along?" He gave me a smug smile. "Because Hathaway was busy sending the police up blind alleyways."

"You wouldn't happen to know where the inspector-general is now?" Blackford asked. I guessed official channels couldn't find him either.

"No idea."

As I opened my mouth, Blackford shot me a look that told me to keep quiet.

"And the others Hathaway had furtive conversations with or spoke to in private?" he added.

"Sir Antony Derwaller, Lord Cecil Isle, and Mr. Damien Reed."

I gave Blackford a look. Those three names again. "Was there anything else you can think of from that conversation?"

"No."

I felt Blackford wanted a private word with Lord Barber, so I thanked him and left the room. I didn't want to go back and face all those happy dancers while I stood on the sidelines, so I looked for a little sitting room to hide in for a while.

When I opened the first door I came to, I discovered Lady Castleley and Lord Cecil in a compromising position.

My mind couldn't take it in.

It was certainly more than a friendly kiss. Their hands pawed each other's bodies. They seemed to be swallowing each other's mouths. And they were cousins. Oh, dear.

They must have heard something. Or perhaps I stood there stunned for longer than I thought. Whatever the reason, they looked my way and then jumped apart.

Lord Cecil laughed. "You should knock first if you don't want to be offended."

Lady Castleley said, "You needn't look so surprised. And you needn't tell my husband. It won't do you any good and may do you a great deal of harm."

I saw her hand shake as she adjusted her neckline.

She was afraid I'd tell Lord Castleley, no matter what she said. Here was my opening to stop her hurtful comments. "Perhaps a truce is in order. You stop belittling me at every opportunity, and I won't tattle every chance I get. Do we have an agreement?"

"Fine. You had already stopped being amusing." Her voice dripped scorn.

"So have you." I turned around and walked out, shutting the door firmly behind me. It might not have been a great response, but I had what I wanted. Lady Castleley's silence.

Was Lady Castleley supporting Lord Cecil? Was he trying to find the gold or get the reward so he could be independently wealthy? Or perhaps so he could afford to spend time in London society with his cousin without having the necessity of employment?

Seen up close, Lord Cecil could have been the man who jostled me on the pavement. He could also have attacked Miss Munroe. Was he the killer? Was he killing in his search for the gold or to protect the gold?

I went back to the ballroom, afraid of what other secrets I might encounter behind other doors. Blackford joined me a few minutes later, in time for another waltz.

Overall, we had a lovely time at the ball, and then we both enjoyed the ride in the carriage. Before we reached Sir Broderick's door, I said, "I don't think Lord Barber was telling us the whole story."

"I don't believe he was lying to us."

"I don't either. I believe he was being reticent since he was being questioned by a female. I know you're busy, but do you think you could meet Lord Barber at your club tomorrow afternoon and ask him the same questions? I think he probably can tell you more details than he'd bother to tell me, and something may be important. Would you please?"

"I'm lunching tomorrow at my club. He's a member. I'll ask him to meet me after lunch."

"Oh, thank you. I just know it's going to prove important." If not for the reason I was leading Blackford to believe.

* * *

The next morning, I stopped at Mrs. Allen's in the hope that Eugenie Munroe was there. The landlady sent me off to the park, saying Eugenie had gone out to enjoy the fine weather.

I searched the closest park and came up empty, so, grumbling at wasted time, I headed toward the British Museum by way of Bloomsbury Square. I found Eugenie in the square, sitting on a bench in the shade with her knitting needles flying.

"Miss Fenchurch," she greeted me. "Have you learned more about Lord Burke or my uncle's killer?"

I gave her a hard stare. "I've learned enough to know you haven't told me everything."

"What do you mean?" Her hands stilled, and I could now see she was working on a blue woolen vest.

"Gold was stolen, your uncle was killed, you and Mr. Burke rushed around Cairo searching for clues to the identities of the thieves, and you traveled back to England on the same ship as the man you suspected of your uncle's death, Mr. Hathaway. Then you found Hathaway dead on the Southampton docks. Now you're searching for Mr. Burke rather than trying to learn what steps the British government is taking to find the thieves and your uncle's killer. Could this be because there is a reward involved?"

She looked away.

"You're after the reward, not the killer."

She faced me, snapping, "Find the gold and you'll find the killer."

"You think Burke will find the gold first and take the reward, cutting you out. That's why you're so determined to find him."

"I could use the reward. Who couldn't? But I want to see my uncle's killer hang."

"But there's more, isn't there? What haven't you told me? Do you think Mr. Burke killed your uncle to make his way easier to the reward?"

"No." Her eyes blazed with fury as she faced me. "He didn't kill my uncle and he didn't kill Mr. Hathaway. He was worried that if I traveled on the *Minotaur* alone with Mr. Hathaway, he would kill me. Just like Mr. Hathaway killed my uncle. Mr. Burke was so worried he broke out of jail to make it to the ship before it left Alexandria."

"He what?" She hadn't mentioned this before. "Why was Mr. Burke in jail?" I sat next to her on the bench, wanting to hear every word.

"Someone, I suspect my uncle's killer, framed Mr. Burke for his murder. The Egyptian police arrested him after most of the Europeans had left Cairo following the Queen's Birthday celebration. We had just finished deciphering one of the messages my uncle took from Mr. Hathaway and were trying to book passage on the ship mentioned in the note."

"The *Minotaur*?"

"Yes. I went ahead and booked my passage so I could follow Mr. Hathaway and then took the train to Alexandria. There was nothing more I could do in Cairo."

"So you just left him there in jail." And I thought she loved him.

"Mr. Burke knew what I had planned, and I knew he was resourceful. He switched identities with a fellow Irishman arrested for public drunkenness. When they were brought in front of the magistrate, the other man was released. Mr. Burke took that man's papers and left, while the other man went back to the prison awaiting the arrival of the British consulate official."

"So Mr. Burke is still wanted for murder in Egypt?" Was it with justification, and what did that mean for Hathaway's murder?

"I imagine so. I don't think he'll go back there any time soon." She gave me a mirthless smile.

"So he escaped the prison by using another man's name and rushed off to Alexandria?"

"Yes. He just barely made it onto the ship."

She seemed to hesitate then. I thought about what she had said before and asked, "Did Mr. Burke search Mr. Hathaway's cabin?"

"Yes." She appeared to relax as she added, "His entire cabin, as well as his extra trunks and crates in the passenger cargo hold. No gold. No more incriminating messages. Nothing."

"Was the ship crowded?"

"Yes. A lot of British government officials and their families and servants were returning from India on the *Minotaur* before it stopped in Alexandria."

"So not many people you knew from Cairo made it on board?"

"Very few. Lord Barber was on board, along with his valet, Hathaway, and a couple of young clerks from the Residency. I got the last cabin."

She suddenly turned away from me as her mistake sank in and I realized what she had been hiding. I raised an eyebrow as I asked, "Where did Mr. Burke stay?"

"He hid in my cabin. He was a stowaway."

"And this is why you've been so anxious to get in touch with Mr. Burke since your return to England. You aren't afraid he killed your uncle for the reward." I hated the phrase even as I used it. "He ruined you."

She shoved her knitting into her bag and jumped up from the bench. Looking at me through narrowed eyes, she snapped, "Good day, Miss Fenchurch."

Before I could say another word, Miss Munroe sobbed, rushed down the path, and crossed the park.

I headed back to Sir Broderick's, considering Miss Munroe's unfortunate state while avoiding the few men on the pavement wearing capes. Tall, short, thin, heavyset, it didn't matter. I kept my distance. Would she ever speak to me again, I wondered as I stepped away from a stooped, gray-haired man in a cape, now that I knew her secret?

If anyone learned she was unchaste, she would be shunned. No decent man would marry her. I should have assured her no one would learn of this from me.

When I returned to Sir Broderick's, Jacob told me he and two others were set to be gas inspectors that afternoon at Lord Barber's. Someone was on watch to make sure both Lord and Lady Barber left.

"Will Lucy manage her job? We can't do it without her."

"I've talked to her," I told him. "We'll come up the side street and wait in the garden."

"We'll open the back door for you," Jacob said. "Good luck."

We had a light luncheon in case of nervous stomachs and then traveled to Mayfair by omnibus. "Are you ready, Lucy?" I murmured as we walked from the side street to the gardens behind the Barber residence.

"I'm going to try my best. I don't want to let you down." She kept hunching and lowering her shoulders and clutching and unclutching her fingers.

"There's no shame if you don't succeed," I told her, hoping to calm her nerves. "None of the rest of us could do this."

"Oh, don't say that." By the quiet wail in her voice, I knew I'd said the wrong thing. "I don't want you depending on me. I don't know what I'm doing."

"Neither do the rest of us. It's different every time.

Every investigation brings us a new problem. But if we're stopped, you're acting as my companion in calling on Lady Barber."

She looked at me wide-eyed. "But she won't be there."

"No. It's merely our cover story." I bent over, pretending to examine some flowers while keeping an eye on the back door. Once Jacob and the Archivist Society gained access to the house to check for any misregulated mantles, he would open the back door. That would be our signal to walk in and head for the study.

When I saw the door open, I felt my body stiffen. Time to begin. "Come on."

CHAPTER SIXTEEN

We went in the darkened house and up to the first floor, where we'd been told Lord Barber's study was. The safe sat on the floor against the back wall behind his large, well-polished desk.

Lucy sat down on the thin carpet and immediately began to work. After a moment, she stopped. "I need a glass."

I started to leave for the kitchen, but Jacob opened up his workman's satchel and handed her a clear water glass. She gave him a smile and got to work.

In no time at all, she called out that the first number was eight. Then she began turning the knob in the other direction. I glanced at the clock on his fireplace mantel. Only five minutes had passed. We were in good shape.

I stood there, not wanting to make a sound and distract Lucy as she listened for the tumblers to make the noise that said they'd connected.

Time seemed to drag, and every moment we were in there increased our chances of being caught. I kept an eye on the door, watching as Jacob patrolled the corridor. He and the other Archivist Society member inside made comments to each other that would lead anyone listening from outside to believe that they were, indeed, checking on every gas lamp and fixture in the house.

Already I was hearing a woman's voice that I thought was the housekeeper, Mrs. Smith, complaining to the man guarding the door.

Twenty minutes passed, and still Lucy hadn't been able to find the second number. We knew from using this technique before that anything past a half hour multiplied our risks.

At twenty-two minutes, Lucy called out fifteen.

One number to go.

Were we going to get inside the safe before we ran out of time? And what would we find inside? Would it be worth the chances we were taking?

I didn't want to leave here without knowing.

At twenty-nine minutes, Jacob came to the doorway and mouthed, "Wrap it up."

"Give her another minute or two," I mouthed back.

He shook his head. "The housekeeper is threatening to come inside."

"Lucy," I whispered.

She turned around, her eyes wide, as she opened the safe door.

I moved forward and crouched down to look inside, expecting to see gold coins. I saw gold, but none of it was in coin form. It was ancient-looking jewelry. Gold and gems in necklaces and masks and wrist cuffs and rings. And little gold statuettes, one I recognized as Bastet.

Lucy set some of the pieces on the rug so we could see what was behind them. More jewelry. More statues.

No gold coins.

"Quick, put them back, shut the door and let's go," I whispered, shoving the goods back inside the small space.

Lucy moved quickly. The safe was locked and we were in the hall when we heard two voices, one male and one female, coming from beneath us. I turned Lucy around and moved us both back into the study and eased the door shut.

Lucy immediately ducked behind the desk and I hid behind a well-stuffed sofa.

I heard Mrs. Smith, the housekeeper, saying, "You could have fixed a dozen leaks..." as her voice came closer to the door.

"It was up on the next floor. The room doesn't appear to be used much. They're the most dangerous kind—no, ma'am, the next floor," I heard Jacob say.

"I must check on the study before I go up and approve your workmanship. And you'd better not have dripped solder on the carpet."

"No, ma'am."

I heard the door open. I was amazed that she didn't hear my heartbeat pounding like a brass band in my chest. How would I explain this to Blackford? Oh, he wouldn't cancel the wedding because of this. Would he?

I started to see spots before my eyes. Either my corset was too tight for squatting behind couches or I was terrified.

I heard her steps pass me toward the safe. *Oh, please, Lucy, become invisible. Don't make a sound.*

I knew I was ruined.

"All right, now show me this gas burner that has caused all this commotion." I heard her footsteps march across the room and out the door.

"Governor burner," Jacob said. A moment later, the door shut and the footsteps moved toward the stairs.

I came out like a flash as Lucy peeked out from under the desk. I helped her up and we stuck our heads out into the hall.

All clear. We tiptoed partway down the stairs when we realized the maids were in the basement level. We'd never make it to the back door. I could hear Mrs. Smith's voice coming closer as she berated Jacob.

I grabbed Lucy's hand, hurried back up the steps and dragged her out the front door. Shutting the front door softly, we walked away sedately, as if we'd just been for a visit.

No one would pay attention to us if we looked like a lady and her maid out making calls.

It wasn't until we reached the corner that we stopped and released the breaths we'd been holding.

"Well done, Lucy. Let's call a cab."

"Good idea, miss. My knees are shaking."

* * *

We all met at Sir Broderick's for tea and scones. Lucy and Jacob were ravenous, and I discovered I ate two before I realized it.

"So there was no sign in the safe that Lord Barber

was involved in the treasury theft," Sir Broderick said.

"Exactly. Whatever he's involved with, it has nothing to do with Mr. Munroe's investigation. There's no reason why he would attack Miss Munroe or kill Mr. Hathaway or Mr. Reed."

"So we can eliminate Lord Barber from our inquiries?" Sir Broderick asked.

"Yes." I felt like a weight settled on my shoulders. One down, too many to go, and Blackford would be furious when he heard about this.

It wasn't until we were in the coach heading to that night's ball that Blackford said, "Barber only had one thing to add."

"What was that?"

"The gold left the vault a full minute early. Munroe seemed to find that important."

"It is if the person sending them off from the basement vault deliberately sent them early to hide the delay when they knocked the one guard in the head. Who sent them off?"

Blackford shook his head. "We'll have to find out."

"Can I ask you something and have you promise not to be angry?"

"That question makes me angry."

Oh, dear. "Why does Lord Barber have ancient Egyptian gold jewelry and statues in his safe? Did he bring them back to sell? Is that his new source of income? And how did he get them?"

He leaned back and stared at me, his eyes cold and his expression stern. "How would you know that?"

"We were told the gold coins from the theft were in his safe. They weren't, but this was what we found."

"Do you have any idea what would have happened if you, an almost-duchess, had been caught breaking into Barber's safe?"

"Not something I wish to contemplate."

"No. It is not."

"And you're not going to tell me where he got all those gold artifacts or what he plans to do with them."

"No, I am not."

It wasn't the first time he'd caught me wrong-footed. "I'm sorry, Blackford. I tried to take a shortcut on this investigation to wrap it up quickly and get on with wedding things, and it backfired."

"Promise me you'll never do anything like that again."

"What do you mean by, 'like that'?"

"Georgia," came out as a growl.

"I promise not to break into any more houses."

"Or businesses, or schools, or churches—"

"I would never break into a church."

His expression didn't change. "Or any building that doesn't belong to us."

There was no help for it. "I promise."

"I'm serious, Georgia. I couldn't have talked your way out of this. I would have been considered part of it."

"I'm sorry. I haven't become used to being responsible for more than just myself and my own reputation."

"All right. We won't say any more about this."

Blackford left me on my own at the ball without waltzing with me first. I knew he was angry, and I guessed he needed time to cool down.

I didn't see anyone I wanted to spend time with, and my fount of trivial conversational gambits was sorely tested.

I did find myself face-to-face with Simon Prescott. His thin blond face seemed to be a mirror image of his sister's. After our bows and curtsies, I asked, "Are you and your sister twins?"

"Why, yes. How did you guess?" he asked.

"There seems to be a strong resemblance between the two of you."

"Many brothers and sisters look alike," Simon told me.

"That's true. But you appear close in age, too."

"Half an hour in our case," he told me. "Have you seen Sylvia tonight?"

"No. Didn't she come with you?"

He peered in every direction. "She told me she had something to do and she'd meet me here. I'm worried. She should have been here by now."

"I'm sure she'll—"

"Oh, there's the delicious Lady Anne Honeywell. Excuse me." Nearly knocking me over as he interrupted me, Simon made quick work of reaching the lady's side. A lady who would have an absolute fortune settled on her.

I suspected Mr. Prescott had already forgotten his concern for his sister.

I didn't see any of our leading suspects, and most of the attendees seemed ten years younger than me.

I couldn't wait to leave.

Blackford and I finally danced one waltz near the end of the evening. We made up in the carriage, and then Blackford said, "There's a reason I want you to stay away from investigating Lord Barber. Can I trust you to accept it has nothing to do with the missing treasure?"

The answer came to me in a second. "There's another investigation involving Lord Barber, and you don't want me to compromise it. I'm right, aren't I?"

He nodded and then said, "You know nothing about it, and we're going to keep it that way."

I nodded. I didn't have time to investigate further. The wedding was less than two days away.

When we arrived back, too soon, at Sir Broderick's, it was to find both him and Mrs. Hardwick waiting up for us. Really, this was taking chaperoning too far.

To my surprise, Sir Broderick turned his attention to Blackford. "Your house called again, Your Grace. They ask that you please call back the moment you arrive. You have a visitor who is most insistent on seeing you tonight about the investigation. He refuses to leave."

"May I?" He headed for the stairs.

It was my investigation, too. I lifted all that fabric in my wide skirt and raced up the stairs behind him to Sir Broderick's study.

He put the call through, and I could tell at once by his expression that something was wrong.

When he set down the receiver, he said, "Lord

Burke is my visitor. He went to visit Miss Munroe about dinnertime tonight, hoping to explain to her his change in plans and offer to check on the status of the investigation into her uncle's death. She never returned to her rooms after she went to the park this morning."

My heart sank. "Oh, no. I saw her in the park this morning. She was knitting. And then we argued and she ran off."

"Which park and which way did she go?" Blackford asked me as we walked down the stairs.

His visible anxiety fed my worries. "She was in Bloomsbury Square and headed toward the junction of Bloomsbury Way and Theobald's Road. I don't believe she knows anyone in London, having lived in a Yorkshire village all her life. Well, except for her years in Oxford and her time in Egypt."

"What time did she leave you?"

"It wasn't quite yet eleven this morning."

He nodded. "If you'll excuse me, I'm going home to speak to Burke and see what our next steps will be." We hurried down the staircase together.

"Of course. Good night, and be careful." I squeezed his hands when we reached the bottom.

"By all means, be careful. You have a wedding in a matter of some hours," Sir Broderick said from where he waited for us in the hall. "Some hours" was stretching the point and he was smiling, but I don't think he was being completely humorous.

Blackford was one of the most capable, observant people I knew, but he took too many chances. Suddenly,

I had visions of my wedding day turned into a day of mourning.

Regrets filled my mind. Delaying giving Blackford an answer to his proposal. Delaying the wedding until summer, when he wanted to get a special license and marry immediately. If we made it to our wedding day in one piece, I vowed I would never make him wait for anything ever again.

He leaned over and kissed my cheek. "Do you want me to telephone and let you know what Burke can tell me, no matter how late I may ring?"

"Please. I'll wait in the study for your call. I'd be too curious to go to sleep until you tell me all the news." *And I know you're safe.*

I walked to the door holding hands with Blackford. Once outside he turned on the step and said, "Two nights from now, you'll be living in Blackford House." He smiled into my eyes. "You could listen from the next room if you wanted."

I stared back at him. "And I'd know you were safely home."

His kiss was brief. "I'll telephone you." He squeezed my hand, took the front steps two at a time, and climbed into the carriage with a leap.

I stood in the doorway and watched until his carriage disappeared around a corner. Then I shut the door and went back into the parlor. "Sir Broderick, you don't mind me waiting up for his call in your study?"

"Not at all. But why not wait with us in here for a while?"

"Yes," Mrs. Hardwick agreed, picking up her embroidery again. "He has to get home and question this man. Now, is there anything else we can do for you for your wedding day?"

I decided to try one more time. "I'd like Sir Broderick to be there. Are you certain you won't come?"

"I'd love to be there, too, Georgia, but my muscles have wasted in the time I've been stuck in this chair. And there are steps and other obstacles between here and the church."

"Blackford has footmen. Surely they could help you. And Jacob, and Sumner, and some of the Archivist Society members and—"

"I won't be lugged around like a sack of potatoes." Sir Broderick slammed his hands on the arms of his wheeled chair. Then he took a deep breath to calm himself. "I'm sorry, my dear, but I'll get to see you dressed for your wedding as you leave for the church. That will do." He smiled at me. "I'm very proud of you. I hope you know that. And your parents would be pleased. He's a good man."

"I wonder how long it will take us to get used to calling you 'Your Grace'?" Mrs. Hardwick said.

"I can't imagine getting used to hearing you say it," I replied. The change in my relationship with my friends was one of the things that had slowed my acceptance of the duke's proposal, and my friends had helped me accept that in all the important ways, our friendships wouldn't change. "Now, if you'll excuse me, I'll go up to the study and wait for Blackford to ring."

Nearly an hour after he left, the telephone jolted me away from the book I was reading. I picked up the receiver immediately and put it to my ear.

"Georgia," Blackford's voice rumbled out, causing my heart to jump in a very nice way. "Burke is with me now. He went back to Mrs. Allen's house to discover Miss Munroe had not returned since you were there. He crisscrossed the neighborhood looking for her without luck."

This wasn't the behavior of a sensible vicar's daughter. Worry, tamped down for a time, now flared. "This doesn't sound good."

"I realize it's late, but may we come over? Between us, we might be able to come up with a plan of action. And," he lowered his voice, "I would be able to see you again."

"Please come over. I'll be waiting."

Sir Broderick and Mrs. Hardwick were coming up in the lift as I left the study. I told them about our telephone conversation and added, "I'll send Humphries off to bed. I can let them in and lock up the front door after they leave."

"Do you want Sir Broderick to join you?" Mrs. Hardwick asked. Not an official member of the Archivist Society, she never offered to sit in on meetings, but I knew it meant she would also stay up, waiting in the next room.

"No. I'll tell you both what I learn at breakfast."

Shortly after I went downstairs I heard male voices on the front steps and let Blackford and Burke in at their knock. After I shut the door, Blackford led the way in, taking my arm without a warm glance or even a smile and escorting me to the parlor as if we were merely acquaintances. One of his less appealing ducal traits.

Mercifully, I only saw that trait in the presence of others.

Lord Grayson Burke followed us and then began to pace across the parlor. "I went back to the boarding house about nine, certain Miss Munroe would have returned, to discover Mrs. Allen had received a note from her saying she had run into a friend from Oxford and had gone home with her. Saying not to worry, and she'd be in touch later. The note was a forgery. A bad copy of Miss Munroe's handwriting."

"Are you certain or is this wishful thinking?" I asked.

"I'm certain." He crossed his arms.

"Still, I'm going to send a telegram to her father in the morning, asking for information about her college friends," I said.

"Not that it will do any good." He paced across the room.

"A necessary step, but I agree. I doubt it will lead us to her. She told me she didn't make any real friends at school, being a 'charity student,' as she put it."

"It's worth the little effort it will take," Burke agreed, "but we must fan out across London, searching where every lead may take us." His tone sounded as if I were too simple to think of this myself.

Did these aristocrats pick up that arrogant tone of

voice the instant they received their title, or was it bred into them? I felt blood leave my head as I thought, *Will my children all sound like this while still in the nursery?* God help me, I didn't want to dislike my own children. I'd have to make sure they had as normal a childhood as possible.

I jerked my thoughts back to the missing Miss Munroe. "We need to get the Archivist Society looking for her in the morning. In the meantime, have you contacted the police and the hospitals? There may have been an accident."

"I have, and the responses so far have been negative," Blackford told me.

"Were they willing to take a missing persons report? If not, we could ask Inspector Grantham." I thought we'd need every available set of eyes looking for her if we were to find her quickly and bring her home safely.

"They took our statements and issued a missing persons watch," Blackford assured me.

It looked more and more like she had been abducted. And I was the one who'd sent her running off after I'd insulted her. "I'll lead the hunt since I was the last one to see her."

"Georgia, won't you have other, more pressing duties to attend to tomorrow?" Blackford sounded more than a little annoyed. "And now that you've been warned off—"

I held his stare. "No. She may have traveled to Egypt, but I found her to be an innocent vicar's daughter. Alone in London, she could be in serious trouble."

Burke was still pacing. "And the killer could be someone she knows and trusts from her time in Egypt. I've been in touch with Lord Cromer, the head of the British mission to Egypt. He said since he returned to England, he has received several letters of resignation from his staff. This includes practically everyone that Bradley Munroe worked closely with at the Residency: the head of the police, the liaison to the treasury, the chief clerk, the secretary of the mission, even the vicar."

"Anyone we can eliminate? Or any we should pay particular attention to?" I asked.

Burke gave a single nod. "Colonel Gregory, head of the Egyptian police. Officially, he reports to the khedive, the Egyptian ruler. He was in a good position to plan and carry out the theft, and he thwarted my investigation at every turn. We don't like or trust each other," he added ruefully.

"What started that?" I asked.

"He was stationed in India with me years ago. A young lady we both fancied died of a snakebite after running through a garden at a party. Gregory blamed me for her death, since she had been speaking to me shortly before she ran off.

"After that, Gregory hounded me. When he wouldn't stop, I was finally forced to resign from the army. I took a position as a royal colonial investigator. I didn't see or hear anything more from Gregory until I arrived in Cairo to investigate the theft at the Egyptian treasury.

"From his position as head of the police, Gregory tried every trick he could think of to block my investigation. I thought it was because he was still angry with me, but now I realize he was well situated to commit the robbery."

"Do you think he has the gold now?"

"If he is in London, I can't think of any reason for him to be here except to collect the gold Hathaway smuggled out. He has no family. He wasn't supposed to leave Egypt for another two weeks. Lord Cromer heard from the khedive, who is furious. Colonel Gregory will not be welcome back in Egypt, and his was a good position."

I stared at him. "Perhaps he would come to London to continue his persecution of you. Or perhaps he thinks you have the gold."

Burke was about to deny it when I saw him reconsider. "It's possible Gregory might do either of these things," he said with a nod.

"Anyone else from this group of resignations who might be behind the theft?" Blackford asked.

"It could be anyone. I suspected Hathaway, but he's dead." Burke shrugged as he marched across the room again.

I interrupted to say, "You didn't kill him, did you? Miss Munroe's account of what happened in Southampton was somewhat disjointed. And she feels she has a reason to protect you."

Burke found Hathaway dead. Aveneil had been investigating Burke when he was killed. He was the right size to be our mysterious man in a cape. And I didn't trust him.

CHAPTER SEVENTEEN

"No." Burke looked from me to Blackford. "No, blast it. I only lost sight of him for a minute, and when I found him, he was on the ground and a figure was running out the other end of the alley between the storage blocks. The figure had too much of a head start for me to go after him. I saw to Hathaway, but it was no good. He died of his head wounds a few moments later."

"Go on, then," Blackford said. "The vicar, the secretary of the mission…"

"The vicar suffered from some tropical illness and has come home to England in poor health. Besides, he's a vicar."

The man had a lot to learn. "We'll excuse him from a role in the theft due to his poor health and probable lack of relevant knowledge, not because of his membership in the clergy. What about the liaison to the treasury?"

He looked at me, his eyes wide with surprise. "Barber? But he's not in the country."

"Oh, no, Lord Burke," I told him. "Lord Barber's not only in London, he was burgled by a gang I suspect was looking for the gold. They had no luck. They were sent by Lord Cecil Isle."

"Are you certain?" Blackford asked.

"Yes. Lord Cecil told me yesterday."

"Why didn't you tell me?"

I picked at a flounce in the skirt of my ball gown, unwilling to answer as freely as I would have liked in front of Lord Burke. "We were otherwise occupied."

Blackford cleared his throat and I thought I saw one curl spring up at the nape of his neck. "So you consider Lord Barber a possibility."

"He's another good choice. He's an impossible prig, and his second-in-command, Lord Cecil Isle, would do anything for money," Burke said. "Either is a good possibility, except they were accusing each other while we were still in Cairo."

"Perhaps they were working together and the accusations were just a smokescreen," I suggested.

"If it is, they've fooled everyone."

And then I remembered what Miss Munroe had said. "Lord Barber was on the *Minotaur*, as were you. So why are you so surprised to learn that he was back in England?"

"I didn't know he was on our ship. I was a stowaway. I was avoiding everyone. I couldn't go out on deck or to the dining room, so I wouldn't have seen him."

I supposed that made sense. "Did Mr. Munroe tell you the cart bearing the gold left the vault a minute early on its trip to be handed off to the Caisse?"

"No. But that implicates the Egyptian guards." Burke frowned.

"Their accomplice, who gave one of the guards a bloody nose, could have been English. The ghost, or whoever it was, must have come out of somewhere," Blackford said.

"The tax records room. Of course. Hathaway," Burke said, nodding as he considered the possibility.

"Exactly." Blackford sounded pleased.

"Miss Munroe told me about your escape from jail and stowing away in her cabin on the *Minotaur.* What she didn't tell me was whether you—" I glanced at Blackford.

He gave Burke a withering stare.

The man turned red and stared at the floor. "There was a terrible storm in the Atlantic off the coast of Portugal. We thought the ship would break apart and sink, and we were going to die. It was mutual at the time, but I've felt like a cad ever since."

The only sound in the room was the ticking of the clock. I don't know what the men were thinking about. I understood Miss Munroe's sense of abandonment. How dare Burke hide from her. "And now you are courting Miss Prescott, who sees you as a way to get a title, even if you don't have enough money."

Burke's eyes widened before his chin rose pugnaciously. "Miss Prescott and I are just friends, as I am with her brother."

"You may have to explain that to her. Or, if you don't, figure out how to pay the bills she sees as her right to owe for all the things she wants as Lady Burke."

"I'll deal with Miss Prescott," came out through

clenched teeth.

"We can't do any more tonight. Begin the Archivist Society efforts in the morning, and I'll go speak to Cromer. Please," Blackford added, taking my hand, "remember that the day after, you are to be married at ten in the morning."

"I'll remember. I hope this will be a short search, because I won't be able to sleep tomorrow night. Good night, my love."

"Goodnight, my duchess."

* * *

I tossed and turned the rest of the night. When I came downstairs in the morning, Adam Fogarty had already arrived to join us for breakfast. He sat down with a heaping plate of eggs and sausage and toast and said, "The part of the Yard that deals with visiting ranking police officers didn't know Colonel Gregory was in town. I've passed the word around at several precincts that we're looking for him."

"Excellent." I finished my tea and rose. "I'm off to Sir Antony's house. On the basis of our raid yesterday and whatever Blackford isn't telling me, I think we can dismiss Lord Barber from our list."

"So where does this leave us?" Sir Broderick asked.

"Lord Cecil Isle and Sir Antony Derwaller, unless Fogarty's colleagues can find Colonel Gregory. Nobody can fall off the face of the earth that completely." All our efforts so far hadn't led to him. Then I remembered a snatch of conversation from before Damien Reed was shot. "Mr. Reed said he met with him here in London a week or so ago at his club."

"That doesn't mean he's still here," Fogarty said.

"It doesn't mean he isn't. I'll see you later. I'm off to talk to the Derwallers."

"Be careful, Georgia. I don't want the mystery man attacking you again," Sir Broderick said.

"Do you want me to go with you?" Fogarty asked.

"No. Enjoy your breakfast. I'll be fine."

"After breakfast, I'll start checking my sources and see if anyone's heard of this Colonel Gregory," Fogarty assured me.

I hurried over to the address in South Kensington that their daughter had given me for Sir Antony Derwaller and his wife. Despite the early hour, I readied my calling card and marched up to their door, knocking on it loudly.

It was still cool out, their front door shaded by the angle of the roof and the sun, which was still hours away from its zenith. The house itself was like its neighbors, four stories and a basement, with the basement entrance under the front stoop. I could hear sounds from the open basement window and see the open draperies through the ground floor bay window. Unlike my last visit here, the servants, at least, were stirring.

A maid, as shown by her uniform, answered the door.

I didn't give her a chance to speak. "I must see your mistress as soon as possible. A young woman of her acquaintance, Eugenie Munroe, has gone missing, and we fear for her life."

"Let her in," I heard a woman's voice say from inside the darkened hall.

As I stepped inside and my eyes adjusted to the dimmer light, I made out the face of Lady Derwaller.

"Let's go into the morning room."

I followed her down the hall to the door closest to the back stairs. I suspected the steps led down to the backyard and the basement. Was Sir Antony in the dining room with its resolutely shut door? "I understand you borrowed this house from some acquaintances in the Foreign Office who were in Cairo with you."

"Yes," Lady Derwaller said as she opened the door, "actually, we met the—" Her voice ended on a shriek that nearly drowned out the crash from inside the room.

A moment later, a man I judged to be nearly the same height as Blackford, dressed in a black cape with the collar pulled up around his face and a black silk top hat pulled over his brow, shoved Lady Derwaller to the side with an elbow to her upper chest. I leaped forward in a foolhardy attempt to stop this theatrical burglar, swinging my handbag at his head.

I'd barely connected when he shoved a gloved hand against my face, thrusting my head back. His arms were longer than mine. Unfazed by my blow, he dashed unscathed down the half-flight of stairs and out their back door.

I stumbled backward a few steps before I fell into the side wall. By then the man was gone.

If he was the killer and Miss Munroe's abductor, I'd done badly against him again. But he hadn't managed to keep his face averted the whole time. With one small glance, I knew it was Lord Cecil Isle.

Catching my breath and rubbing my neck, I said, "Are you all right, Lady Derwaller?"

She nodded, her eyes wide with shock.

"Get your mistress a cup of tea with plenty of sugar," I shouted to the maid. "Lean on me." We stumbled the few steps into the morning room. After I brushed shattered pieces of porcelain—had it been a statue of some kind?—onto the floor, I sat her on the nearest chair.

She leaned her head against the high, heavily stuffed back and shut her eyes for a moment. When she opened them, she said, "Who was that man?"

"I don't know," I lied. "Did he do any damage beside breaking that—what was it?"

"A statue of some Egyptian queen. It belongs, belonged, to the lady of the house. She loved that statue. It was quite valuable."

It was rubble now. Like Lord Barber's statue of Aphrodite. Lord Cecil was still searching for the gold.

The woman looked around. "Nothing else appears to be missing or damaged." The maid brought in a steaming cup of tea and Lady Derwaller took a long drink. "And what are you doing here?"

I didn't wait to be asked to sit. My neck hurt and I was feeling a bit shocked myself. I brushed shards of porcelain off another chair and collapsed. "I'm sure you met Eugenie Munroe while you were in Cairo."

"Yes. A very nice young woman."

"She's been kidnapped here in London and we believe it has to do with the theft of the gold from the Egyptian treasury."

"I thought Cairo was bad, but London is even more dangerous. I can't wait until the wedding is over and we can leave."

"Your daughter's wedding," I said weakly. Mine would occur in a matter of hours, and here I had been, confronting a possible killer. My whole body shook for a moment.

Lady Derwaller didn't seem to notice. "My daughter is getting married next week. The next day, we head for Norfolk."

"Why Norfolk?"

"Sir Antony is a distant cousin of the current Earl of Marshment. He has been chosen to be the earl's new land agent. We are so looking forward to a quiet life in the English countryside we grew up in."

Easy enough to check, and if true, eliminated another suspect. Anyone who went to that much trouble stealing a fortune and killing to keep it wouldn't be taking a job as a land agent.

"Did Miss Munroe mention knowing anyone in London?"

"No. Her relatives are in Yorkshire. Miss Fenchurch, are you all right? You look quite pale."

I felt faint, but I dismissed her comment with, "It's the shock. Have you seen Miss Munroe since you came to London?"

"No. And you say she's in danger?"

"Yes. Can you think of anyone she would turn to for help?"

"Possibly Mr. Burke. He was helping her investigate her uncle's death. You know about that?"

I nodded and was glad to find my neck didn't protest. "Did Mr. Munroe say anything about the gold theft to you or your husband?"

She set down her teacup. "He said nothing to me. Excuse me while I see if my husband's up yet."

She barely left the room before she walked back in with a middle-aged man who was a bit on the short and stocky side. The look of shock on his face as he glanced around the room at the powdered and pebbled porcelain pieces convinced me he didn't have any prior knowledge of this attack.

"Are you ladies quite all right?"

"Yes. As soon as I opened the door, he came running out, pushed us out of the way, and dashed out the back door," his wife told him.

"Why was he here? What did he want?" Sir Antony asked the room, looking about in confusion.

"This seems to be happening to various members of the British delegation stationed in Cairo this past year. I think there's some connection with the missing gold," I told him.

He looked perplexed. "I'm sorry. Who are you?"

Lady Derwaller made the introductions. I nodded, not trusting my legs to curtsy while his wife explained that Miss Munroe was missing, possibly kidnapped.

"You were at the center of things in Cairo at the

time of the theft. Tell me what happened," I said, lowering myself back into the chair.

He brushed off a seat and sat to face me. "Everyone was in a dither after the theft. The entire city was like a treasure hunt at a children's party." He sighed. "Except that people died."

"Who's your favorite for this thief?"

"Oh, Hathaway, no doubt. We were both on the committee to readjust the tax rates and burdens facing the Egyptians. Hathaway was named chair of the committee, although I don't know why." He looked at me and gave his head a small shake.

"That's neither here nor there," he continued. "I had the feeling something was going on during April, but I had no idea what. I just had a vague feeling that something was amiss. Then came the first of May and the theft. I had my suspicions, you understand, but no proof. None whatever."

"Did you tell this to Mr. Munroe?"

"Yes. His own suspicions ran that way, but if he could prove it, he didn't tell me. And then he was killed."

"Were you familiar with the storage for the Egyptian tax records in the treasury building? I understand the storeroom was off the hall that the gold passed through on its way from the vault to the reception room where it was handed over to the Caisse."

"Yes. We used those records to make our recommendations as a committee to improve the Egyptian tax system. We were in and out of there at least daily." I could see when the idea struck him. "The storeroom was searched for the gold, but not until a week after the theft."

"And the gold could have been moved out of the treasury in that week?" I asked.

"Yes. No one thought to look for the gold inside the treasury building for days after the theft, and then only because Mr. Munroe insisted. Everyone was checking boats and trains, even camels, leaving Cairo."

"In light of the theft, did anything you overheard in April make sense or point to a particular person?"

"No. I wish it had." He ran a hand through his thinning brown hair. "Then I might have been able to prevent Mr. Munroe's death."

"I've been told you had an argument with Mr. Munroe in the street outside Shepheard's Hotel the day before he was murdered."

"Where did you hear that?" His tone was full of bluster.

I kept my own tone detached. "Is it true?"

He reddened. "Yes."

"What was it about?"

Sir Antony folded his arms over his chest and leaned back. "My daughter convinced his niece to take her to the souk. Just the two of them, without a chaperone or a male guard. They were gone for hours. Munroe was beside himself. Nothing happened to the girls, but he blamed me. He was very protective of Eugenie."

"Would you have allowed your daughter to go into the souk alone?"

"Alone, no, but Eugenie speaks fluent Arabic. I didn't think they'd get into any trouble. And they did take one of the maids with them," he added, as if this solved any problem of propriety.

"Was this the only time Miss Munroe went into the souk without a male escort?" Something I wanted to ask Eugenie, if we could find her.

He shrugged. "So far as I know. Munroe certainly acted like it was."

"Was the souk that dangerous?"

"Alone? Eh, possibly. In pairs? And with a maid? I wouldn't think so. My wife used to shop there with only our trusted housekeeper to do some of the translating."

"Any idea who Munroe's murderer is?" I hoped he had some idea.

"None. I'd guess the thief, since everyone knew Mr. Munroe was leading the investigation into finding the gold and the thieves. He'd said he was sure the head of the thieves was an Englishman, and our country would eventually have to pay if the gold wasn't recovered. That didn't make him popular with anyone at the Residency."

"Including Lord Cromer?"

"Especially Lord Cromer. I heard him tell Mr. Munroe not to say that unless he could back it up with facts. Munroe said he hoped to have his proof soon."

"When did he say that?"

"A day or two before he was killed. Hathaway and I were standing outside the door waiting to give a report. We could hear every word. Hathaway turned bright red and looked like he wanted to kill Munroe then and there." Sir Antony looked at me and colored. "I don't mean to imply—"

"But you thought it, didn't you?" I asked.

He loosed a deep breath and nodded. "Yes, I did. But Hathaway's dead. Anything he could have told you is lost."

"Who did Hathaway often talk to during that period? Or socialize with?"

"Colonel Gregory, for one. I found him in our office a few times talking to Hathaway when no one else was about. And then there was Lord Cecil Isle. The two of them could play cards all night. Other than them, Hathaway didn't seem to have many friends. He spoke to Lord Barber frequently in Barber's office, but all they seemed to do was argue."

As I left their home, I ruled out Sir Antony, but it didn't get me closer to Eugenie's prison. There were still too many possibilities.

Including that I had once again faced Lord Cecil, possibly the killer, only to be easily brushed off by him. I was determined he wouldn't get away so easily next time.

CHAPTER EIGHTEEN

Once I returned to Sir Broderick's, annoyed that Lord Cecil could get away so easily, I spent the morning packing and sending trunks to Blackford House. I hoped the mindless tasks would set my brain free to figure out where Eugenie had been taken. She wouldn't have set off on her own overnight.

Sergeant Fogarty arrived much earlier than I expected. I hurried down to the front hall, saying, "You've learned something."

"Not something I wanted to learn. A young woman was found dead early this morning in a mews in Mayfair."

My heart tipped over. Miss Munroe.

"She was wearing a ball gown. And in her dancing shoe was an Egyptian gold coin."

My heart righted itself but my brain could find no way out. "Cynthia Finch? The woman who supposedly stole it from the coin shop?"

"As soon as I found out, I contacted Inspector Grantham. We showed a photograph to the coin dealer," Fogarty said. "It was the young woman who came to see him. Scotland Yard has identified her as Sylvia Prescott."

Her brother had been looking for her at the ball the night before. "What happened to her?"

"She was stabbed to death."

I sat on the stairs and stared at him. I was certain of two things. The thief was still in London killing people to protect his identity, and Miss Munroe was in even graver danger.

And then I remembered Lord Burke's words from the night before. *I'll deal with Miss Prescott.* Was he protecting his claim to the reward, which he needed so badly? Or did Miss Prescott have a hold on him that he didn't want to honor?

If that was the case, could Miss Munroe be next? She certainly had a right to have a claim on him after what happened on the ship.

Fogarty left to continue his investigation, assuring me that Inspector Grantham and the Yard were working on the case. In answer to my request, Emma came over as soon as she could. The baby hadn't thrown off her posture or her gait yet, but her stomach was definitely leading the way. Of course, being Emma, she was still the most beautiful woman in any gathering.

"I got your message. Where are we going, Georgia?" Emma asked as she walked past me to greet Mrs. Hardwick with a familial hug.

"I'm going to the last place I saw Miss Munroe yesterday morning and ask all the omnibus conductors and hansom cab drivers I can find if anyone saw her. She was wearing an exotic-looking bright red silk shawl and she is young and pretty, with brown hair and dark brown eyes."

"I'll be glad to go with you. I'm tired of Sumner telling me to rest while he writes."

"Not until you stay for a bite to eat," Mrs. Hardwick said. "You need to feed the babe."

After we ate, Emma and I set off to Bloomsbury Way and Theobald's Road. We split up the vast number of vehicles that passed us at the last place I saw Miss Munroe. We questioned every cabbie we could stop and all of the omnibus drivers and conductors. Emma and I hadn't worked together on an investigation in nearly a year, but old habits served us well.

Emma's blossoming middle and undiminished beauty meant every cabbie and driver was solicitous of her. The sparkle in her eyes told me she was enjoying this change in her routine.

I was grateful for her assistance.

Even with this extra help, it took us over an hour to find a conductor who remembered Miss Munroe by her flame-red silk shawl. Emma and I climbed aboard the omnibus and rode next to the conductor.

"I thought she'd get run over crossing the street like that, her red shawl flying out behind her. She was in such a hurry she didn't look out for carriages or wagons and nearly was run over twice before she reached us. Those drivers had to pull up on their teams pretty quick, I can tell you."

"Who was she running from?" I asked.

"Why, she wasn't running from nobody. She was following someone. Someone in a hansom cab. She'd seen the passenger and was after him. Told me he had disappeared before and she wouldn't let him do that again. I guessed he was a male admirer."

"Did she say anything else?"

"Only that he wasn't an admirer."

Blast. That could be Burke, or possibly she figured out what happened in Cairo. This didn't give us a clue. "Where did she go?"

"Rode with us as far as Grays Inn Road. The cabbie turned left there, so she hopped off and jumped on a bus heading that way."

"Do you remember which route was painted on the outside of the omnibus?"

"Caledonian Road. I thought it was odd since that neighborhood can be rough. Dangerous if you're not careful about how you go. Could be she didn't have to go that far. Ah, and here you are."

"Thank you so much." Emma and I climbed down and began the process again. Now the questioning was limited to all the drivers and conductors on the omnibuses painted with the route "Caledonian Road."

It went faster this time. I thanked Providence that Miss Munroe wore that bright scarf in this smog-scarred town. It only took six omnibuses before we found a driver who remembered her.

"Sure, I'll take you to where I dropped her off. It's not a usual stop, but she was insistent. The hansom cab she was following turned in around there somewhere. Now you sit down, missus," he added, addressing Emma.

A man leaped up and gave her his seat. She thanked

both men and gave them a glimpse of her beautiful smile. She sat, I think gladly, and gave a sigh.

We rode longer this time. We were on Caledonian Road when the driver pulled the bus over. "She got off here."

"Here" was just before we crossed the Regent's Canal. Beyond the shops along Caledonian Road were brick row houses, and beyond them on our side were old brick warehouses backing up to the railyards along both sides of the canal. On the other side of this main road were houses as far as I could see.

"Who was in the cab?" I asked.

"I don't know. I lost sight of it. I don't know why she thought it pulled in here. She was watching it closely, I suppose. I was watching out for traffic and passengers and pedestrians stepping out into the road. Doesn't leave no time for watching cabs."

"Thank you. You've been most helpful, taking us this far in her journey," Emma said. We climbed down, Emma giving the two men her thanks again, and stood on the pavement looking around.

"I guess we begin by asking in these shops. We can hope she stopped in one of them for an address or directions," I said. "I'll take the other side of the street and you can have this side. Shout if you find anything."

Emma nodded and walked into the first shop, a greengrocer. I crossed the street, avoiding being knocked down by a cab and then a wagon. The first shop I came to was a butcher shop. I walked in to find a young man, little more than a boy, behind the counter.

"I wonder if you can help me," I said. "I'm looking for a friend who may have come by here yesterday asking for directions. She's an attractive young woman and she was wearing a bright red silk shawl."

"A stranger to this neighborhood?"

"A stranger to London."

"No strangers when I was in here yesterday."

The next shop, a newsagent with some sweets and tobacco displayed, was operated by an older woman. She'd been at her sister's and her husband handled the shop yesterday. He was at the racecourse today and wouldn't be back for hours.

And so it went. I'd asked in every shop for a block in each direction before I crossed back to join Emma, again dodging traffic that seemed to want to flatten me.

"Any luck?" I asked.

"No. You'd think everyone would have noticed that red silk. I can't wait to see it myself."

"Same here, because that would mean we'd freed her." I was hot and tired. I needed to sit down and think.

"Let's take a cab back and tell the rest of the Archivist Society what we learned. Maybe someone will have an idea what to do next," I said. "And Emma, thank you. This went way beyond what I could expect."

"I'm still a member of the Archivist Society and I still want to do my bit. Thank you for asking me." She linked her arm in mine. "It reminded me of the old days. Before marriage and the baby. It reminded me I'm still my own person."

"I think that may be why I took on a case so close to

the wedding. I don't want to let go of me. Of my talents."

"You won't, Georgia. Don't worry." She gave my arm a squeeze. "Now, let's find that cab. I'm tired."

We crossed the street to head back into town and I noticed cabs and wagons stopped for her; the driver of one lifted his cap. Emma was young, blonde, and beautiful. She'd always stopped traffic.

We returned to Sir Broderick's to find some of the Archivist Society members, including Sumner, Fogarty, and Jacob, as well as Blackford and Lord Burke, waiting for us. Burke leaped to his feet as we entered the drawing room and said, "Did you find her?"

He looked behind us, and when she didn't appear, his shoulders slumped.

Sumner had jumped up as well, but he'd gone directly to Emma and asked if she felt all right. In his eyes, the rest of us didn't exist.

"Fogarty, are you acquainted with the constables at the station closest to Caledonian Road and the Regent's Canal?" I asked.

"A few of them. Why?"

"We traced Miss Munroe's travels as far as that spot, where she alighted from an omnibus. That was the last sighting of her, and none of the shopkeepers we spoke to remembered seeing her yesterday, morning or afternoon."

"Well done," Sir Broderick said.

"Did you try some of the houses around there?" Burke asked.

I turned and glared at him. I think one or two others

did the same. Jacob said, "Which ones do you think they should have called at? There are hundreds in the area. Thousands."

Burke shut his mouth, but he gave Jacob an irritated look.

"We've ruled out Lord Barber and Sir Antony Derwaller. Unless there is someone else you want to add, I believe our list of thieves and murderers is down to two. Lord Cecil Isle and Colonel Gregory, who was last sighted in London a week ago." I looked around. No one made any other suggestions.

"Where would Isle hide Miss Munroe?" Blackford asked. "He's living at the St. George Club. Trust me when I say there is nowhere to hide a lady, or a female of any description, in the St. George Club."

"I know somewhere else he might hide her. Fogarty, if you'll talk to the constables at the Caledonian Road station and see if anyone on our list has a connection with that area, I'll check on the most likely place for Lord Cecil to hide a woman."

I took a deep breath and continued. "Lord Cecil burgled Sir Antony Derwaller's house this morning. He knocked me over, but not before I saw his face."

"Good grief, Georgia, stay home," Blackford said.

Before I could reply, Mrs. Hardwick came in and said, "We're just putting tea on the table. Please, everyone have something to eat. You'll need to keep up your strength for what may be a long search this afternoon and evening."

We all murmured agreement except Burke. "Thank

you, Mrs. Hardwick, but I'm going to the last place Eugenie was seen. If I learn anything, I'll send a message."

"Wait. Lord Burke." I hurried after him.

He paused by the front door.

"Have you been told they found Miss Prescott murdered this morning?"

"Yes. With one of the Egyptian coins in her possession. What was she doing?" Burke sounded as baffled as I felt.

"She showed a great interest in this investigation. Could she have found the thief?"

"I don't know how. Fogarty, who told me about her death, also told me the address the seller of the coin used was fake."

"Perhaps she kept trying coin shops in the hopes he'd try to sell some more. Perhaps she saw him and followed him. Was she resourceful enough to do that?"

"To get her hands on a fortune? She'd do that and more."

"I'll have the Archivist Society check more coin shops. Maybe we'll get lucky."

"We don't have time for that. We must find Miss Munroe."

As he turned to leave, I stepped in his path. "Last night you said, 'I'll deal with Miss Prescott.' What did you mean?"

"That I'd talk to her." He looked away and then back at me. "I certainly didn't plan to kill her."

He nudged me aside. I watched in shock as Burke

strode out of the house, shoving his hat on his head. What did he hope to accomplish on his own? Did he think he'd have better luck than the rest of us, or did he already know where she was?

No, he couldn't know. He seemed genuinely worried about Miss Munroe's fate. But he was the right size to have been her attacker. "Someone needs to follow him. To make sure he does go to Regent's Canal."

"You don't trust him?" Blackford asked.

"No. I think he's in the clear for Mr. Munroe's murder, but he could be guilty of trying whatever means are necessary to find the gold and claim the reward."

One of the Archivist Society members said, "He doesn't know me. I'll go," and hurried away.

Jacob watched his friend leave as he shrugged and said from the dining room doorway, "I'm with you, Mrs. Hardwick. Come on, Adam, you can talk to the constables after we eat."

"After all that running around today, I'm hungry," Emma said. Sumner and she walked arm in arm into the dining room.

"Georgia?" Blackford asked.

"Let's have tea and then I'll find out if my idea of where Lord Cecil could hide Miss Munroe is any good." If she wasn't there, I was out of ideas, and I didn't want to admit defeat.

"May I give you a ride somewhere?" he asked, his hand on the small of my back.

I was tempted to lean into his touch, even if I couldn't feel anything through my corset except a slight pressure. "Please. Your presence might be useful."

Luncheon was a quiet affair. Sir Broderick sat in his wheeled chair at the end of the table closest to the burning fire, even during this warm weather. Mrs. Hardwick, who had no use for heat in midsummer, sat at the other end of the table, open windows at her back. The rest of us took places on either side, but we ate without speaking.

Jacob ate with the enthusiasm of the young, but I don't think the rest of us noticed what we ate, when we remembered to lift our silverware. We were worried about the missing young woman and what the death of the other young woman meant for our investigation.

Fogarty said he'd round up some help and have them check all the coin shops.

Blackford didn't ask where he was escorting me until luncheon was over and we were in his carriage.

"Lady Castleley's," I told him.

His eyebrows rose. "And you want me along in case Lord Castleley is present."

"I don't want him to hear what I'm going to ask his wife."

He leaned back with a sigh. "We're not going to have secrets from each other, are we, Georgia?"

"Only when they involve presents. I like those to be surprises." I gave him a big smile.

"Agreed. Our only secrets from each other will concern gifts for the other." He smiled back. Then he turned serious again. "You think Lord Cecil is hiding Eugenie Munroe at Castleley House?"

"It would make sense. Lady Castleley and Lord Cecil are kin. Closer than most kin." I wouldn't tell him what I'd seen at the ball. "Lord Cecil was involved in the burglary at Lord Barber's and this morning broke into Sir Antony's house, I suspect in a search for the gold. And if Lord Cecil Isle asked Lady Castleley to keep Eugenie Munroe safe in her house, never letting her outside because of some danger or threat, Lady Castleley would do it with no hesitation."

The rest of the ride was quiet, with the two of us curled up in a world of our own. It ended too soon with our arrival at Castleley House.

I climbed down into Blackford's arms and then we walked together up the wide walkway to the front door. The garden was magnificent. The windows gleamed. The shutters shone with fresh paint.

It didn't look like a place Miss Munroe, or anyone, would be held against her will.

We went up to the front door, rang the bell, and handed our calling cards to the stiffly formal butler. Blackford's calling card, when he glanced at it, unbent him sufficiently to show us into the drawing room.

He left us then and I circled a drawing room full of marble busts and porcelain figurines, tiny ships in glass curio cabinets, and scraps of papyrus writings framed and hung behind glass. The crisscross pattern on the wooden floor was repeated on the green papered walls. The room might as well have been in a private museum and demanded solemnity. It didn't appear to be a room that attracted warmth.

I was glad I didn't give voice to my thoughts since a moment later, Lord Castleley came into the room. "This is early for a visit, Blackford." He didn't appear any friendlier than he had at the ball.

"A young woman is in danger and Miss Fenchurch thinks Lady Castleley may be able to shed some light on her hiding place."

Castleley kept his gaze on Blackford, never glancing my way. "Isobelle? That seems highly unlikely."

"It may be, but I'd like to put my questions to her. Privately." I kept my voice lowered as I wondered if he'd glance my way.

"What could you do for her that Isobelle can't?"

My hope lifted. That sentence sounded like Miss Munroe was here. "That remains to be seen. May I speak with your wife? Alone?"

After a long pause, Castleley walked over and pulled the bell rope. A moment later, the butler returned.

"Take this woman to Lady Castleley."

I followed the man out and up the front stairs. We went down a short hall where he knocked on the door at the end before slowly turning the knob. What Lord Cecil had said I should have done at the ball.

I hadn't, and I had learned a great deal.

"What is it?" I heard from inside as the butler entered the room.

"His lordship asked me to bring this woman—"

I stepped around the butler. "Lady Castleley. We need to talk."

"No, we don't. Show this—"

I interrupted her with, "Did your cousin ask you to keep Miss Munroe safe? Or did he just tell you to keep her out of sight?" The room had two large windows overlooking the gardens, giving a breathtaking view. It was hard to picture anyone being held against their will in this house.

She sat up from the reclining sofa she lay on, her jewel-red dressing gown flowing down her slender body. I gave a second's thought to how awful I would look in that color with my auburn hair before she said, "What are you talking about?" She waved the butler out of the room.

When he shut the door behind him, I walked over and said, "A young woman, Eugenie Munroe, is missing. She is the key to finding the gold Lord Cecil is looking for. She's in danger, unless you know where your cousin has hidden her."

Something flickered behind her pale eyes. Jealousy? Curiosity? "I know Cecil is trying to find some stolen gold, but I've heard nothing about this Miss Munroe."

"Has he told you the finder's fee for leading the police to the gold is 100,000 pounds?"

I saw a stunned expression cross her face before she said, "Sit down."

I took an overstuffed chair in a pink material and faced her. From here, the view out the windows was of the top of a large apple tree. "At this point, we've narrowed it down to two people who could have the gold and would want to hold Miss Munroe hostage. Your cousin is one of them. We have no interest in the gold.

We only want Miss Munroe set free unharmed."

"We?"

"The Duke of Blackford, the Archivist Society, and me."

She nodded. "I know Cecil wants the gold. I had no idea finding it was worth so much. Does Miss Munroe know where the gold is?"

"No. She only knows a friend of your cousin had the gold when he was murdered."

She fell for my trap, nearly leaping from the couch. "Murdered? Do you mean Cecil could be in danger?"

"If he doesn't have the gold and is trying to find it, yes, he's in peril. If he has it, everyone in his way could be in danger. Several people have been killed trying to take possession of the gold."

She sank back down. "The idiot. Yes, he's trying to find it, but he hasn't found it, and he isn't holding this woman hostage."

I stared at her. "Are you certain he doesn't have the gold or the young woman?" I decided to try one more trick. "He was the man identified as the one who stole my handbag to slip a threatening note inside."

CHAPTER NINETEEN

"Yes. Cecil is childish and selfish and greedy, but he's not a killer and he doesn't have the gold. If he had the treasure, he'd have bragged to me about it. He did brag to me about stealing your handbag." Lady Castleley gave a smirk that quickly dissolved as I raised my eyebrows at her.

Inwardly I cheered. One mystery solved. "I thought he had. I'm not after the gold. It's not worth dying for."

"It would be if you'd grown up in a marquess's home where nothing you saw would ever be yours. Please believe me, Cecil had no intention of hurting you. He only wanted to frighten you off."

"He did more than that when he shoved both Lady Derwaller and me and destroyed a statue of an Egyptian queen. Fortunately, neither of us was seriously hurt."

"Oh, Cecil wouldn't—"

"I saw his face," I shouted. Lowering my voice, I said, "He didn't tell you about that, did he?"

"No," she admitted.

"Now a woman's been kidnapped. The stakes have risen and we won't be frightened off. If Lord Cecil continues playing games, he will get hurt." I gave her a hard stare.

Lady Castleley blew out a sigh. "You were right. If he had the woman, he'd bring her here for me to hide." She rose and called for her maid. "If you find Cecil, don't hurt him. He isn't the villain you seek."

She told me to wait as her maid had her dressed and coiffed in record time. I wondered if Lucy and I would ever work in such harmony.

Then Lady Castleley joined me at the door and we walked downstairs together to the drawing room where Castleley and Blackford still stood a dozen feet apart. "Is the young woman here?" Castleley asked, his expression thunderous.

"No," his wife said with a charming pout. Castleley must have fallen for that expression at one time.

The butler hovered near the door, trying to listen for orders and look invisible at the same time. I didn't envy him his job.

"There you have it. Now, you've taken up enough of our time. Good day." Castleley's glance at me was murderous.

I considered pouting, glanced at Blackford, and decided it would be wiser to avoid acting like this simpering woman.

The butler opened the door for us, and Blackford and I left. Once outside the house, I said, "It's up to Fogarty now. Everything is pointing to Colonel Gregory. But Lord Cecil was my handbag thief."

"Just to give you a note? Aren't there easier ways?" Blackford asked.

"Lord Cecil seems to like to play pranks."

Blackford grumbled before he said, "Back to Sir Broderick's?"

"Yes. Fogarty will head there as soon as he gets a location for our missing colonel."

Once we'd climbed into the carriage and were on our way, I said, "Why do people like the Castleleys hate me so much? Is it only my birth into a middle-class family?"

"You're a reminder that you are rising in social circles by who you are and what you've accomplished, and not a title some ancestor earned. And the more people who do as you've done, the less room there is for impoverished aristocrats to live their empty lives without paying for their fun."

He took my hand in his. "Look at the peers who are married to American heiresses rather than the daughters of English peers. And then think about the number of fathers who worry about their daughters marrying a man without a title, without a fortune, or not marrying at all."

"So it's not personal." I heard the tone of wonder in my voice. "It's because they don't believe I deserve to marry the most eligible bachelor in England. They believe you should marry someone more like them."

He put an arm around my shoulders and pulled me close. "If I were willing to marry someone from my own circle, I'd have done it long ago."

I glanced up at him and he nodded, a small smile crossing his lips. "Once we're married and have a family, they'll forget they ever had any objection to you. There will be someone else to earn their ire. Someone else who'll commit the same sin."

I relaxed into his embrace. Those murderous glances and snide comments would soon go away.

After learning Fogarty hadn't returned with the colonel's address, Blackford left to take care of business, telling us to call Blackford House when we heard from the retired policeman.

I asked and discovered no one had heard from Burke or his Archivist Society tail, either.

I tried to pack. I tried to read. I found I was getting nothing done as I paced. In prior times when all I could do was wait, I'd spent the time shelving books in the bookstore or helping customers. I doubted Grace, who was handling the bookshop efficiently on her own with Frances Atterby's help, would appreciate me interfering the day before my wedding.

I couldn't make social calls because I wouldn't be available the second Fogarty returned to Sir Broderick's. I couldn't go out for a walk and enjoy the nice weather. I couldn't drop in on Lady Westover and Aunt Phyllida because they didn't have a telephone. There was a telephone at Blackford House, but Blackford wanted to get some business conducted and the servants were readying the house for the wedding breakfast and didn't need my interference.

Word came back that Burke was asking at houses and shops along Caledonian Road and its side streets. He hadn't kidnapped Miss Munroe. His worry was genuine.

I paced the study carpet until Sir Broderick threw me out. Emma was home resting after our busy search, Sumner was writing, and Jacob was at the law office.

These days, Jacob was presumably working. He'd found a profession he liked almost as much as lock picking, and he kept busy in the office studying the law.

Later, after hours that felt like days, I heard a knock at the door.

I rushed to the front hall to find Humphries holding the door. Fogarty came in rubbing his knee, saying, "I found the house. It was rented two weeks ago to Mr. Hathaway."

"Hathaway died longer ago than that. He couldn't have rented the house." A moment later, I felt sure I knew who had used Hathaway's name.

Fogarty grinned at me and I smiled in return. This had to be the place. I nearly jumped up and down with joy. We should find Eugenie Munroe and the gold there.

"The renter matches the description of Colonel Gregory. And he's been to two other numismatic dealers selling Egyptian gold coins. They identified him from his photo. And a young blonde woman was there asking questions just before he arrived in one shop."

"Miss Prescott could have seen him there." Which meant Burke was innocent. "Let me call Blackford House. And leave a note for the Archivist Society to follow us." I ran up the stairs, my feet flying with joy.

"And call the Yard. Inspector Grantham needs to know," Fogarty called out.

I picked up the telephone receiver and gave Sir Broderick's quizzical expression an answering smile. "Blackford House, please."

When the phone was answered, "Blackford House, Stevens the butler speaking," I felt deflated.

"This is Georgia Fenchurch. Is he there, Stevens?"

His voice warmed. "No, miss. He's at a club conducting business, but I'm not certain which club. May I take a message?"

"Tell him we've found where Colonel Gregory must be. Please have him call Sir Broderick as soon as he gets this message. He has the address."

"I will, miss."

"Thank you, Stevens. Good-bye." I hung up before I heard his reply.

"Fogarty found him," Sir Broderick said, leaning forward eagerly.

"He was renting under the name of Mr. Hathaway."

"Clever. No one would be looking for Hathaway in connection with the gold or the murders now. He's dead." I heard the grudging admiration in Sir Broderick's voice.

"Fogarty and I are going over there now."

His tone immediately changed to concern. "Is that smart? Only the two of you? Shouldn't you wait for Blackford or Sumner or Jacob or some of the others from the society?"

"We're just going to peer in some windows and find some good vantage points for watching the house. Send over help as it becomes available. We have hours of sunlight left to make our move." I picked up the telephone again and called Scotland Yard.

There I didn't find as willing a message taker. I ended up leaving a long and detailed message for Inspector Grantham that included the address. I asked the constable writing this down to give it to the inspector as quickly as possible. An abducted young woman was counting on him.

"Yes, miss," the constable said, sounding a little doubtful.

"It's important," I told him and hung up.

I scrawled down the address Fogarty had told me for Sir Broderick and hurried downstairs.

The retired policeman was sitting at the dining room table having a cup of tea and some of Dominique's homemade biscuits with Mrs. Hardwick when I came into the room.

"If you're going to spend hours watching this house for any sign of Miss Munroe, you'll need sustenance," Mrs. Hardwick said.

"Sergeant Fogarty will. I've done nothing all afternoon but rest." I paced to the window and looked out through the lace curtains. A breeze blew through the open window and ruffled them into my face. I batted them away.

Fogarty sighed. "I understand your eagerness to get her away safely before you need to get ready for the wedding. Give me a minute and we'll go."

"I'm not trying to hurry you, Adam. I can't settle today. I think it's the wedding."

"Got the jitters, have you? Happens to everyone before the big day." He gave me a wink.

He didn't take long finishing his tea, but then our travel across town in the busiest part of the afternoon took forever. We took an omnibus on the same route as Emma and I had taken that morning, stopping just before the bridge over the canal. There was no room on the top level where the breeze made the ride cooler, so we sweltered in the lower level. Dust and smells came in the open windows and then were trapped inside.

I was glad to get out of the stinking bus into the heat of the late afternoon on Caledonian Road.

"It's this way," Fogarty said, and led me down a side street. We were so close to the canal I knew the buildings on one side of the lane must back up onto the towpath. There were a few houses on the canal side and beyond them was a series of warehouses.

Fogarty walked me down the pavement, saying, "It's the last house there," in a low voice. We walked past the old brick structure, two stories tall with small windows, a slate roof, and fireplaces at each end. Then we took the path past a warehouse that led to the towpath.

From where we stood, to one side of us we could see a basin off the canal and then the York Road and the huge railyards for the terminus for the northbound trains. In the other direction were a few houses and then the bridge that carried the Caledonian Road over the canal. Across from us, warehouses with solid brick walls only had windows up near the roofs to let in light.

"Few places for people to overlook a house on this

street," I said. "Was M. Aveneil's body found along this part of the canal?"

"Yes. A little closer to the basin, I think."

Despite the heat, I shivered. In the middle of the bustling city, here was a spot that probably wasn't looked upon from one hour to the next. I shook off my unease. "What's our next step?"

"Wait for help. This isn't the type of neighborhood where residents take any notice of what happens outside of their doors. If we need help, they won't come to our aid."

"Then I'll be glad when some of the other Archivist Society members arrive." I'd be even happier if Blackford appeared at that moment.

On the ground floor in the back of the house were windows surrounded by ivy. If I could get that close, they were low enough that I could see in. "I'm going to peek inside. You keep watch."

"It's not safe."

"I want to find out if I can see any sign of Miss Munroe."

"Georgia..."

I passed through the gate of the low wooden fence and walked up to stand next to the closest window. By leaning into the ivy and pressing my face close to the glass, I could make out a large black iron stove and a table. The room appeared empty.

I glanced back at Fogarty, who was watching the area. Tiptoeing to the other window, I again stayed out of sight, hidden by the ivy. I pressed my face to the glass with the leaves as a mask. This appeared to be a main room, with a fireplace and a few chairs. Also empty.

Turning around to the sound of a twig snapping, I found Fogarty standing near me with his hands in the air. Another man stood close behind him. A man I'd only seen in a photograph.

Colonel Gregory.

Then I saw the revolver he held. I swallowed hard. The barrel was huge.

It looked like I was facing a cannon.

And I knew if he shot us full of holes, no one would remark on hearing gunshots.

Aiming the gun at me, Gregory had Fogarty take off his jacket. The colonel found his knife hidden in an inside pocket.

There was nowhere to run and hide. But while his attention was focused on Fogarty and his coat, it only took me a moment to open my handbag and snatch the folding knife Blackford had given me. I slipped it up one of my sleeves, which were tight from wrist to elbow.

Gregory threw Adam's jacket at him and said, "Now your handbag, Miss Fenchurch." Wonderful. He knew my name.

I had already clicked the top shut and wordlessly handed it over. He rummaged through it, a scornful look on his face, and handed it back.

Then he aimed the gun at Adam and said, "Walk around to the front door. Don't make me shoot your friend, Miss Fenchurch."

The way he held the gun close to Adam's back, he

knew I would follow his directions. Fogarty was my friend. I wouldn't do anything to endanger him. I had no choice.

As I walked around the house toward the front door, I said, "There are plenty of other people who know where you are and that we are here, Colonel Gregory."

"By the time they realize you're missing I'll be long gone. A million in gold can buy plenty of anonymity for the rest of my life. They'll never catch me."

CHAPTER TWENTY

"We found you," I told Colonel Gregory. "You weren't as clever about hiding under a dead man's name as you thought." Despite the dry weather, there was no one about on the towpath or the side street.

"No. I caught you." His laugh when he said this chilled me worse than the inside of the gloomy old house he pushed us into. The front hall was small, with a closed door on either side and a steep staircase in front of me. The wallpaper was peeling at the edges and water stained. The air was clammy, stale, and smelled of dry rot.

He ordered us both upstairs. "And if you're good, I might let you live."

"How many people have you killed since you stole the gold, Colonel?"

"If I answer that, I would have to kill you both to keep my secret safe." His chuckle made my skin crawl. "Now, move."

The stairs were steep and while I could climb them quickly, Fogarty took his time with his bad leg. I turned around at the top of the staircase, looking for a way to fight back. There was nothing. Just a few closed doors.

He forced us to the door at the end of the short hall and told me to unlock it.

"No."

He lifted the revolver, a six-shooter he'd probably saved from his military days, to fire. Fogarty jumped forward and fought him for the gun.

I yelled "Eugenie" just before the pistol fired, sending plaster down on our heads and filling the small hallway with smoke, dust, and the stench of burnt gunpowder.

In the aftermath, I thought I heard a scream before Gregory gained control of the gun and smashed Fogarty in the head with the side of the weapon. The old policeman went down in a heap.

Gregory pointed the gun at him. In a cold voice, he said, "If you want him to live, open the door."

I unlocked it, pulling the key out as I turned the knob. It was a small, dark, stuffy space without windows. In what light came in from the open doorway, I could see Eugenie Munroe sitting on the floor a few feet in front of me, tied up, gagged, her eyes wide open and her hairdo falling about her ears. Her hat was a short distance away.

At his gesture, I stepped inside the room and stood to one side of the doorframe. He half-dragged, half-threw Fogarty in to a spot near Miss Munroe and slammed the door. I readied my handbag.

Then he reopened it. "Where's the key?"

I smashed him over the head with my bag.

The only effect was to make him angry. He pushed

me against the wall, his hands around my throat. "The key."

I dropped it away from the door.

As he reached for it, I slid past him and ran.

I was down the stairs in a second, but I couldn't open the outside door. Locked. And no key.

I didn't have time to pick the lock.

I had to get out now.

I turned and opened one of the doors, shutting it behind me. I couldn't find a key and his footsteps were pounding down the stairwell. The only window in this room, a small drawing room or dining room, was open but as small as the one in the back. I doubted I could get out this way.

This was it. I was a dead woman.

The only potential weapons I saw were twenty large crates labeled "Hathaway." I instinctively saw a use for the wooden slats. Colonel Gregory was a soldier and a formidably sized man, but I wouldn't give up without a fight.

I would need every weapon I could find against him.

I propped a chair against the door under the knob. Then I tried to pry one of the crates apart with my gloved hands. Where were our reinforcements from the Archivist Society? If they didn't show up soon, we'd all be dead.

Gregory banged against the door, making it shake.

"Help. Help," I yelled out the window.

I had failed to tear the crate apart when Colonel Gregory crashed open the door, breaking the chair.

"That won't do you any good. No one around here notices anything. Safer that way for everybody."

He came toward me, the gun raised, and I picked up the crate. The statue of a cat, supposedly hollow, was surprisingly heavy, but I had strong arms from all the books I'd moved over the years. These had to be the crates Burke and Eugenie had searched on the *Minotaur*.

Swinging it slightly up and down as he looked at me with a smirk, I raised it as high as I could and flung it at the colonel. He smashed the crate to the floor with one fist. Rather than strike him down, the crate broke apart on impact with the stone floor. The statue shattered and the wooden slats of the crate splintered into pieces. Gold coins shot across the room from inside the slats.

I stared at them in wonder before I smiled at the audacity of the plan. "No wonder they couldn't find the gold from the Egyptian treasury in Mr. Hathaway's trunks. It was hidden inside the hollowed-out crate slats. The statues were a red herring."

"I won't let you have the gold," Gregory snarled as he crushed the shards of the statue beneath his feet in an effort to reach me.

I dodged away from him, pushing another crate between us. "I don't want the treasure. I just want to know who killed Bradley Munroe. That's the only reason I've been involved in this."

He aimed his pistol at me. "I killed Munroe."

Keep him talking, Georgia. Help will be here soon. "Because he wanted the gold?"

"Because he was going to take it away from me. It

amounts to the same thing."

"And the Egyptian guards?"

"Hathaway was supposed to knock the one fellow out. He botched it, and the guard wanted part of the treasure to keep quiet. The other wanted more than his agreed-upon fee."

"And then Hathaway got greedy?" I was sensing a pattern.

"He planned to go into hiding with the crates. He changed the plan. My plan."

"And Reed? And Aveneil? And Sylvia Prescott?"

"They all wanted my treasure." His eyes gleamed with avarice. "And now you'll be the next to die."

"Except I don't want your money. I just received what I wanted."

"Nonsense. Every woman wants more."

"I'm about to marry a wealthy man. I'll be richer than I ever thought I'd be. Than I want to be. Keep your gold. I don't want it."

I could see in his eyes when he decided not to shoot, but his pistol, still aimed at me, convinced me not to fight. He pinned my arms back and forced me to march out of the room and up the stairs before I could find a weapon or an escape route.

"I'd kill you," he said in an annoyed tone, his breath making my ear itch, "but I have too much to do to pack up the gold before I leave tonight. If you stay locked up, someone will let you out eventually. At least you'll live to see your wedding day. More than you deserve for the trouble you've caused me."

"You win," I said and relaxed my muscles. Perhaps he'd let his guard down if he thought I was compliant. "Did Damien Reed design the slats for the crates?"

"He built them, too. Brilliant man, but greedy." Gregory unlocked the door to the room where Eugenie and Fogarty were, threw me in, and slammed the door. As I fell on my hands and knees, disoriented by the darkness, I heard the lock click.

"Adam? Eugenie? Are you all right?" I whispered.

Adam groaned. Eugenie gave a muffled shriek. I headed on my hands and knees toward the sound of the shriek. After some fumbling, I managed to get the gag out of her mouth.

"Oh, Miss Fenchurch. Thank you. Can you untie my wrists?"

"Call me Georgia." Untying her was going to take a great deal of trial and error in the dark. "I found the gold."

"Where? And call me Eugenie."

"Inside the hollowed-out slats of the crates containing the large statues of the cats and dogs."

"Bastet and Anubis. They're Egyptian gods."

I was so surprised at being corrected on such a minor point I nearly giggled. Then I remembered there was nothing funny about our position.

As I worked on the ropes binding her hands, I asked, "How did you end up here?"

"When I left you in the park, I walked out to the main street. I saw Colonel Gregory riding by in a hansom cab. He should have been in Egypt. I thought he was following a lead as to who killed my uncle, so I followed him here. He invited me in and told me he hadn't had any luck finding the killer. Then I saw the statues of Bastet and Anubis that Mr. Hathaway shipped home on the *Minotaur*. His name was still on the label on the crates. The next thing I knew I was in here."

"There are twenty large crates downstairs with the statues inside. There could be gold coins hidden in the slats of all twenty." It was an audacious plan to smuggle the gold.

"Colonel Gregory said Damien Reed had the crates built to hide the coins." Then I had another, more frightening thought. "I wonder how many other crates and chests Reed had built to allow all sorts of people to smuggle valuables out of Egypt? And for whom?"

Eugenie didn't seem interested in other smugglers. "Mr. Hathaway shipped his statues in those twenty large crates. We looked all over those crates. And the gold was inside the slats the whole time." She gave a little *aaah*. "No wonder we couldn't find it."

"Colonel Gregory must have been at the center of the theft. And he told me he killed your uncle and the other victims to keep the treasure."

I felt her stiffen for a moment and then let loose a sob. "My uncle thought Mr. Hathaway was the danger. No wonder Colonel Gregory was able to come into Uncle Bradley's room and kill him. But how can we prove it?"

"I don't know," I told her.

"Could we have misjudged Mr. Hathaway?" She sounded worried that she had judged the dead man unfairly.

"I doubt it. Those crates were originally addressed to Hathaway. Gregory and Hathaway were in it together." I was more concerned with saving the living than worrying about the dead.

"Why did you come here looking for me? How did you know I was taken prisoner?"

"Mr. Burke went to your lodgings last night. When you didn't return, he went to the Duke of Blackford, who contacted me."

"Why would a duke contact you about me?"

"I'm marrying him tomorrow. At least I hope I am. Mr. Ranleigh is the Duke of Blackford. Oh, I wish I knew when help will arrive." At that moment I was more frustrated than frightened, since Gregory and his pistol were elsewhere.

"You have help coming?" She sounded as if every statement I made was more surprising than the last. She really was an innocent from a small village.

"Yes. Sergeant Fogarty learned of this address, and we left it behind for the Archivist Society and the police to follow us."

"But how did he learn of it?"

Fogarty spoke up from somewhere nearby in the dark. "After Georgia traced you to this neighborhood, I asked the lads on the beat if they knew where Colonel Gregory lived. When they'd never heard of him, I tried the name Hathaway. They pointed out this house."

"Adam. You're awake. How are you feeling?" My relief filled my voice.

"Thank goodness I have a hard skull and he didn't get in a good blow. I'll live," he said. "I guess it's time I give this up. When it came down to it, I didn't protect you."

"I got you into this. Don't blame yourself," I told him. "Blame me."

It had taken me a while but when I finally succeeded in freeing her wrists, Eugenie said, "Oh, my hands are tingling."

"Are your feet free?"

"Yes. But now we're locked in here to die of the heat. He won't tell anyone we're trapped in this room, and without knowing we're here, how will your friends find us?"

I didn't notice the heat as much as I felt sweat pool inside my corset and could stand a cooling drink. Still, I had to keep up our spirits. Blackford and the Archivist Society and Scotland Yard would rescue us. I hoped. "I told Mr. Burke I'd find you and bring you back. It's up to us to send a signal."

"Why wouldn't he answer my letters? Or see me?" Once I mentioned Burke's name, she didn't seem to hear anything else.

"That's a question I hope you can ask him yourself very soon." I crawled over the rough floor to the door and tried the handle. The knob didn't move. "He's good to his word. We're locked in."

I heard Eugenie moving slowly toward me. "Is the key in the lock?"

I peered through the keyhole and saw a faint light.

"No." I pulled a hairpin out of my drooping hairdo and sat on the floor as I began to work on the lock.

Eugenie must have scooted over since she was sitting next to me. I heard her voice in my ear say, "What are you doing?"

"Trying to unlock the doorknob with a hairpin."

"Where did you learn that?" She sounded eager as she moved closer.

"A skill I needed for my work with the Archivist Society."

"They sound wonderful."

"We are," Fogarty said from behind us, pride in his voice.

We both heard the click a moment before I twisted the knob and the door swung in toward us. Both Eugenie and I had to slide on our bottoms out of the way. The small hallway was surprisingly light compared to our prison, even with the other hall doors closed.

Two men's voices came up the stairs to us. I guessed one was Gregory. Who was the other?

I looked at Eugenie, who shrugged and shook her head.

I held my finger up to my lips to signal for silence before stiffly rising to step out into the hall. I tried the first door on the right, guessing it would lead to the street side of the house. Tiptoeing over to the small window, I saw I was right.

The room was empty except for some wooden furniture. I tried the window and found it opened easily. The room must have been in use sometime recently. I reached down and grabbed the hem of my petticoat, knowing it was sewn in strips of lace and silk. The tiny stitches defied my strength.

I reached up the tight lower part of my sleeve and pulled out my knife. I sliced through the thread and cut off a piece of the hem of my petticoat. Attaching it to the outside of the window, I shut the window to hold it in place. There wasn't much of a breeze, but the shiny white lacy material fluttered like the flag of a whorehouse.

That should gather some notice along this street. I hoped it would also draw the attention of the Archivist Society. Or a bobby. Or Blackford's attention. He'd been fascinated by the amount of lace and silk in my traveling wardrobe. But then, he knew what I'd ordered. He'd paid for my trousseau.

I hoped no one spread the story of an almost-duchess flying part of her lacy petticoat out of a window to signal for a rescue from a killer. The aristocrats who'd already decided I wasn't fit to join their ranks would have a wonderful time retelling that tale to all and sundry. Lady Castleley and Lady Tidminster would make comments about the lacy banner for the next ten years.

Well, let them. I'd had enough of their rudeness. I would marry Blackford and they would have to live with our happiness.

I tiptoed back out into the hall and looked over my companions. Eugenie was bruised and dirty, but she had shaken out her red silk shawl and wore it around her shoulders once more. Fogarty leaned against the wall, a nasty gash down his hairline and blood smeared on his face and ear.

My call for help had to work. I didn't want my friends hurt more than they already were, and we'd shown we were no match for Gregory alone. Worse, there was now a second man downstairs.

I opened a door on the other side of the hall and found an empty room. I crept to the window and discovered that it overlooked the canal. When I tried to open it, the sash stuck for a moment before jerking open an inch or two. Another piece of my petticoat blew in the wind like the first one on the street side by the time I eased the window shut.

When I came out of the room and closed the door, Eugenie mouthed, "Now what?"

I looked at Fogarty. I was out of ideas.

He gestured down the stairs and held out his hand for my knife.

"Door's locked," I whispered.

At that moment, I heard voices and footsteps on the street outside. I hurried across the front bedroom again and looked out the window, Eugenie and Fogarty pressing behind me to see out. Blackford, Sumner, Jacob, and two constables stood out in the street, arguing.

I pulled open the window, sending the lace and silk floating down to the men. "We're in here," I yelled as loudly as I could.

The men all turned to look up at the window where we stood.

"It's Grayson Burke," Eugenie said with a sigh.

"Help us! The gold is here," I shouted. "Colonel Gregory is holding us prisoner."

Blackford's voice came clearly into the room. "Unlock that door, now, Jacob, or we'll break it down."

One of the bobbies blew his whistle.

I heard the two men downstairs shout at each other and move about. Then one set of footsteps came up the stairs toward us.

No. I wouldn't let them kill us. I was determined to face them down.

I still held my knife. I slipped into the hall and pressed my back against the wall as I inched my way to the edge of the stairwell.

The footsteps came closer.

Downstairs, there was a crash. The front door must have been broken open. I took advantage of the distraction and peeked around the corner.

The man on the stairs was Lord Cecil. And in his hand I spotted a revolver.

Did everyone come back from Cairo with a firearm?

I kept watch from the top landing. The Duke of Blackford and Sumner stepped into the front hall and came face-to-face with Colonel Gregory. Gregory stood at the bottom of the stairs, his gun at his side. Blackford held his silver-tipped cane ready in one hand. Sumner held a revolver.

Then I heard Colonel Gregory roar, "What is the meaning of this, breaking into my house? I'll call the constables."

"We brought two with us to charge you with kidnapping Miss Munroe, Miss Fenchurch, and Sergeant Fogarty of the Metropolitan Police," Blackford said, stepping forward. Behind him, I could see Sumner's muscular shape moving to one side of the hall, the gun aimed with a clear shot at Gregory.

Gregory pointed his revolver at Blackford. "I am within my rights to defend my property from thieves."

Lord Cecil Isle cocked his weapon and aimed, also at Blackford. The men in the hall didn't appear aware of him standing near the top of the staircase. I had to act.

I stepped out from hiding and shoved Lord Cecil hard. Off balance, he crashed down the steep stairway, bouncing off his shoulders and hips. His gun went off, shattering the plaster on the wall and making everyone jump at the thunderous noise.

Eugenie screamed.

Gregory swung around and fired.

A second explosion rocked the house. Gunpowder filled my nostrils. Lord Cecil Isle screamed. Blood dripped down the man's trouser leg as he landed in a heap at the bottom of the staircase.

Sumner jumped forward and wrestled with the colonel while Blackford cracked our jailer on his gun arm with the weighed cane. The gun fell to the floor and Blackford grabbed it. The bobbies took Gregory in a close hold as their prisoner.

I grabbed Lord Cecil's gun off a step on my way down the stairs, Eugenie and Fogarty close behind me.

Our way was blocked by Burke, who had come

inside and then ripped away the man's trouser leg. "You'll live, my lord. It's a flesh wound." Nevertheless, he balled up a clean handkerchief and pressed it on the bloody wound.

"He tried to kill me. I want him arrested." Lord Cecil was practically screaming, pointing at the colonel. "And I claim the reward for the gold. All, or almost all, of the gold stolen from the Egyptian treasury in Cairo is in the dining room. It's hidden inside the wooden slats of the twenty crates."

He had everyone's attention now. He shouted, "I suggest you call in the Bank of England. There's a fortune in there. A temptation for any man. Guard it until you can move it to a bank vault for safety. I won't be cheated out of my reward by thieves."

CHAPTER TWENTY-ONE

Eugenie pushed past me and stormed down the last few steps. Gone was the timid young woman who'd grown up in the vicarage. In her place was the woman who'd had the courage to leave home and study at Oxford and then travel to Egypt.

"You?" she snapped, facing Lord Cecil. "I was imprisoned by Colonel Gregory when I found the crates addressed to Mr. Hathaway. And that was yesterday, before you showed up here. Miss Fenchurch was the first to find the gold inside the crate slats. Also before you arrived. We deserve the gold. Not you."

I decided to add to his problems. "We heard you talking to Colonel Gregory before you knew our rescuers were coming, Lord Cecil." Then I turned to our captor. "Did he try to make a deal? His silence for some of the gold, Colonel?"

"Half," Gregory said, sounding disgusted. The sneer on his face was directed at Lord Cecil.

"Liar," Lord Cecil replied. I almost expected to see him stick out his tongue at the colonel.

"Which one of you killed my uncle?" Eugenie asked.

"I have an alibi and I can prove it. Ask the card

players at the British Residency." Lord Cecil was shouting again and clutching his leg above the bullet wound.

"Colonel Gregory told me he killed your uncle, Hathaway, Reed, M. Aveneil, Sylvia Prescott, and two Egyptian guards," I told Eugenie. Then I turned to Gregory. "Didn't think I'd be able to tell anyone before you got away, did you?"

He sneered in return, but he didn't speak.

"We received the translations of the coded messages your uncle took from Mr. Hathaway," Blackford told Eugenie.

"What did they say?" I asked, eager to learn about that part of the mystery.

"They were between Hathaway and Gregory. Hathaway was to switch the casket containing the gold for one with iron nails in the basement of the treasury building. He was to move the gold chest into the records room and then hide it in a box of paper records. A few days later, Hathaway used his position to remove what appeared to be stacks of paper records from the treasury, with the colonel making sure the boxes were not searched. The gold was hidden inside."

Blackford took my hand as he continued. "Damien Reed provided the crates to hide the coins and a place to do the work. Gregory was to make sure no one was caught or arrested."

"But all your dreams have gone up in smoke," I snapped at Colonel Gregory.

"I refuse to say a word. Prove it." The colonel spoke

quietly. Too quietly. I wondered what he was planning. Or perhaps he was tired from all the killing and deception.

"Well, take him off to jail. And get me a doctor," Lord Cecil demanded.

"You should answer for your crimes, too," Eugenie said.

He looked amazed. "Crimes? What crime have I committed?"

"You threatened my fiancée," Blackford said in the coldest voice I'd ever heard.

I heard more men's voices in the street moments before Inspector Grantham entered the small area. He glanced around before he said, "Georgia, I just received your message about Miss Munroe being abducted and brought here, but it appears the Archivist Society has rescued her already."

"Oh, no, Inspector, you're needed here," Blackford said. "They may have rescued Miss Munroe, but we need to have two men arrested for theft, murder, and abduction, and a guard put on a king's ransom in gold until the Bank of England can safely lock it up."

He opened the door and Grantham stepped into the room. He swallowed hard before he turned to the closest constable and issued orders. The bobby hurried away. Then Grantham shut the door, putting his back to it, standing guard.

The constables the inspector brought with him now took charge of both men. Gregory was led away, his wrists bound behind him. Lord Cecil wasn't bound, but he was lifted inside the closed carriage both men would ride to the police station.

"We'll hold the preliminary hearing for both men at Scotland Yard. It's the only place with enough room. And we'll need all of you to accompany us to make statements," Grantham said.

"How did you know Gregory had the gold?" Burke asked, his eyes only on Eugenie.

"He had the statues of Anubis and Bastet that belonged to Mr. Hathaway," Eugenie told him. "The statues I told Lord Salisbury about. It turned out the gold from the Egyptian treasury was hidden in the hollowed-out boards of the crates that held the statues." Grantham stepped aside so she could open the door to the dining room. "Look in here."

"Those are the crates Mr. Reed created according to the coded letters," Blackford told him.

Gold coins glittered in the late afternoon sun where they were scattered across the floor.

* * *

We spent what was left of the afternoon and all of the evening at Scotland Yard. We sat in a large conference room listening as Eugenie and Burke carefully told their stories from the beginning to members of Scotland Yard, the Foreign Office, and the British Treasury.

Each organization wanted separate reports, and a clutch of scribes took down each person's testimony in turn.

I was told Lord Cecil was in another room having

his own preliminary hearing after a doctor had sewed up his wound. At one point, I was called in there to tell them I believed Lord Cecil had stolen my handbag. I gave the chief officer the note that had been placed in my bag.

I also told them he'd admitted to me that he sent other men into Lord Barber's house because he believed the gold was hidden there. While there they destroyed a valuable statue. And that I recognized Lord Cecil as the man who struck me and Lady Derwaller in the Derwaller residence after he destroyed another statue he believed contained gold.

When I left to return to the other hearing, Mrs. Hardwick was telling about cleaning up Lord Cecil after he'd been beaten. Jacob sat waiting to tell what he knew.

When I reached Colonel Gregory's hearing again, I was surprised to see Sir Ralph Wyatt had arrived. He gave me a wide smile as he took his seat by Inspector Grantham and began answering questions. He told the listeners that less than two thousand pounds' worth of gold was missing from the treasure and the rest was in transit to the Bank of England for safekeeping until the representatives from the Caisse de la Dette Publique could assemble in London to carry out their job.

Then he told about decoding the coded letters that spelled out the roles Gregory and Hathaway were to play and using their names.

For the first time, Colonel Gregory glared at the speaker. So far, he had refused every invitation to tell his side of the story.

When Sir Ralph finished, he came over and Blackford rose so he could take his chair. "My dear Miss Fenchurch, it's so nice to see you again. I hear that you've had an ordeal."

I wished I didn't look so bedraggled. "We were lucky. After all the killing Colonel Gregory carried out, he ran out of time before he was able to finish the job and escape."

"Why did he kill so many people? He was a soldier, that is part of their job, but these weren't combatants."

"They all wanted a share, or had been promised a share of the treasure if they were successful in stealing the gold. I guess he wanted to keep it all."

A commotion at the door made us both turn. Simon Prescott burst in and headed directly for Burke. "Where's the scum who killed my sister?"

Burke put a restraining hand on his arm. "In custody."

"Let me at him. I'll get the truth out of him for you." Prescott wheeled around, only to be stopped by constables.

"I'd like to hear about your sister's role in this," Grantham said. "Come over here, please."

Prescott was led to a chair near Grantham, where he sprawled with an arrogant attitude.

"What role did your sister, Sylvia Prescott, have in the theft of the Egyptian gold?"

"None."

"We found a coin from the robbery on her person when her body was discovered."

"It was her property and I want it returned."

"She has been identified as the thief who stole it from a numismatic shop where it had been sold for pounds sterling. It was never hers. Now, please answer our questions, Mr. Prescott." Inspector Grantham sounded like he was reaching the end of his patience.

Prescott lost all his bluster and sat up in the chair. "We learned about the theft and the reward from Lord Burke. Sylvia said she'd rather find the gold and get the reward for herself than have to marry Burke for it." He looked over at his so-called friend. "Sorry, old boy."

Burke shut his eyes and nodded. Eugenie stared at the man sitting next to her as if he were suddenly a stranger and pulled her red silk shawl tighter around her shoulders.

"My sister was clever. She figured out how the thief would get rid of the gold, by trading in a few coins at a time, and so she checked the different coin shops. He'd just been in one. She spotted him and followed. She was supposed to tell me that night at the ball where she had followed him, but he must have spotted her as well. Or she confronted him. Either way, he killed her on her way to the ball."

"When was the last time you spoke to your sister?"

"I spoke to her just before she went out to check more numismatic shops that afternoon, but she'd been home later and left me a message." He pulled a piece of paper out of his pocket and handed it to Grantham.

Grantham opened it and read aloud, "Found him. We can get the reward. I'll tell you about it at the ball."

He handed the note to a constable and turned to Prescott. "Did you know who 'him' refers to?"

"No. I would have found out that night."

"Thank you, Mr. Prescott. We'll contact you later. You may go home."

He rose and stormed out of the room, shoving past Burke on his way.

Weary and tired of sitting, I rose and walked over to check on Fogarty. He sat near the back of the room, one side of his head above his ear now cleaned and bandaged.

Jacob muttered something about missing his dinner, which immediately made my stomach growl loudly. My cheeks heated as Fogarty and Jacob grinned at me.

"Even a duchess can get hungry when locked up by a thief," Fogarty said.

His jovial attitude reminded me of how close the danger had been. I took a shaky breath as I looked at his bandage. "Locked up by a murderer."

He grabbed my hand and said, "It's okay, Georgia. We're all right and the villains are locked up. Hanging will keep Colonel Gregory from ever killing anyone else."

The evening was finished when the various arms of the government agreed on the questions being sent to the Egyptian government once the Foreign Office officially informed them that the gold had been recovered and the Caisse division would proceed normally from London.

"Someone in Cairo must know something about

who made those crates and where," Grantham said. "Reed must have kept records, either here or in Cairo. We'll continue this hearing after we've heard from the Egyptians. The day after tomorrow?"

The other British agencies agreed. I was relieved. I wanted Inspector Grantham at my wedding in the morning since we'd worked together for so long.

"We have enough evidence tonight to go to the police magistrate to request Colonel Gregory be held over for trial for theft and abduction. Are you certain there isn't anything you'd like to say in your own defense, Colonel?"

Gregory only looked at him and glared.

Officials began to circulate around the room. I was surprised at the number of black-suited men among these officials who knew Blackford and congratulated him on his upcoming wedding. The number who then wished me well was gratifying.

Now that we were all released to go to our beds or offices, the Duke of Blackford gave Sumner, Fogarty, Jacob, and me a ride to Sir Broderick's in his carriage.

Jacob nearly jumped from the carriage when we reached Sir Broderick's house and hurried inside. Fogarty followed more slowly, limping on his bad leg. When Sumner climbed down from the carriage, Blackford said, "You know that I'm counting on you in the morning."

"You won't be sorry," his sometime employee said with a grin and then handed me down to the pavement.

"Our wedding's tomorrow—" Just then, the church

bells up the street began to toll twelve. "Oh, it's after midnight and bad luck for you to see me now," I said.

"It was just a little while ago that I found myself breaking down a door to rescue you. You were glad to see me then." The corner of his mouth quivered in an attempt to hide his smile.

"We were doing a good job of rescuing ourselves. Weren't we, Sergeant Fogarty?" I called out, but Adam was too far away to hear. "Besides, that was yesterday."

I liked the old wedding customs. "I shouldn't see you now. Today. It's bad luck for the groom to see the bride on their wedding day."

We didn't need any bad luck, not after what we'd been through the last few days. And thank goodness, it looked   like   we'd   make   it   to   the   altar.

CHAPTER TWENTY-TWO

"Then turn around," Blackford commanded. "I'll see you at the church at ten." Then he quietly added, "My duchess."

"I'm so glad the day has finally come," I said with a shiver of excitement. I found that I meant it more than I expected. More than I hoped.

This marriage was going to work because we were going to make it work. And hang Lady Castleley and her awful cousin Lord Cecil Isle. At least he was currently locked up. I hoped it would do him good.

It didn't appear that he'd killed anyone, so he wouldn't hang.

"Until the morning." Blackford tapped at the top of his carriage with his cane and I heard the wheels start rolling down the cobblestones behind the click of horses' hooves.

Sumner wished me well and turned to walk the short distance home to where Emma waited. I was certain she had stayed awake to find out what happened. Fogarty and I went inside Sir Broderick's, where Mrs. Hardwick exclaimed over his injury and hurried off to get him a cup of hot, heavily sugared tea.

I was relieved to see she had returned safely, but I suspected a friend of Fogarty's from the police force had seen her home after she'd given evidence at Scotland Yard.

At Sir Broderick's signal, Jacob stopped entertaining him with the events at the house by the canal until Mrs. Hardwick returned.

"Where is Miss Munroe now?" he asked me.

"Lord Burke insisted on seeing her safely home to her lodgings," I told Sir Broderick. "He may not have wanted to see her in London before, but he's changed his mind."

"I hope it's her courage and not her sudden wealth that has turned his head," he replied.

"Her wealth?" Jacob asked, his face screwed up in puzzlement.

"Think of it. She seems to have the best claim to the reward for finding the stolen gold. Burke could use that to rebuild his burned-down castle," Fogarty said.

"How are you doing?" Sir Broderick asked him, staring closely into his face.

"I'm sore and a little headachy, but I'm sure Mrs. Hardwick will soon have me right as rain."

When Mrs. Hardwick returned with his cup of tea, she clucked over our escape and rescue and rang for the maid. "I imagine you'll want a cold supper," she added, and ordered bread and meats along with tea to be served to all of us in the dining room.

No one could reply to that over Jacob's enthusiastic "Yes."

I found I was trying to hold in a yawn. The day's events had worn me out, and tomorrow would be an even bigger day. No, it was tomorrow already. My wedding day.

The thought almost took away my appetite. Almost.

* * *

Despite my fatigue, I tossed and turned for most of what was left of the night. When I rose stiff and grumpy in the morning, I tried to enjoy a soak in the tub. Despite the warm weather, the servants had built a fire in the fireplace in my room and set the tub next to it.

I found I couldn't relax, even with rose petals in the water. Now that the time had come, each second seemed to drag. I couldn't wait to say, "I do."

Once I felt cleaned up from my ordeal the day before, I dried and put on my combinations. Then Lucy began to lace me into my corset. "Aunt Phyllida and Lady Westover will be there this morning?" I asked before gasping out, "Not so tight."

"That's the way Lady Arabella wanted them," Lucy said.

"I don't. They can be snug without cutting off my circulation," I grumbled.

"Today they can't. You have to look perfect. You're getting married."

"Not if I can't breathe."

Lucy loosened the strings enough that I could take in sufficient air to say my vows.

"Of course they'll be there," Mrs. Hardwick said. "Everyone knows where they're supposed to be and when. You just worry about looking beautiful."

"Is everything ready for the wedding breakfast?"

"The duke is having his staff take care of that at Blackford House. You have nothing to worry about."

"I will if they don't like the idea of having a bookseller for a mistress," I said.

Emma came in and I introduced her to Lucy. After all these years of dressing myself with the help of Emma, Aunt Phyllida, or Mrs. Hardwick, having a lady's maid was a strange concept. I knew it was inevitable, and Lucy seemed to understand my hesitation. We'd probably manage quite well together if she'd just allow me to breathe.

Especially since the dress she'd made for herself from the navy blue fabric was lovely, and she knew how to break into safes.

Emma pushed me onto the stool in front of my dressing table to work on my constantly falling hairdo, telling Lucy all the problems she would encounter dressing my hair. The two of them talked about me as if I couldn't hear them.

Long, curly locks of reddish hair fell in front of my face as Emma continued her efforts while she talked. "I heard what you said," she told me when she paused from complaining about the challenges my curls provided. "The staff at Blackford House won't have a bookseller for a mistress. They will have a well-respected duchess who owns a bookshop and investigates with the Archivist Society. What is there not to love?"

She gave me a big smile. I held tight to the hope Emma was right.

We had tea and toast to hold us over until the breakfast. I could barely eat, but Emma polished off hers and mine before we began to get me dressed for my big day. After Emma, Mrs. Hardwick, and Lucy found there wasn't enough room for the three of them around the gown, they took turns fussing over my appearance.

Sir Broderick came in twenty minutes before the wedding, sunk into his wheeled chair more than usual and wrapped up in a blanket. I thought at least his color was good, but I gave Mrs. Hardwick a concerned look.

If he were ill, I'd spend my entire honeymoon worrying about him.

To my raised eyebrows, she said, "He's been feeling the cold so much for the past day."

"I hope you'll feel better now that you get to see me in my bridal gown," I told him, twirling around to show off my train.

"I feel better just seeing you here in front of us safe and sound. After yesterday..."

"That was yesterday. All is well today," I told him, and I found I believed it.

"And I came to wish the bride every happiness." He rolled over and took my hands. I saw a bit of jacket sleeve and shirt cuff and knew he couldn't have been feeling too poorly if he'd bothered to fully dress.

"I wish you would come."

"I know you want me to attend, but it would take an act of God or Parliament to get me down the front steps." He changed his scowl into a smile. "You look beautiful. Your parents would be so proud."

"Thank you." I was trying hard not to cry, and Sir Broderick's eyes were glistening. He was the closest thing I'd had to family for many years.

"Here. Put this in your shoe for good luck. It was in your mother's shoe on her wedding day." He handed me a silver sixpence.

Then I did cry. "I thought we'd lost it."

"I put it away when you first came here after their deaths. I knew you'd need it someday."

I bent over and hugged him, and then slipped off one shoe to place the narrow bit of silver under the arch of my foot. As soon as I stood up, my helpers began to fuss with my dress again.

"Do you have something old—?" Emma began.

"This locket. It was Blackford's grandmother's." I fingered it on a thin chain around my neck. "My dress is new. I've borrowed a handkerchief from Mrs. Hardwick. But blue?"

Emma tied a blue ribbon around my wrist. "It's from Aunt Phyllida."

"And with the silver sixpence in my shoe, I'm ready." I gave a deep sigh. I felt ready.

For Blackford. For marriage. For the future.

At a quarter to ten, we went outside to the stares, the waves, and the cries of "God bless you" from neighbors and passersby on the street. The carriage Blackford sent to carry Mrs. Hardwick, Emma, Lucy, and me to the church had arrived. We climbed in—but headed off in the opposite direction from the church.

I grabbed at the door handle. "Where are we going?"

"To Fenchurch's Books."

"It's closed today." I began to panic. It was a good thing Emma ate most of my breakfast.

Emma grinned at me. "That's where it all began. We need to go past there. For good luck."

Traffic in London being what it was, I was afraid I'd end up being late for my own wedding, but Emma and Mrs. Hardwick kept reassuring me. Nevertheless, I kept fussing. I wanted to get to the church. I wanted the service to be over. I wanted to be Blackford's duchess.

We finally arrived at St. Ethelbert's, one block down the street from Sir Broderick's townhouse, at five minutes past ten on the church's tower clock.

The footmen helped me down last, and then I walked the short distance to the first three steps, across the portico, and then up the last step while Emma, Lucy, and Mrs. Hardwick fought to keep my train off the newly swept stone walk.

I blinked as I entered the dark sanctuary after the bright sunshine outside. Then I saw the building was crowded with people staring at me. Every pew was full, even the balconies that normally seated the servants and lower classes. It was my wedding day. Let them stare. I was marrying Blackford.

As I took two steps forward on the wide stone-paved center aisle, looking up at the bright stained-glass windows over the altar, the pipe organ began to play. Glorious music filled the church.

"Georgia."

I looked over at Jacob, and then down into the smiling face of Sir Broderick. "How—?" My heart did a flip in surprise.

"I'm to walk, or rather, wheel, you down the aisle in place of my dear friend, your father." The blanket was gone. Instead, I could see his waistcoat of dove gray matched his gloves, and his high silk hat was as black as his frock coat. Someone had attached a bouquet of daisies and white roses to the back of his wheeled chair. But none of this was as lovely as the smile that lit up his eyes.

"But how? You said—"

"Getting me here is Blackford's wedding present to you, Georgia. He knows how much it means to both of us. Now, go marry that man before he gets tired of waiting for you. You arrived five minutes late." He held out his hand, and I took it.

I looked down the length of the aisle and saw Blackford standing there waiting for me. For an instant, I considered running down to join him.

Jacob helped Sir Broderick wheel the chair down the worn stones until we reached the front, while I glanced at the faces filling each pew. The entire Archivist Society was there, along with friends from the bookshop and a wide selection of aristocrats and diplomats. Inspector Grantham gave me a wink. Lady Castleley and I exchanged stares. She looked faintly disgusted as she glanced at Sir Broderick. I passed Lady Westover and Aunt Phyllida in the first row, who both mouthed, "Hallelujah."

And then I reached the front and stood next to Gordon Ranleigh, the Duke of Blackford. My very soon-to-be husband.

I handed off my flowers to Emma. The vicar began speaking. Jacob wheeled Sir Broderick behind us and to the side. Sumner handed Blackford the ring and stepped away.

And then it was just Blackford and me as we faced the vicar. I recited the right words at the right time, all the while staring into Blackford's dark eyes. I noticed his hair curled at his collar, a sure sign he was nervous.

We held hands and it seemed as if the vicar would speak forever. Blackford slipped the ring on my finger. The vicar finally said, "I now pronounce you man and wife."

We kissed, but what I wanted to do was jump up and down and throw my arms around Blackford.

As our lips parted, he whispered, "My beloved duchess."

"Thank you for my wedding present. For making it possible for Sir Broderick to be here. You. Are. Perfect. I love you so much."

The organ filled the church with a spirited tune, and I was Georgia Ranleigh, Duchess of Blackford.

Blackford and I headed down the aisle on our exciting new adventure. A different type of partnership. Marriage. I thought I'd burst with all the love and joy in my heart.

I was the luckiest woman in the world.

If you enjoyed The Detecting Duchess, here is a FREE SHORT STORY about Georgia and Emma during an investigation that takes place nearly ten years before The Detecting Duchess. Use this link to get your free short story, The Missing Brooch.
https://dl.bookfunnel.com/p1g2xi20n3

For a change of pace, here is a sample of
A Memorable Christmas Season
A novella
Set in London during the Regency
Read on…

A Memorable Christmas Season will
appear in
Christmas Revels IV arriving in
Autumn 2017

CHAPTER ONE

Susanna Dunley, Dowager Countess of Roekirk, directed the footmen to replace a few more branches of greenery on the banister and then nodded her approval. As the footmen cleared away the last of the fading greenery, her son's wife, Rose, hurried toward her, her face a mask of misery.

"Rose, what's wrong?"

"I—I just cast up my accounts. I don't think I can go through with it now. Not tonight of all nights."

The girl burst into tears and Susanna gathered her in her arms. "Hush, now. The ball will be the best of the year. Your first party will be a crush and will make your reputation as a hostess. Everything is ready. Except us."

Susanna felt the girl's arm. "You're freezing. Is it that cold in your room?"

She nodded and sniffed as she straightened.

"Let's go upstairs. Sit by the fire to warm yourself before you dress for the ball. You'll feel so much better once the guests begin to arrive." Susanna led the girl upstairs while mentally checking off all the tasks that needed to be done to put on a successful ball in the week between Christmas and Hogmanay.

All those of the ton in town for the Christmas season had been invited to the ball. Many of them were Scottish like Roekirk, his wife, and mother and unable to go home, as the roads to the north were impassable.

Once Christmas Day and Boxing Day were past, there had been nothing planned until the Duke of Derwin's New Year's Eve gala. Rose had carefully chosen the perfect date. December 28th.

Susanna hoped it would take both their minds off the date.

"Your first time hosting a Christmas ball. Your first Christmas as a married woman. I know you're nervous," Susanna said as they reached the first floor landing. "It will be fine. Wonderful. Don't worry. Just warm up and get ready."

Rose had nearly opened the door to her room, but before entering, she dashed down the hall after her mother-in-law. "Are you sure the house looks all right? Will the musicians be here on time? Oh, I should check the food—"

The girl would make herself sick again if she didn't calm down. "Rose, all will be well. Relax. Take a deep breath. Now, go make yourself even more lovely. And wear Roekirk's Christmas gift to you."

"Those emeralds are so beautiful. Yes. Yes, I will." Rose skipped down the hall and went into her room to dress.

This ball would go a long way toward helping Rose find her feet. Rose only lacked seasoning, and seasoning was something Susanna could supply. And once Rose was confident in her role as countess, then Susanna could—dear heavens, be what? Dowager. An ugly word for someone without purpose.

Now was not the time to study the future.

After long years of practice, Susanna and her lady's maid quickly readied her for the ball. She'd had time to read a chapter of a gothic novel before there was a scratching on her door. Her maid opened it and Rose walked in.

Susanna gave her an encouraging smile. "Oh, is it time to go down, Rose?"

"I think so. I heard Richard on the stairs a little while ago."

"I suspect to get into the brandy ahead of time. He hates balls. So like his father." The thought of the late Earl of Roekirk ruined Susanna's tranquility. She snapped her book shut.

Rose looked at the ornate mantle clock and said, "It's only twenty minutes until the guests will arrive." Susanna glanced over to see she was bouncing on her toes again.

They went down the broad staircase together and lingered in the front hallway for a minute, until Birdwell, stationed near the door, cleared his throat.

"Perhaps we should check each of the main floor rooms to make sure all is in readiness. One never knows where guests might wander during a ball. Especially young guests." Susanna smiled and started on her tour.

Rose followed, a blush on her cheeks. Does she think we don't remember our courting days when we get older, Susanna wondered? Thoughts of summer days in the glen when she was younger than Rose warmed her face.

The front drawing room, red fabric on walls and cushions blending nicely with the holly on the mantle and over paintings, was pristine. The music room, ebony furniture and ivory walls and draperies, was cheered with the fire in the grate and improved with mistletoe over the doorway and the mantle. The mauve and rose dining room had the chairs removed. The long table was set for the buffet with punch bowls at either end. Under the chandelier, the silver sparkled from many polishings.

Without saying a word, the two women walked past the closed door to the study. Richard was in there.

They went on to walk around the ballroom once. The floor had been waxed until it reflected the candles in the chandeliers. Most of the chairs in the house were against the pale blue walls. A great deal of greenery balanced over the draperies closed against the chill of the winter night.

Susanna entered the morning room first. The yellow walls and upholstery made this a charming room in the morning. Tonight it was dreary, without Christmas decoration or fire.

"I don't think anyone will come in here," Rose said and walked off.

Next was the library, all leather and paneling touched with mistletoe on the mantle and a fire in the grate. The card room, in shades of green, was set up for two tables of card play. Susanna had decided the blue drawing room hadn't been redecorated for a hundred years, but tonight she found it slightly less hideous with liberal helpings of greenery and red ribbon.

"The servants have done a wonderful job, haven't they, Rose?" the dowager asked.

"Yes," Rose answered as she turned toward the front hall to await the first guests.

"Just the green drawing room left," Susanna said and started in that direction.

With a sigh, Rose followed. "Do you think anyone will bother wandering that far from the party? There won't be a fire in there tonight and the draperies are closed against the cold, hiding the lovely view of the garden you so prize in the summer."

"You must be thorough," Susanna said. She opened the door and felt cold air tumble out the door and strike her where she stood in the warmer hall. The cold breeze from the room made her suspect the French doors to the garden were ajar. "Perhaps we should have a fire laid in here?"

Susanna reached for a candelabra from a table in the hallway and stepped forward. In the flickering light, she could see a hand on the arm of a high-backed chair. The chair faced away from the hall, toward the drapery-covered French doors.

Had one of the guests arrived early? But why would they come back here? Had one of the servants thought this was an appropriate place to bring her guests?

"Good evening," Susanna said as she reached the

chair. Then her hand holding the candelabra shook so violently that light rolled up and down the walls.

She took a step back with a gasp. "Don't come any closer, Rose. Could you please fetch Birdwell?"

Instead of obeying, Rose moved to stand next to her mother-in-law and looked down on the man. An arrow stuck out of the breast of his deep red and blue waistcoat.

The deep red was blood.

Rose wailed, "This will ruin everything," before she collapsed in a heap.

Susanna looked down at the unconscious body of her daughter-in-law and thought, "What a wretched time for that silly girl to faint." Leaving the door open, she hurried to the front hall, hoping none of the guests chose this moment to arrive.

They had five or ten minutes, at the most, to rectify this disaster.

Fortunately, no guests were in sight and Birdwell was still there. "Find a footman to take your place and come with me," she told him.

At that moment, the bell rang and a footman, unaware of the tension flooding Susanna, opened the door. A man walked in, shaking the cold and snow from his broad shoulders, and Susanna thought for a moment she might faint.

Will? In her house? After all these years?

Pull yourself together, girl.

"Lord Keyminster, what brings you here?" Susanna said with a curtsy on shaking legs.

He swept her a low bow. "The new countess invited me to the ball tonight. I came early, to allow you to deny me entrance without embarrassment."

"I would never turn you away." Susanna realized with a shock that she had spoken aloud.

"My thanks, milady. Shall I leave now and come back at a better time?" His face had aged thirty years, there was gray in his dark hair, but his smile, wicked and wry, hadn't changed a jot.

A plan half-formed in Susanna's mind. "No. As long as you are here, you can perform a great service for me, as a leading diplomat and as a friend."

With another bow, he said, "I am at your service."

"Please, follow me. Birdwell, bring more light. We'll have need of you."

Susanna turned and hurried toward the green drawing room, certain the men would follow. Birdwell was paid to follow orders. She had never been certain why Will Marsden, now the Earl of Keyminster, did anything.

As she entered the green drawing room, the door open as she had left it, the countess groaned and sat up. "Good. Rose, pull yourself together. Your guests will start arriving at any moment. Do you want me to call your maid?"

"No, I'm all right." Then she looked horrified. "But what do I tell the guests?"

"If they ask, tell them I will join them shortly. A minor household emergency is keeping me from them at present. And tell Richard nothing."

Unfortunately, the silly girl looked at the chair, the hand still draped over the arm, and gasped as she slid on her bottom away from the dead man.

"Come, come. You'll ruin your dress that way. Be brave, Rose. Rise and put a smile on your face." Susanna stood by her, bent over with a smile, offering her hand.

Lord Keyminster gave Rose, Countess of Roekirk, his hand which she took. Susanna stood by while he helped Rose to her feet, and she rewarded him with the coquettish smile that had won her husband, Richard, the new Earl of Roekirk.

Enough of this. Susanna ignored her jealous annoyance, took Rose's hands and said, "This is the ball you've been planning for weeks. Go and enjoy it. Lord Keyminster and I will take care of this. Now, not a word about what you've seen. Smile. Have fun. Enjoy your ball."

"I'll go up the back stairs and repair the damage before I come back down the front staircase," Rose said with a weak smile.

"Very wise," Susanna said to encourage her as she walked her to the door. Once the girl was on her way up the stairs, Susanna shut the door and turned to the two men. "What do you make of this?"

"I have no idea how he gained admittance, milady," Birdwell said.

Lord Keyminster lifted the man's chin with one hand and held a candle close with the other. "Do you know him?"

He was perhaps forty, with light brown hair and a

thin face. Blood—where had that come from—had trickled onto his collar, and death had robbed him of any individuality. She shook her head. "I didn't make up the guest list. Good heavens, I didn't know you had been invited."

"He's Sir Benjamin Atwell."

"The traitor?" Susanna felt her eyes widen as she looked at Lord Keyminster. It was getting hard to think of him by his relatively new title while depending on him to help her rid herself of an unexpected corpse. "Why, the scoundrel. I know him only by reputation, but he wouldn't be admitted to my house."

Sometimes she found it easier to ignore that she was the dowager countess. It was no longer her house. And ignored that she unfortunately did know him. She took a breath and continued. "Didn't he sell British battle plans to the French, causing the deaths of scores of British soldiers?"

"Something like that." Keyminster glanced down and shook his head, a motion she remembered all too well. "The question is why murder him here?"

"Everyone in the ton who's in town will be here tonight. Perhaps they wanted to be in the crush when the body is found."

"How did he get here? Birdwell, is it? How would he find this room here in the corner of the house?"

"Perhaps from outside, milord." Birdwell walked over and pulled aside the draperies covering the window facing the dead man. Behind it was a French door leading to the garden.

Will, as he'd always been in her mind, walked over and examined the door handle. "Easily forced." He opened the door, sending in a wave of bitter air. "The snow on the ground outside has been churned up here. Was the staff outside this room for any reason?"

"No, milord. The rear staff entrance is on the other side. There's not any greenery here that they would have cut to decorate inside."

Will stepped outside, peering at the snow glittering from the light coming from the room. Susanna stepped outside the door, trying to ignore the cold.

"There are three sets of footprints coming to this door and one going past it and back again. What is back there?" Will asked.

"A shed." Susanna shut her eyes when she realized what that meant.

"What about this shed? And come inside before you freeze." He swept out his hand for her to proceed him. Then he pulled the door shut and locked it before Birdwell closed the draperies again.

Fortunately, the rug by the door was large enough for them both to wipe the snow off their shoes.

Shivering, Susanna hugged herself for a moment before standing gracefully. "We keep gardening supplies in the shed. We also keep the bows and arrows and targets in there for summer archery practice." Susanna put her hand on Will's arm. "Someone knew all this and brought this man into my home to kill him. Why?"

Author's Notes

The historical basis of The Detecting Duchess is sound. Egypt almost went bankrupt in the years before 1897, and their European creditors set up the Caisse de la Dette Publique to take twice yearly payments from the Egyptian treasury and then divide it among the creditors. The Caisse was set up the way I describe it in this story. One of the two payments in 1897 was on May first. There was at that time a commission run by the British and the French to modernize and equalize the Egyptian system of taxation. The titles used in this story are correct, although the people who held these positions have no similarity to the characters in this story with the exception of Lord Cromer, the consul-general, who held that position for many years. The inspector-general of the Egyptian police at that time was a British military officer, but usually held the rank of general.

Queen Victoria's birthday was celebrated with parades and fireworks and parties on May 24 in Cairo as well as the rest of the Empire. After that date, the social season for Europeans in Egypt ended and anyone who could headed back to Europe to avoid the intense desert heat in the summer.

The theft and the characters involved are fictitious. In 2017 dollars, $1,000,000 would equal about 55 pounds of gold. An amount an old lady could move around in a wheeled case. Using current exchange rates, that would make a million British pounds weigh a little over 70 pounds in gold. However, the value of one million pounds sterling in 1897 expressed in 2017 US dollars must be multiplied by a factor of 135. For this, I am using a calculator created by Eric Nye, Department of English, University of Wyoming, called Pounds Sterling to Dollars: Historical Conversion of Currency.

Multiplying the 55 pounds by 135 gives us a weight of almost 7500 pounds. Two men with a wheeled cart wouldn't be able to move it, and transporting it to England the way I used in the story wouldn't be feasible.

And that, gentle reader, is why we ask you to willingly suspend your disbelief and follow us into the thrills and excitement of the story.

About the Author

Kate Parker grew up reading her mother's collection of mystery books by Christie, Sayers, and others. Now she can't write a story without someone being killed, and everyday items are studied for their lethal potential. It's taken her years to convince her husband she hasn't poisoned dinner; that funny taste is because she can't cook. Her children have grown up to be surprisingly normal, but two of them are developing their own love of literary mayhem, so the term "normal" may have to be revised.

Living in a nineteenth century town has inspired Kate's love of history. Her Victorian Bookshop Mystery series features a single woman in late Victorian London who, besides running a bookshop, is part of an informal detective agency known as the Archivist Society. This society solves cases that have baffled Scotland Yard, allowing the victims and their families to find closure.

In the Deadly series, Kate has brought her imagination forward forty years to a rapidly changing world before World War II. London society more closely resembles today's lifestyle, but Victorian influences still abound. Her sleuth is a young widow earning her living as a society reporter for a large daily newspaper while learning new skills and exploring her increasingly perilous world.

As much as she loves stately architecture and

vintage clothing, Kate has also developed an appreciation of central heating and air conditioning. She's discovered life in coastal Carolina requires her to wear shorts and T-shirts while drinking hot tea and it takes a great deal of imagination to picture cool, misty weather when it's 90 degrees and sunny outside.

Follow Kate and her deadly examination of history at www.KateParkerbooks.com

And

www.Facebook.com/Author.Kate.Parker/

CPSIA information can be obtained
at www.ICGtesting.com
Printed in the USA
LVHW050713090419
613451LV00022BA/360